SHAMEFU

Bets knew that the Earl of Burlingham made no secret of his scandalous life and loves. Drinking, gambling, womanizing, debauchery—all were on the ever lengthening licentious list that the infamous earl flaunted before the shocked eyes and wagging tongues of the *ton*.

But now Bets was shocked to discover the secret that Burlingham successfully hid from the world. Despite his glittering title and dazzling looks, the earl was in desperate need of funds—and in frantic search of a rich bride to rescue him from drowning in a sea of debt.

Bets, too, possessed a secret—a secret that was quite as unsuspected. She was as impoverished as this man who was ardently employing his charm and skill to make her his wife.

Bets knew that she had to tell the earl the truth before it was too late for him to find another financial angel—or before he sealed her lips with kisses.

The Fourth Season

The Fourth Season

by

Anne Douglas

A SIGNET BOOK

SIGNET
Published by the Penguin Group
Penguin Books USA Inc., 375 Hudson Street,
New York, New York 10014, U.S.A.
Penguin Books Ltd, 27 Wrights Lane,
London W8 5TZ, England
Penguin Books Australia Ltd, Ringwood,
Victoria, Australia
Penguin Books Canada Ltd, 10 Alcorn Avenue,
Toronto, Ontario, Canada M4V 3B2
Penguin Books (N.Z.) Ltd, 182–190 Wairau Road,
Auckland 10, New Zealand

Penguin Books Ltd, Registered Offices:
Harmondsworth, Middlesex, England

First published by Signet,
an imprint of Dutton Signet,
a division of Penguin Books USA Inc.

First Printing, January, 1995
10 9 8 7 6 5 4 3 2 1

Copyright © Anne Bayless, 1995
All rights reserved

 REGISTERED TRADEMARK—MARCA REGISTRADA.

Printed in the United States of America

Chapter One

Robert Francis Frederick Farnsworth, Earl of Burlingham, only son and heir of the sixth Marquess of Fleet, awoke in his London town house with a raging headache, not helped by the intrusive pounding on the door of his bedchamber.

"Come in," he managed, and groaned.

"I cannot, your lordship," said the voice of Geordie, his butler/footman/valet, muffled by the heavy door.

"Hell's bells! Whyever not?" Rob struggled to sit up, then sank again and dragged the pillow over his ear. "Go away!"

"You locked the door, your lordship," said Geordie.

Rob had heard that despite that pillow. "So?" he said groggily.

"Sir, you have a caller." Geordie was yelling now. "Your friend Hazleton. He insists he must see you."

Rob forced himself to sit up and threw the offending pillow across the room. It had not far to go, for the opposite wall was not more than ten feet away. The stark bedchamber held only the bed, a wardrobe, a small chest that served also as washstand, and a tiny fireplace. Any more furniture and there would hardly have been space for an occupant. Ah, the indignities of being rolled up, he thought for the hundredth time as he headed for the washbasin to throw cold water on his face. He suddenly realized he was fully dressed except for neckcloth and boots.

Eventually he staggered to the door and turned the

key. Geordie heard and immediately opened the door. Behind him stood Thomas Hazelton.

"Hazleton, eh? Wake a man out of a sound sleep, will you?" Rob grumbled, rubbing his eyes. "Could it not wait? What time is it?"

"Noon, you slugabed," said Hazleton, frowning. Rob had never seen him look so serious. "Are you ready to face the music, or do you plan to leave town?"

"Face the music?" Rob rubbed his head. "What are you talking about? I fear my head is still fuzzy. Geordie!" he called to the servant, just disappearing down the hall. "Strong tea! *New leaves,* mind! With brandy! This instant!" He colored at the inference that tea here was not always brewed with fresh leaves. Hazleton showed no sign of having noticed.

"You know that you will never be able to lift your head in this town again," Hazleton said sternly, moving to sit on the edge of the bed. "Why no chair in here? Good God, man, every bedchamber needs a chair."

"Where would I put it?" Rob asked reasonably. "What do you mean about lifting my head? I have lifted my head in all the best places. Unfortunately I do not seem to be able to lift it properly at the moment." He rubbed the back of his neck and stared at Hazleton with bleary eyes. "What is the matter with me?"

"The usual, no doubt," Hazleton said crossly. "Look here, friend, you are in deep trouble. I mean it. What do you intend to do about it?"

Instead of answering, Rob tottered to the door, opened it with a crash, and yelled down the hall, "Geordie! This minute!"

He returned and sank down beside Hazleton. Rob yawned and punched his friend ineffectually on the shoulder. "Now," said Rob, "tell me what I am supposed to have done."

"Good God! You mean you don't remember?" Hazleton turned and swept his gaze over the man sitting beside him. "You do look pretty bad," he said. "Slept in your clothes, did you? I did not wait to help put you to

bed when I brought you home. Geordie said he would
take over." He continued to stare at Rob.

"You had better tell me the worst," said Rob in resig-
nation.

"In a nutshell, you arrived at Almack's last night very
drunk, insulted Mrs. Drummond Burrell's gown, and
passed out at her feet."

"I did? Surely not. Egad, I was afraid you were about
to tell me I had knifed someone or been caught out
cheating at cards," said Rob, feeling somewhat better.
"Why was I even talking to Mrs. Drummond Burrell?
Starchy female. Not my type. I do not believe a word of
it."

"But dozens of people saw you! Heard you! Whatever
came over you?"

"Damn! Wish I could remember. How was Mrs.
Drummond Burrell's gown? That bad?"

"Robert! I don't even remember what the woman was
wearing. Something blue, I think. Who cares? That is
not the point. You have insulted a patroness of Almack's
and of course you will never be permitted to go there
again. I'm sure all London has heard of this by now.
Rob, you have just removed yourself from polite soci-
ety."

"Pooh." Rob managed a weak laugh. "Nine days' wonder. It will all blow over when something else comes
along."

"It certainly will not endear you to the mamas of all
those delectable chits on the marriage mart," Hazleton
said sternly.

"Ah! Tea! Will you join me?" Rob greeted Geordie
with as much enthusiasm as he could muster, given his
condition. The tray Geordie bore held a brandy decanter
as well as tea things. Rob poured for them both, then
added a generous dollop of brandy to his own cup. His
hand was steady.

That is odd, he thought. Drunk enough to pass out and
this morning my hand does not shake as it usually does.

Something peculiar here. I can't remember a thing after I set out for Almack's. . . .

"I have things to do," he told Hazleton when the tea was gone. "Come back for supper, will you? My head should be clear by then. Glad you came," he said as his friend departed. "Have Geordie let you out. Noon! I must be up and doing." He smiled, but the smile did not reach his eyes.

He sank back on the bed and put his head in his hands. What could this mean? What had he done?

He remembered having a single glass of wine—yes, perhaps it had been refilled, once only—at his favorite neighborhood tavern before going on to Almack's. He had needed that drink to give him courage for the task he had set himself. It was imperative that he settle on a wealthy, or at least comfortably fixed, young chit and arrange to marry her as soon as possible before Dors Court fell into complete ruin. Before his aging parents ran out of paintings and plate to sell in order to buy food. Before the whole world learned that his own pockets were to let and the facade of wealth and ease he struggled to maintain was only that, a facade.

He had been putting off the search—it was so much easier to continue to attend the races, play cards, drink with his fellows—but he could put it off no longer. He dreaded having to dance attendance on a bevy of empty-headed misses, pay them wholly false compliments, and what was far worse, give up, at least for the moment, his thoroughly enjoyable pursuits.

The search promised to be difficult, considering his unsavory reputation. He remembered his vow last night to have no more to drink the entire evening (not that he would find anything at Almack's) so that he could be at his charming best when he looked over the crop of young ladies. He had even dared hope that not every protective mother would draw away, nose in the air as if she had encountered a bad smell, when he approached.

He rubbed his head, where the ache was becoming almost bearable. He had to think. He recalled leaving the

Friend at Hand in his curricle, headed for Almack's. He was to meet Tom Hazleton there. Tom, second son in a wealthy family, had no black marks against his name. He had agreed to lend what assistance he could in pointing out possible candidates for Rob's suit. Rob's circle of acquaintances among the fairer sex was limited, considering the reluctance of so many to have anything to do with him. Lord, did they really believe all that nonsense? Surely two duels—and he was pushed into them against his will, he thought righteously—a few small altercations, an occasional example of overimbibing and dallying with lightskirts—were not so unusual? Did not half the young bucks of the *ton* do much worse? He tried to dredge up from his faltering memory his arrival at Almack's, where he had not been in years. He drew a blank.

"Geordie!" he roared. "A bath!" When he heard no response he slammed out of his chamber and called down the stairs. "Geordie! I have places to go and people to see! Now! Today! Not next week, you old goat."

Geordie approached dejectedly from the back of the cramped little house. "No more coal," he reported. "Want a cold bath, your lordship?" He looked over his big, misshapen nose at his master and smoothed his thinning hair.

"God almighty," said Rob. "Send someone out to get some. Put it on my account. I seem not to have the money on me."

"Who's to send?" Geordie asked.

"Don't we have a footman?"

"Not since last week. Don't you remember? Or was you too squiffed? He left 'cause he hadn't been paid—told me he had a new post somewheres else. Jemmy Parsons, it was. A good man." Geordie gave his master an accusing look.

"You mean the staff is down to—what? Two?" Rob gripped the stair rail to hold himself up. He did not need another calamity.

"Just me and Mrs. Burket, and that boy what thinks he's a groom," said Geordie.

Rob considered. No time to worry about baths and staff now. He had to make an effort to whitewash his reputation, and fast. His and his family's future depended on it.

"Never mind," he told Geordie. "Lay out some clean clothes so I can be off." He returned to his chamber on leaden feet. The task before him was daunting, and he dreaded it.

But his usual ebullience could not quite be stifled. He wished he could remember what Mrs. Drummond Burrell's face had looked like when he had remarked on her gown. He chuckled.

It did not take long for word of the incident at Almack's to spread all over social London. Lady Bets Fortescue learned of it from her mother, Elizabeth, Dowager Countess of Stanbourne, who had it direct from one of her bosom bows. The friend had actually been present at Almack's at the time. The incident had been the *pièce de résistance* of her Thursday At Home.

"Oh, Bets!" Lady Stanbourne was so distraught she removed her turban only to put it back on her head instead of the lacy cap she wore in the house. "What am I doing?" she muttered, looking in confusion at her cap. Then, turning to her daughter, she burst out, "I fear I have the most dreadful news. Whatever shall we do?"

"What is it, Mama?" Bets was all solicitude, though she could not imagine her mother would learn anything dire at Lady Stafford's. The ladies in attendance traded *on dits* over their teacups, shuddering delicately at the peccadilloes of those not present. Perhaps old King George had died?

"Burlingham is ruined," said Lady Stanbourne. She drew a much-twisted handkerchief from her reticule and wiped her eyes.

"Burlingham? That—that rakehell?" Bets frowned. She was to mourn the ruin of a man she had never met?

A man who, she had been led to believe, had been headed straight to perdition for years? "What is that to us?" she demanded.

She led her mother toward the morning room, the most cheerful room in the house because it got the sun. Only now it was afternoon, and the sun had moved around to the other side of the house. The room still looked cheerful, with warm yellow walls and blue-and-white upholstered chairs. Bets sat Lady Stanbourne at the table where Bets did the household menus and accounts and took a chair opposite, pushing aside a pile of papers.

"Please explain to me how Burlingham's downfall could affect us," she asked her mother, patting that lady's hands as they gripped the mangled handkerchief. "I confess I am all at sea."

Lady Stanbourne sniffed. "He—he arrived at Almack's last night quite drunk," she reported. "One cannot imagine how he came to be admitted. He accosted Mrs. Drummond Burrell—Mrs. Drummond Burrell, of all people! She must be the—the snippiest patroness Almack's has!—and ridiculed her gown. Then he collapsed in a heap at her feet and had to be carried out. Corned, pickled, and salted, as they say! Oh!" She wiped her eyes.

Bets had met Mrs. Drummond Burrell a time or two and had not been pleasantly impressed. She could hardly stifle a grin at the picture of that lady's comedown. But what had this to do with her?

"Are we to go into mourning, Mama? Why are you so upset?"

"Bets! I had Burlingham in mind for you." Lady Stanbourne raised tear-stained eyes to her daughter's face.

"For me! Good heavens!" Bets recoiled. Her own mother could do this to her? Foster an alliance with a man about whom no one had a good word to say? Had they come to this? "No! I cannot believe it! It is just as well he is ruined. Now, I pray, you will forget it. Mama, I am sure I . . ."

"Oh, yes, you are sure," Lady Stanbourne said scathingly. "You have been sure for what is it—three or four years now? Bets! You will soon be three-and-twenty! You are in your fourth season! We cannot afford to—to—"

"Yes, Mama." Bets sighed. She shuffled through the pile of papers on the table, noted in passing that it was mutton again tonight, and gave her mother an assessing look. "I am well aware that we *cannot afford*. Nevertheless I beg leave to settle my own future. The gentlemen of the *ton* cannot all be fops and fools. Or rakehells, for that matter. Burlingham indeed! What in heaven's name made you think of him as a candidate? We do not even know him! He would make the most wretched of husbands."

Lady Stanbourne steeled herself and said, as if she had learned it by heart, "He is an earl. He is the only heir of the Marquess of Fleet. He stands to inherit Dors Court, in Dorset, which I understand is an estate of some magnificence. He is a well-made man of the right age—somewhere in his late twenties, I believe—and he is unmarried, not affianced so far as I have heard. It stands to reason that he will settle down once he is wed."

"Settle down once he is wed?" Bets laughed, a harsh laugh with no humor in it. "Why should you think so?"

"One can hope," said her mother. She looked almost cheerful for a moment, then her face fell. "But now I do not know—this faux pas with Mrs. Drummond Burrell—"

"Good riddance," said Bets. "Mama, I have been meaning to ask you. Must we have our tea from Fortnum and Mason? It is precious dear there, and we could do so much better somewhere else—"

Lady Stanbourne drew herself up and became the imperious matriarch she had once attempted to be, before the Stanbourne fortunes had vanished. "We have certain standards to maintain," she said.

Bets knew it was hopeless. "Yes, Mama," she said.

She rose and headed for the kitchen to remind Molly

that teatime was nigh. Lady Stanbourne looked after her in dismay. A tall, slim, graceful girl with an abundance of brown hair—despite its tendency to curl—with an animated face that was near beauty when she smiled: Why could she not attract an acceptable suitor? Suitors she had had, but none she would have as a husband. And now, in her fourth season, the numbers were fewer and fewer. Lady Stanbourne disliked exceedingly having to subject the poor girl to another season, for she knew there was talk. But how else to snare a well-to-do husband?

Lady Stanbourne scanned the familiar morning room. It looked fresh and bright as always. Their house, in Knightsbridge Terrace in the village of Knightsbridge, just outside London, was a fine house, if small, and most of the signs of their penury were well hidden. No one knew, she felt sure, that the late earl, her husband, had left them in such straitened circumstances. He had been wealthy; everyone knew that. Now they lived on the quarterly pittance doled out by Lady Stanbourne's stepson, Godfrey, son of the first Countess of Stanbourne. Godfrey had never accepted his father's second wife or the daughter born to them. Godfrey had explained that his father's fortune had dwindled alarmingly because of unwise investments on the 'Change, made by the late earl while possibly of unsound mind during his last days.

Lady Stanbourne had no head for finances, but was doing her level best to live carefully. Five years it had been, five long years since she had lost her beloved husband. She and Bets had moved immediately to London, to the house left her by her parents. A year of mourning had delayed Bets' come-out. Now here she was, nearly three-and-twenty, in her fourth season, and seemingly no nearer to finding a wealthy husband than ever.

Lady Stanbourne dabbed at her eyes once again. How could the girl be so particular? It was the outside of enough! On the other hand, she had to admit that if it were not for Bets, she herself would be near desperate. Bets had quickly learned how to live on a pittance. She was not above helping with the housework, taking on tasks that their two servants—the poorly trained Molly, who lived in, and the cook, who came by the day—had no time for. Bets ran the house and oversaw their finances, with Lady Stanbourne permitted only a bit of spending money.

Molly and Bets arrived with the tea and a few poor biscuits. Lady Stanbourne had had better at Lady Stafford's At Home so refrained from the biscuits. She put on a cheerful face and bent her thoughts toward some other gentleman of the *ton* who might be enticed into offering for her daughter.

Maybe Arthur Percival could be brought up to scratch. Bets was engaged to go driving with him that afternoon. He was not as good a prospect as Lady Stanbourne would have wished, but at least he seemed interested.

"Bets, you must be all that is pleasant and amiable with Mr. Percival," Lady Stanbourne said sternly. Her face had the look of a general leading his troops into battle, a look that seemed incongruous on such a small, fluffy woman. "Please, I beg of you! Do not treat him as if he were a little boy and you his mama. Oh, I know you!" she went on as Bets, indignant, tried to interrupt. "You will tell him he should have worn a warmer coat, or try to straighten his neckcloth. Bets, young gentlemen do not like that in young ladies. They get enough of that at home! You must pretend you think him all that is strong, and masterful, and perfect, and hang on his every word."

Bets broke into peals of laughter, narrowly missing spilling her tea. "Hang on every word of Arthur Percival's?" she cried, wiping her eyes. "Spare me! His deepest thoughts concern the state of the weather. 'Will we have rain today?' or 'I do believe it is a little warmer,' or 'Perhaps I should take an umbrella.' Mama, I do not wish to waste my time on Mr. Percival. He lacks two farthings to rub together in any case. I am going only because *you* accepted the invitation for me. Did you not see the look I gave you? Heavens!"

Lady Stanbourne looked stricken. She had been told that there was a very real possibility that Arthur Percival would become a baron one day, his older brother, the heir, having contracted a wasting sickness.

"Please!" she begged. "Be nice to him."

"Very well, I shall try," Bets agreed. She finished her tea and carried her cup and her mother's to the kitchen, then made another trip for the biscuit plate.

"Should I wash up?" Lady Stanbourne heard Bets ask as she met the maid, Molly, outside the morning room. Molly mumbled something that seemed to indicate Bets would not be needed.

What was the world coming to when the daughter of an earl was reduced to clearing the table and offering to wash dishes?

Burlingham managed to pull himself together after Hazleton's departure and leave home soon after one of the clock. He took time only to run hurriedly through his small pile of invitations to be certain he was not promised somewhere. His social life was going to have to wait until he made a start on solving the mystery of the Almack's incident.

He noted he was expected to attend the Purtwee ball that evening. The Purtwees were relatives; Rob's great-grandfather and George Purtwee's great-grandmother had been brother and sister. That made him and George third cousins, but they had never been particularly close. Rob decided not to bother sending regrets.

His first destination was the establishment where he had drunk wine before going to Almack's, in case the lass who had served him could provide any information. He entered the Friend at Hand to find it nearly deserted. The maid who had served him was not to be seen. He sat down at a table near the back and stretched his long legs before him, the picture of relaxation.

"McNally," he greeted the innkeeper, who came to take his order, "how are you keeping? May I buy you a drink?"

Anne Douglas

"Certainly, my lord," said McNally, a small, middle-aged man with a slight limp. "What will you have?"

"I do not believe I shall have what I had last night," said Rob easily. "By the way, what did I have last night?"

"Dunno, my lord," the innkeeper replied. He gave Rob a quizzical glance. " 'Twas Tessie that served you, if I remember right." He pondered. "Had to have been Tessie. Maudie hadn't come in yet. Damned wench was late. Said she tore her dress and had to go back and change. Ha! Another tale like that and I'll have to turn her off."

"Yes, it was Tessie. Where is she now?" Rob asked mildly.

"Ain't come in yet," said McNally. "What'll you have, my lord?"

"A brandy," said Rob, crossing his legs and staring at his toes. "Is Tessie not your daughter?" he persisted.

"Nah," said McNally. He spat, then turned fiery red as he realized he was in the presence of a gentleman. "She's me brother's girl," he said as he limped after a brandy for the gentleman and an ale for himself.

Rob drummed his fingers with impatience on the scarred table. He could sit and drink in the Friend at Hand all afternoon—he had done so on more than one occasion—but he wanted information, and he wanted it now. Did McNally himself know anything? It was hard to tell. Despite being a regular customer he could not count on any loyalty from the dour innkeeper. Rob owed him money.

When McNally returned, carefully balancing the drinks as he limped up to the table, Rob smiled in welcome and waited for the man to speak.

"Heard you pulled the wrong pig by the ear last night," McNally said jovially. Rob detected a hint of malice. "Pot valiant, was you? God damn! I didn't think you was so bad off when you left here. Made a couple of stops elsewhere, did you?"

Rob glared. "No, I did not make any other stops.

Come, McNally. What was in that wine Tessie gave me?"

McNally looked injured. "What do you mean?" he demanded. "Dunno what wine you ordered, but I'd have you know the Friend at Hand never waters the wine—never puts nothing in it—what are you accusin' me of?" He had hardly sat down before he sprang up again and gripped the back of his chair, resting his weight on his good leg. Rob noticed his knuckles were white.

"Sit down, sit down." Rob waved the man back into the chair. "I am not accusing you of anything. I just thought . . . perhaps . . . Tessie . . ."

"What about Tessie?"

"What time does she start work?"

"Whenever I needs her, that's when. She'll be upstairs helpin' the missus until the crowd comes in."

"I would like to talk to her."

"Oh, you would, would you? Don't you be gettin' any ideas about Tessie. You want to see her, you come back later and buy another drink. And your lordship, sir, it'll be for coin next time. I got to cut off your tab. Sorry, sir, you owes me seventy-six pounds, six shillin's, fourpence. When d'you plan to pay up, sir?"

"Seventy-six pounds!" Rob roared. He caught himself. It was hardly sensible to shout out his debts. "McNally, you blithering idiot," he said in a more normal voice, "how could I owe you seventy-six pounds?"

"And six shillin's, fourpence," said the innkeeper. "There was that time you was feelin' good and bought for everybody. Remember? Not a month back. Not to mention all the drinks before and since."

Rob put his head in his hands. His sins were catching up with him, no doubt about it. He was sure McNally had inflated the bill for the round of drinks he had bought after betting on the right horse—for once—but he had no proof. His town house had no coal, and no footman. He still had no idea what he had drunk the night before.

He held on to his temper with difficulty. This was no

time for his customary arrogance. "Might I have a look at last night's accounts?" he asked in a pleasant tone. "They might tell me what I had to drink, since Tessie is not here to remind me. For God's sake, man, this is important!"

McNally chuckled. "The day Tessie marks down what you blokes gets to pour down your gullets'll be the day pigs fly," he said. "She cain't read nor write, your lordship, sir. Lemme show you." He limped back to an office behind the bar and returned with a shabby accounts book, its pages stained with spills of food and drink, and opened it to the last filled page. "See?" he said, and spread it before Rob's eyes.

Under "Tess" was a series of stroke marks. Nothing more.

"She makes one mark for beer, ale, stout, porter; two marks for wine," said McNally.

"If she remembers," said Rob in disgust. "Tell me, what if someone orders whiskey or gin? Or rum?"

"Three marks. We don't get much call for 'em."

"Very well. Now may I see my own account? This seventy-six pounds you say I owe?"

"And six shillin's, fourpence. Certainly, your lordship, sir." McNally scurried back to the office with his account book and returned with a bundle of papers pinned together. Rob flipped through them. There was his signature, all right, "Burlingham" scribbled on each one. He realized for the first time that his purchase of several rounds of drinks a month earlier had cost him fifty-one pounds ninepence. Fifty-one pounds! That was more than his servants got in a year. Two pounds should have been ample, but there was his signature. God, he thought. How bosky was I when I signed this? Did I even look at it? Were all those jolly patrons demanding the finest rather than their ordinary ale? He was certain McNally was cheating him unmercifully, but he had no way to prove it. It could have been one pound or a thousand; he didn't have it. But last night's chit was the vital one.

He finally found it. Four strokes. Two glasses of wine. A dead end.

"Where did you hear about my—my little problem of last evening?" he asked McNally, who was nervously eager to get away.

McNally's face was bland. "Oh, some swells was in here talkin' about it last night after that Almack place closed up," he said.

"What swells?" Rob demanded.

"Didn't know 'em," said McNally. He refused to meet Rob's eyes.

"What did they look like?"

"Like swells! All dressed up, they was, in prime twig."

"How many?"

"Two or three. I forget."

"I am sure you do. So long ago, of course. How could you remember how many at this late date? Yet you remember what they said. That is odd, is it not?" Rob felt like shaking the man until his ratty wig fell off.

"What's it to you?" McNally was indignant. "Two, three—what's it matter? Now I come to think of it, there was two. Yes, just the two. Now, you feel better?"

"Oh, yes," said Rob. "I feel ever so much better. Were they tall? Short? Fat? Thin? Old? Young? Come, McNally, tell me."

"I never noticed, *sir*. Too interested in what they was sayin'. Wished I'd of seen you, your lordship! You must of been a sight!" McNally laughed.

Rob rose and gave McNally his haughtiest stare. "Put this on my account," he said airily and left before McNally, hampered by his bad leg, could catch up with him for a coin—or a signature.

He was on foot, and not far from Hyde Park. He walked aimlessly toward the park, lost in thought.

Chapter Two

It certainly would not *do* to set her cap for Lord Burlingham, not that the opportunity was likely to arise. Bets was upset at her mother at the very idea, but considering how unlikely it was they would ever meet—the scoundrel, no doubt, would leave London in disgrace—she decided not to dwell on it but rather to enjoy her drive with Arthur Percival as best she could. She did not think it likely.

She would have been bored with Mr. Percival but the opportunity never offered. Bets was too busy hanging on for dear life to the seat of the phaeton he drove. Mr. Percival, staying in London at the home of his older brother, had borrowed the raciest of his brother's carriages, no doubt in the mistaken notion of impressing her, Bets thought. She could not remember seeing a more inept driver.

Her companion had discussed the weather, past, present, and future, from every aspect as he drove the short distance from her home in Knightsbridge Terrace to Hyde Park. His conversation tended to be disjointed, however, as occasionally he needed to think of his horses and thread his pair through the traffic. When they reached the park, he seemed to think the horses would know what to do and gave Bets his undivided attention.

"High steppers, ain't they?" he said proudly as the horses, no longer held to a walk, broke into a trot. "Needed the exercise. M'brother's poorly, y'know. Hasn't left the house in weeks. Asked me to take 'em out and welcome. What's the matter, Lady Elizabeth?"

Belatedly he noticed her tight grip on the edge of the seat. "Never fear, I'll get you safely to . . ."

He suddenly realized, too late, that the phaeton was heading straight toward a pair of gentlemen riders engrossed in conversation as they ambled in his direction. No horse worth its salt would collide willingly with another horse, but Arthur Percival apparently did not trust his pair. He pulled hard on the reins, so abruptly that the horses came to a sudden, jolting stop. Bets found herself flying through the air, coming to rest on the grass verge with her head in a border of budding daffodils.

She couldn't breathe. She couldn't breathe! Panic-stricken, Bets lay motionless until finally, with a great gulp, she was able to get her starved lungs working again. She looked up into a concerned face. She expected Arthur Percival, but somehow she had got that wrong. This was not Arthur Percival.

"Miss! Are you hurt?" asked a tall, rangy gentleman with coal black hair and eyes to match. His face was a face young maidens dream of, all planes and hollows with a straight nose and straight black brows. The brows were drawn together in a worried frown as the gentleman bent over her. "Please do not try to move. We must be sure no bones are broken."

Bets wiggled her arms and legs. Bruised and aching, perhaps, but surely no lasting damage. Then she remembered her skirt. Was she decent? Had her skirt flown up? She reached down to adjust it, then tried to sit up.

The stranger smiled, and she was struck by the sight of his teeth. Perfect, white teeth except for one front tooth that lapped slightly over its fellow.

"You obey well, do you not?" said the man. "Not to worry. Nothing visible but your ankles, and very fine ankles they are. May I help you sit up, if you are sure you are all right?"

"Where—where is Mr. Percival?" Bets asked as he clamped strong arms under hers and gently pulled her up to a sitting position.

"If you refer to your escort, he fell off the other side,"

said the man. "Is he worth rescuing? Should we not just leave him there? He deserves it. Such a clodpole!" He looked toward the heap of disheveled clothing on the other side of the path just as the heap pushed itself dazedly to its feet.

"Ah, Burlingham," said Percival. "Would you take care of the lady while I rescue the damned phaeton? It's m'brother's, you know and he would . . ."

"At your service, you beef-witted cawker," said Rob. He ducked in a semblance of a bow.

"You—you are *Burlingham?*" said Bets in amazement. "I thought you looked familiar—I have seen you—but we have never met."

She held up her arms for him to help her stand, but he failed to take them. "Rest awhile," he said, and dropped to the grass beside her, settling comfortably with his arms around his knees and his feet in the daffodils. "Yes, for my sins, I am Burlingham," he admitted. His face grew serious as he looked at her. "And you? Why have we not met?"

"I am Lady Elizabeth Fortescue," said Bets. "I—I really do not know why we have not met."

"No doubt your mama has done all in her power to prevent it," Rob said bitterly. He brightened. "But now we have, have we not? May I assist you home? You will not wish to trust yourself with that cork-brained Percival, will you?"

Bets looked around. Arthur Percival was trying to lead the agitated horses, still pulling the phaeton, toward them. The light carriage, empty, bounced and jiggled. A curricle and three horsemen had stopped to see what was the matter. Bets had not even been aware of them. She saw no horse or carriage that might be Burlingham's, however.

"I would be grateful," said Bets, "but where is your carriage?"

"I am on foot," Rob replied. "I live not far from here. I will simply go home for my curricle. Where do you live?"

"Knightsbridge," said Bets. She waited for his reaction. Knightsbridge was not as fashionable an address as she could wish, even if the Duke of Wellington's elder brother, the Marquess Wellesley, lived there when he was in England. Not that she had ever met him.

"Knightsbridge! How convenient." Bets noted that Burlingham seemed actually pleased. "Are you sure you are quite recovered? It might be better for me to escort you home on foot than to take time to walk to my house, get the carriage out, and have the horses put to. I could hardly invite you in for a restorative, of course; it would not do for you to enter my bachelor establishment."

He smiled at her and again she noticed his single lapped tooth. She decided it was quite beguiling.

"Thank you. I shall be glad of your company," she said.

He rose lithely and pulled her up. She ached in numerous places but seemed whole. Her gown was not, however. Grass stains were the least of it. Ground-in dirt, rips—what would Mama say? She had so few gowns; this pale yellow one was the best of the year-before-last's crop. But she had met Burlingham! Her earlier dark thoughts about him vanished. He seemed so friendly, so helpful, so *handsome*. Surely he could not have insulted Mrs. Drummond Burrell as Mama had said. Surely it was a tale some wicked rumor-monger had invented. She felt no hesitancy in letting him escort her home. Anything was better than another ride in Arthur Percival's phaeton!

"Here! Where do you think you are going with her?" Percival shouted as they started across the grass toward the edge of the park. "Burlingham! Come back here!"

Rob tucked Bets' arm in his. "I am taking her home, you jingle-brained chub," he called back. "Home *safely*. You hear?" He turned and escorted Bets out of the park. He decided Arthur Percival was beneath his further notice.

Thank God she lives close, he thought. If we had to go to my town house to get the horses and carriage and she had seen how I am living . . . She doesn't seem to know about the incident at Almack's, so maybe I have a chance. . . . She must be the daughter of the late earl, and I am sure a fortune is involved. . . .

He beamed upon Bets. She returned an uncertain smile.

Bets tried to avoid limping. She had twisted her ankle when she fell from the phaeton, but she refused to admit it to the Earl of Burlingham. She had insisted she was not injured; she would not back down now. If he learned of it he probably would feel he had to leave her in the park in that dolt Percival's care while he went to his home after a carriage. She did not intend ever to speak to that dolt again.

Rob strolled carelessly along, Bets' arm resting on his. The attitude was all that was proper, but he felt her fingers grip his forearm a little more tightly than necessary. Was it by chance or by design? He felt warm all over. Then he noticed a slight lurch in her stride and with it came a pang of disappointment. It would seem her protests of being whole and hale were somewhat exaggerated and she actually needed his support. He slackened his pace but kept going, stopping only to toss a coin—one of his last!—to the crossing boy, who swept them a passage through the droppings littering Knightsbridge.

He'd be damned, he thought, if he would leave her in the park in that numskull Percival's care while he went for his carriage. The numskull probably would have the effrontery to suggest driving her home in his phaeton. Not only would her life be in danger, but Rob would not learn where she lived and would have to go to a deal of trouble to learn her direction, when he had many other things on his mind.

"Are you sure you are unharmed?" he asked, smiling down at her when Knightsbridge had been safely crossed. An untidy lock of hair flopped in his face and he blew at it ineffectually. The arm that was not supporting hers held his hat, somewhat the worse for its sojourn in the daffodil bed. He had inadvertently sat on it when he dropped to the grass to comfort her.

"I am fine, thank you," she said, "only a little shaken up, I fear. But home is not far. You know Knightsbridge Terrace? We are in Knightsbridge Terrace near to the Sloane Street corner. I will show you."

Her eyes were fixed on that errant lock of hair, still in his eyes. She was seized with an impulse to brush it back for him when she remembered her mother's remark about Bets' habit of trying to mother her admirers. Somehow she didn't believe her impulse was maternal, but she refrained.

"Are you here for the season?" Rob asked. "I am surprised I have not seen you before."

"Yes—no—I am here for the season, but I am here all the time," she said. "We live here."

He stopped for a moment and removed her arm from his so he could look straight at her. "You live here? Are you not the Earl of Stanbourne's daughter? I thought his seat was in Suffolk."

"Ah, yes, Suffolk." Her gaze grew dreamy for a moment. "Yes, Papa was the Earl of Stanbourne, but he has been gone more than five years. My brother Godfrey is the earl now. My half brother, I should say. He is indeed in Suffolk. So is my other half brother, William. But Mama and I live here. The house was left to her by her father." And thank God for that, she added silently, or we might have to depend for a roof over our heads on Godfrey's charity, of which he has precious little.

"How delightful it must be for your admirers," said Rob. "They can find you in town in season or out. Though I suppose you do go to the country when things pall here."

"No," she said. "We stay here."

Rob placed her arm on his once more and they strolled on. Bets tried to forget her painful ankle and her disheveled appearance. She prayed they would meet no one she knew. Several pedestrians gave them searching looks, but they were strangers.

"You are taking part in the season, you say?" Rob persisted. "I shall look forward to seeing you here and there, now we are acquainted."

He was not planning to leave London in shame! Bets' heart gave a little leap. She was more certain than ever that his supposed insult to Mrs. Drummond Burrell was vicious gossip; he was all that was polite and solicitous. But to fall down drunk at Almack's! That was hard to countenance. Too many people had seen that happen, according to Lady Stanbourne. Yet he showed no signs of overindulgence the night before; a little tired, perhaps, but quite clear-eyed. She knew well what a man recovering from a bout of drinking was like. Had she not had to contend with her brother William many a time? She had no liking for such.

"That would be delightful," she said. "I look forward to it. And here, your lordship, is my home."

She had steered him to a tall, narrow brick house overshadowed by much larger and more ornate houses crowding it on either side. Rob paused and looked keenly at the Fortescue house. Set back far enough from the street to permit a garden in front, now a riot of crocuses, hyacinths, and just-emerging daffodils, it was a little jewel of a house.

"Neoclassic," Bets remarked as she stood beside him. "By an admirer of Henry Holland's work. Not Holland himself, I fear. My grandfather had it built in 1788. Mama was married from here. Will you come in? Mama will wish to meet you and thank you for rescuing me."

"Delighted," he said.

His gaze swept over the house as they approached the dark green painted door flanked by white Ionic columns. Bets frowned at the sight of white paint flaking off the columns in a couple of places, but her escort seemed unaware of them. Bets reached in front of him and clapped the brass lion's-head knocker.

Nothing happened.

Bets frowned and knocked again. Finally the door opened. Inside stood Molly, wiping her hands on a stained apron.

"Oh, 'ello, miss. Back so soon? Lor, what 'appened to your gown?" said Molly.

Bets cringed.

"Take his lordship's hat and tell Mama we have a guest," she said quickly. "We will be in the sitting room. And some refreshments, please."

Molly took Rob's battered hat and held it out in front of her to give it a thorough examination. "Wot'd he do?" she asked, smiling. "Tramp on it?"

"That will do, Molly," Bets said sternly. She dared not look at her escort. "Please notify Mama immediately."

"Yes'm," said the maid. She dropped the hat on the hall table and disappeared toward the back of the house.

Leading the Earl of Burlingham toward the sitting room, Bets stole a glance at his face. What he must think of the inept maid! To her surprise he was clearly amused.

"She is new," Bets said, trying to overcome her embarrassment. "Mama is trying to train her. I hope you can forgive her impertinence."

"By all means," said Rob. "Most of us have servant problems, I believe. Or so my friends with families tell me. In my bachelor establishment I have need for fewer servants, and those I have, have been with me long enough to know their duties and my preferences." There, he said to himself. She will have no reason to wonder at my sparse staff, should she ever learn of it. He smiled genially.

"Please sit down," Bets invited as she chose a chair for herself. Remembering the rip in the blue silk-upholstered seat of one of several occasional chairs placed around the room, she sat in that chair, spreading her skirt to hide the rip. That gave her a full view of her skirt front. Heavens! How could she have forgotten the condition of her gown since her fall?

"Oh, dear. I must change—" she began as the earl

took a comfortable chair near the fire. Then her mother entered the room.

"Bets!" Lady Stanbourne shrieked. "What in the world happened to you?" She ran to her daughter and put a hand under Bets' armpit to help her rise. "Are you injured? What happened?" Suddenly she became aware of another person in the room.

"Who are you?" she demanded, turning to stare at the earl. As he and Bets began to speak at once, she gulped and said in a weak voice, "I beg pardon, your lordship. Welcome to our home, your lordship. My! How pleasant to have the Earl of Burlingham come to call. May I offer you some refreshment?"

"I thank you, my lady," said Rob, bowing. "First, I am sure, you will wish to see to your daughter. She suffered a nasty fall in the park. No"—at her look of distress— "she tells me she is not injured. She will tell you all about it. I shall gladly wait here while she repairs her dignity and changes her gown. Lady Elizabeth, do you wish assistance up the stairs?"

"No, thank you," said Bets, grasping her mother's arm and hurrying her out of the room. "We shall be back shortly. Molly will bring you some refreshment."

They left the door ajar as they departed. Rob heard Bets tell her mother, "You should have pulled the bell rope," and Lady Stanbourne answer, "But you know it is not working." Their voices grew fainter as they moved farther away and he settled back in his chair to wait.

Suddenly out of the silence he heard Lady Stanbourne's high voice shouting, "Molly! Brandy for the earl!"

In short order, Molly, looking frightened, brought him brandy.

Rob studied the sitting room as he sipped. The furnishings were in excellent taste, Sheraton most likely, he guessed, with a fine, thick Axminster rug under all. One of the most impressive articles in the room was an antique clock more than two feet tall, with gilded face, black Roman numerals on a white ground, and black lacquered wood case trimmed in gold. Miniature Corinthian columns with gold bases and carving supported the roof, adorned with gold finials and swags. It stood on the mantelshelf and quite overshadowed the landscape painting hung behind it.

Rob crossed his legs and smiled over his brandy. There was no question that this family had money. Just as he finally made up his mind he had to find a chit with plenty of the ready, the chit had virtually fallen in his lap. And not bad-looking, either.

"What happened to you?" Lady Stanbourne demanded as she and Bets mounted the stairs. "Were you hurt? Your poor gown! Oh, dear, I wonder if it can be mended."

Bets recounted her drive with Mr. Percival and its disastrous end. "I turned my ankle, but nothing serious," she assured her mother. "But just think! Had I not gone driving with that—that nincompoop, I should never have met Burlingham. Mama, he is all that is polite and considerate. I cannot believe he behaved so to Mrs. Drummond Burrell. Are you sure it happened?"

"I had it straight from Lady Stafford," Lady Stanbourne replied. "She saw it with her own eyes. So, I believe, did many others. There can be no doubt it happened."

"Did she actually hear what the earl said?"

"Well, no, I believe not, but she had it directly from Rupert, Lord Stafford."

"Oh, Rupert," Bets said in dismissal. "One believes only half of what he says. He probably got it from someone who got it from someone else who got it from someone else who made it up out of whole cloth."

"Has Burlingham mentioned this?" Lady Stanbourne asked as she went to Bets' wardrobe for a fresh gown. No maid, no abigail here; Molly, a maid of all work, was presumably busy getting brandy for his lordship.

"Oh, no," said Bets. "Nor have I." She began undoing the buttons on her yellow gown. She looked down ruefully. Perhaps an appliquéd band around the skirt would hide the damage? She rather thought not.

"While you wash off the grime I will endeavor to do something with your hair," her mother offered. "We must not keep Burlingham waiting." She steered Bets toward the washbasin. "Oh, Bets, is he not divine? If I were five-and-twenty years younger . . . He does seem interested, does he not? You see, my idea was not so bad after all. Now if he can just live down this incident at Almack's . . ."

"Mama, you are jumping to conclusions. I own that he has been everything that is kind, but what gentleman would not be under the circumstances? Please! I promise not to act motherly toward him if you will promise not to throw me at his head." She rubbed a wet flannel over her face and arms as her mother endeavored to pick grass out of her hair and subdue it into order with a brush.

"There now," Lady Stanbourne said at last. "You should do. Oh! I forgot your stockings. And your slippers! I had hoped your peach gown would hide them, but when you sit down . . . We will take no chances. I shall go downstairs and act the hostess until you are ready."

Full of happy anticipation, Lady Stanbourne descended to the drawing room. She found the earl comfortably relaxed where she had left him, his brandy glass empty and the decanter at his side alarmingly low. Her heart sank. So it was true that Burlingham drank too much.

He rose and smiled, waiting until she was seated, then poured himself another tot. "Will you not join me?" he asked.

"Ah—no, thank you," she said. "I will have Molly should bring some tea." She reached for the bellpull, then thought better of it. Burlingham kept a perfectly straight face. "I will just go and see what is keeping Bets," she said, and ducked out."

Soon Bets and Lady Stanbourne returned, followed by Molly with tea. Once the ladies were seated and had poured tea for themselves, Rob sipped his brandy. No one spoke. Both ladies were watching him, little smiles on their faces, apparently waiting for him to break the silence.

"Excellent brandy," he said finally, staring down at his glass. "You are fortunate to have it, what with the war and all. I am down to my last three kegs and shall have to find myself a gentleman soon, I fear."

Three kegs! Lady Stanbourne was startled. Her poor cellar held no more than three bottles of brandy, and if she entertained Burlingham once or twice more she would have none at the rate he was going through it.

But she smiled and agreed that the difficulty of obtaining French brandy was certainly an inconvenience.

Burlingham next complimented her on the antique clock on the mantelshelf. "I have never seen one like it," he said. "It must be very old and valuable."

Lady Stanbourne was all smiles again. "Yes, indeed," she agreed heartily. "From 1675 or thereabouts. One of my father's dearest possessions. It should be striking the hour in a few minutes. It has such a melodic tone! Made right here in London by one Henry Jones; it has his name on the back. I have no idea of its worth but I am sure it is considerable."

Rob wondered how much it would bring from a moneylender. He wished it were his to pawn.

"Ladies," he said, rising, "I must be off; I have a guest coming to dine. Lady Elizabeth, would you do me the honor of driving out with me tomorrow? I assure you I do not drive a phaeton; I have only a curricle, and you shall be safe with me. Will you take the chance?"

"I should enjoy that," Bets answered, trying not to appear too eager.

"At five," he said, and took his leave, carrying the battered hat. Bets watched from the window. He smiled up at her and began to whistle as he strode down the street.

Chapter Three

Rob and Tom Hazleton had shared the best that Mrs. Burket could put together, which was not much—damned stringy mutton, Rob thought—and were sitting over a brandy in Rob's minute "library." This all-purpose room he called library because it did contain a single bookcase full of dusty volumes that he had brought from Dors Court. He cast a jaundiced eye at the bookcase as the two men sat before the fireplace. The array of leather bindings looked impressive. He planned to read those books some day if mold and bookworm did not get them first.

"You have never been in the Friend at Hand with me, have you?" Rob asked. He had told Hazleton all he remembered of the night before.

"Not I," said his friend, smoothing his green pantaloons. "Beneath my touch."

"Then you can do me a favor. About this barmaid, Tessie. I think she drugged me last night. She was off duty when I was there this afternoon, and old McNally—who is her uncle, by the way—refused to call her. Perhaps you could sweet-talk her into admitting something."

"Ha! As you well know, sweet-talking barmaids is one of the things I do best." Hazleton smirked. "Why, I could tell you—"

"That is why I asked you, you daft addle-cove. Have another brandy. Two more kegs in the cellar." Rob reached for the decanter.

"Is that to be your bribe? I sit here before a fire made

up exclusively of brush and twigs and soon to breathe its last, and drink two kegs of brandy? I suppose after the first keg I would fail to note the lack of fire."

"Damn you, Hazleton!" Rob did not like to be twitted about his poverty, a state that he made every effort to hide. Of course Tom Hazleton knew; they had few secrets from each other. It rankled just the same. Rob rose and paced the room, stopping to kick a long, crooked branch farther into the fire.

"Sorry, friend. I could not resist. I am so enamored of your library, you know." Hazleton smiled and accepted more brandy. "You do understand that I shall have to bribe this Tessie with coin. Am I to provide the coin?"

"Could you? I promise to pay you back when my ship comes in. By the way, I do believe I have found that ship. Fell into my lap, you might say, this very afternoon." Suddenly Rob's gloom vanished.

"Bully! You won at White's? Or was it a cockfight? Congratulations."

"Oh, no, it was a filly."

"A ship fell into your lap but it was a filly. I have difficulty picturing this. What race did you bet on?"

"I mean a filly in skirts. Have you ever heard of a Lady Elizabeth Fortescue?" Rob asked, his face alight.

Hazleton gave his friend a keen glance. Showing actual enthusiasm over a lady? That was hardly Rob's way. Willing wenches, drink, races, boxing matches, gaming tables, more drink—those were what held Rob's interest. He had rarely bothered with the balls and parties and dinners that attracted the *ton* during the season; vastly boring, he had insisted. Until recently. Now, as Tom knew, Rob had made up his mind to find a wealthy lady and marry her posthaste. But he had never shown any enthusiasm at the prospect.

"Lady Elizabeth Fortescue. Hmmm. Any relation to Hugh Fortescue, Earl of Fortescue? He is Lord Lieutenant of Devonshire and so forth and so forth. He would be about the right age to have a daughter on the marriage mart. How did this very-well-endowed chit happen to fall in your lap?"

"No, no, wrong Fortescue. Her father was Earl of Stanbourne and the seat is in Suffolk. Her father is dead but she and the dowager countess live in a most handsome small house in Knightsbridge. I rescued her when that oaf Arthur Percival took her driving in his brother's phaeton and she fell out. His fault entirely! Fortunately she was not hurt, only shaken up. It happened in Hyde Park and I was nearby. She has agreed to go driving with me tomorrow. A most comely wench, Tom." Rob's eyes sparkled with anticipation.

Hazleton was still cogitating. "Is she taking part in the season?" he asked at last.

"Oh, yes."

"Is she tall, lots of brown hair, brown eyes, very animated?"

"You have her exactly."

Hazleton fiddled with his quizzing glass, framed in green enamel. "Rob, I hate to tell you this. I truly do. Your Lady Elizabeth is in her *fourth season*. It is the talk of my mother's friends. She must be two-or three-and-twenty by now. Her doting mama keeps trotting her out for inspection in the vain hope she will take. Why she does not go quietly away and potter among her roses or look after her brother's children or something, I have no idea. It must be horribly embarrassing for her."

Rob knitted his brows. This enchanting girl—hardly a girl, he amended—a failure on the marriage mart? How could that be? Surely her wealth would find her a suitor even if she were a fright to look at, which she certainly was not.

"You have met her, I trust?" Rob asked. "Why do you think she does not take?"

Hazleton laughed. "Yes, I have met her, and believe me, Rob, she is all yours as far as I am concerned. She's the mothering type. Or should I say smothering? If there is anything I cannot stand, it is to be mothered. How would you feel if a young lady constantly worried about your collar, or your neckcloth, or whether your handkerchief is straight, or whether your ears will get cold because your hat does not cover them properly? I ask you! I suppose one could stomach it in a wife, if one were so foolish as to take a wife, but . . ."

"She did not treat me so," Rob said stiffly.

"No? She will. I also understand she is vastly particular. Particular! How can she be particular in her *fourth season?* Yet I hear she has discouraged several possible suitors before they ever got so far as to ask for her hand. Richard Beauchamp, for one. Told me so himself."

"He did not mind that she mothered him?"

"I believe he was willing to put up with anything if he could just lay his hands on some of that Stanbourne fortune. By the way, she does dance well. You willing to dance, Rob?" Hazleton chuckled. This was more amusing by the minute.

"I have not forgotten how to dance," Rob said gruffly. "What do you think, my friend? Am I a better prospect than Richard Beauchamp? I think I could put up with a bit of mothering if I had to." He frowned, considering.

"Do you know Beauchamp?"

"No."

"Let me assure you, you are a better prospect." Hazleton ticked off his fingers. "He has, one, no chin; two, a circumference greater than Prinny's; three, interests confined to Egyptian antiquities. Oh, yes, and four, no money."

"Your Number Four sounds familiar," Rob said ruefully. "Now, Tom, have another brandy and then, if you please, make yourself acquainted with Tessie. I will spend a quiet evening at home. Still don't feel top of the trees. Damn. I was supposed to go to the Purtwee ball tonight. They will not miss me. Probably invited me just because we are cousins. Come by when you have anything to report, will you? Use your fatal charm on Tessie."

Once Hazleton had left, Rob prepared for bed. He had not been to bed so early in years, he was sure. His last thoughts were warm ones of a tall, brown-haired lady who would ride in his curricle with him. He would have to spruce up the young stable lad to act as groom—no, as tiger. Billy would never be convincing as a groom. As a proper tiger? He had to laugh.

Burton, Lord Purtwee, glanced over the glittering Purtwee ballroom, lit by hundreds of candles in Venetian chandeliers. It was late, well past two of the clock, and some of the guests were beginning to leave though the small orchestra was still playing. He turned to his son, George.

"Haven't seen Burlingham all night," he remarked. "I suppose he is in the card room?"

"He never came," said George. "I kept watch. Wanted to see if he could hold his head up after that dreadful incident at Almack's." He grinned. "Maybe he has gone back to Dorset with his tail between his legs."

"Oh, I don't think that would be enough to send him out of town," said his father. "What is there for him in Dorset?"

"Not much," George agreed.

George began to consider his next step.

Chapter Four

Friday morning gave promise of being a beautiful day. Bets' ankle was better. She went out to the back garden once breakfast was over to see what, if anything, was coming up, now spring was near. Most of summer's blooms were still napping beneath the soil, but a few green shoots held promise. To her delight a blackbird was singing lustily in the shrubbery, and she soon saw the reason——the dull brown female, showing no interest as she ran over the ground in fits and starts, searching for tasty morsels.

Bets saw in her mind's eye the profusion of blossoms that would fill the garden beds in summer, and sighed. She and her mother shared a love of gardening and often worked together with trowel and spade, happily tending their favorites. But their favorites were all flowers; not a vegetable was to be found in the back garden. This year was going to have to be different. If they could raise some of their own vegetables, they could save a tidy sum.

The back garden, though more extensive than the front plot, was still small. Grandfather Bonner, Lady Stanbourne had told her once, had not been interested in gardens. He had felt himself lucky to be able to buy the narrow strip of land between two impressive houses in Knightsbridge Terrace. He had sold his foundry in Birmingham that made iron plows and other farm implements with the intent of living in London like a gentleman in his declining years, though he was only three-and-fifty at the time. He wished to give his only surviving child, the adored Elizabeth, a chance at a good marriage, which he believed could be found only in London, and he had succeeded. He and Grandmother Bonner had had eight happy years there, Lady Stanbourne had reported, sniffling, before his death. Bets barely remembered him. Grandmother Bonner had felt ill equipped to go on alone and had spent her last years with the Fortescues. Papa had been very good about it, though Godfrey and William considered it one more imposition brought about by Papa's foolish decision to marry Elizabeth Bonner.

Why could her half brothers not see how happy Mama had made Papa, Bets often wondered. Lady Stanbourne, for all her diminutive size and fluffy appearance, ran their home with efficiency, entertained with aplomb, and was ever kind and friendly to the two half-grown boys who came with the marriage. They had resented their stepmother from the first and had never changed their minds.

Bets went back into the house for a string to measure dimensions for a possible vegetable bed. Would the wallflowers have to go? Her mother's beloved roses? Cabbages instead of lilies?

Molly, washing the breakfast dishes, wiped her hands on her grimy apron and rummaged in a drawer to find string for her mistress.

"Here, ma'am," she said, holding out a tangle of string saved from some package or other. "This be enough?"

"That is fine," said Bets. "Molly, I am expecting a gentleman this afternoon. Would you be sure to wear a clean apron? And you might save time to help me dress."

"Yes'm," said Molly.

Bets repaired to the back stoop to untangle the string. It took her thirty-five minutes, by which time she had lost all interest in measuring for vegetables. It was much more delightful to think about her coming drive with the notorious Burlingham. Would he be as friendly and attentive as he had been when he rescued her in the park? Would he be sober? What would they talk about? She felt tongue-tied at the thought; she knew virtually nothing about all the subjects he was said to be interested in—racing, for heaven's sake, or wagering on boxing matches, or—no, she would not think about it—wenching!

So naturally she thought about it. So far as she had been able to work it out, it consisted of men paying attention to women of less than spotless character. Kissing them, perhaps? She was unable to see why a gentleman would wish to do that, when there were so many fresh young girls of good families available. She had been kissed once or twice, and the process did not seem to be particularly exciting. Why did gentlemen find it so pleasurable? Bets shook her head in confusion. She supposed she could ask her mother. Lady Stanbourne never discussed such things with her. Apparently a lady was expected to *know* these things instinctively.

Wondering whether Lord Burlingham would ever try to kiss her, Bets wound the string neatly around her fingers, rolled it off, and returned to the kitchen. The vegetable garden could wait.

"Kindly put this away so it does not tangle again," she instructed Molly, who was desultorily wiping a plate while looking out the window.

"Yes'm," said Molly, setting the string on the freshly wiped plate before reaching for a saucer.

Bets went off to confer with her mother, not about kissing but about what she should wear to go out driving.

Feeling like a new man after a night's sound sleep, Rob rose, ate a scanty breakfast, downed a small tot of brandy, and repaired to the mews behind the fine house next door. He hired stable space from his neighbor, his own house having no stable and no place to build one. His stable hire would be due in a few days. It was imperative that he pay on time, for his neighbor, a minor viscount, had threatened to turn out his three horses—two carriage horses and a saddle horse—and take possession of his curricle should he be late again.

"Billy!" he yelled. "At once, Billy! No time to waste!"

" 'Ere, gov'nor," said a scrawny, bedraggled ragamuffin appearing from the stable. His clothes, clearly intended for an adult, were tied on with a rope around his waist, and he was barefoot. Hair and face were a uniform gray.

Rob paused to look at the boy. How in heaven's name could he be turned into a smart-looking tiger by afternoon? There was also the curricle, though surely it was in better shape than the boy.

He groaned and wondered whether the pursuit of a wealthy lady was worth all this bother. Bother? Hard work was what it was, hard, unrelenting work, plus a web of deceit that must be carefully spun, with no second chance should he forget himself and reveal his poverty, or trip himself on his own lies. He preferred to think of them as slight stretches of the truth; he did not like to admit he was preparing to tell a whole bundle of lies. Must be getting a conscience at this late date, he thought, and chuckled.

"Let us take a look at the rig," he told Billy. "I am to drive out with a lady this afternoon."

"A *lady?*" said Billy in surprise. "Didn't know you knew any, gov'nor, or I mean, your lordship. Carriage is right up to snuff. I greased the axles just yestiddy."

"And wallowed in the grease, I have no doubt."

"Your lordship! I never!"

"Very well. Let me just see if the squabs are clean, or at least presentable." Rob directed Billy to sit on the tongue while he climbed into the two-wheeled vehicle to examine the seat. It had once been a very fine curricle, but time had not been kind. The cushions were stained with what looked suspiciously like brandy, or was it port? The leather had lost its sheen and was quite worn in places.

Rob climbed down again and thought. "Run in and

ask Mrs. Burket if she has a shawl," he directed Billy. "Maybe we can hide the worst."

Billy ran off joyfully. When he did not return in half an hour, Rob, who had been examining the wheels and found them to his satisfaction, stalked angrily after him.

In the kitchen he found Billy sitting at the table, a plaid shawl around his filthy shoulders, ravenously stuffing down bread with butter and jam while Mrs. Burket, the cook and housekeeper, looked on benignly.

"Poor lad's fair to starve to death," she announced. "Look at 'im! Breath of air'd blow 'im away."

Rob sighed. "So I see," he said. "May I have the shawl?" He pulled it gingerly from Billy's shoulders, taking care not to dislodge any of Billy's dirt with it, and went out alone to the stable. The shawl would cover the worst of the squabs, he decided. He draped it as artfully as he could and moved to talk to his horses while he waited for Billy.

When Billy returned, jam added to his other stains, Rob decided to call on the boy's pride, if he had any.

"You would not wish to appear as you do now when acting as the Earl of Burlingham's tiger, would you?" he asked.

"Oh! Gov—I mean your lordship—*you're* the Earl of Burlingham, ain't you?"

"I am, and you know it."

"Then why'd you say it like that, as if 'e was some other cove?"

Rob grimaced. How to explain to this dirty little guttersnipe? "What I mean is, you would not wish to appear as you are for any earl, or any gentleman about to drive out in his curricle, would you?"

Billy looked down at his clothes. "All I got," he said. "Don't 'ave shoes."

"We shall have to take you in hand. Have you ever had a bath?"

Billy cowered, fear in his face. "Oh, sir! Please, sir! I like to died, that time they made me take a bath in the workhouse! That was afore I come to you. They said I 'ad to be clean or you wouldn't take me. That weren't true, were it? You'd 'ave taken me anyhow, wouldn't you? Oh, sir, the water was so cold, I like to died, I did." His face crumpled at the memory, and Rob was afraid the boy was about to cry. Of course, tears running down his face might give an indication of his true skin tone. . . .

"How about warm water?" Rob said kindly. "With warm water, a bath can be very pleasant. Come. Geordie will help."

"I don't wanna!" Billy yelped. Rob had to take him by the ear as if he were a three-year-old to propel him back to the house and into the kitchen.

The saga of Billy's first warm bath was told and retold for weeks afterward. It took place in the kitchen, close to the source of hot water (a small supply of coal had been obtained), in a large washtub. Mrs. Burket offered to help but her offer was declined to avoid embarrassment to Billy. Geordie did his best, with Rob holding the unwilling Billy, who showed surprising strength in his efforts to get away. An estimated gallon of water got on the floor. The cat, Caterine Purr, tried to lap up some of the spilled water and was roughly jostled when Rob, fighting to hold on to Billy, slipped in the puddle.

Finally Geordie pronounced it done; Billy was lifted from the tub, wrapped in a sheet, and his hair was vigorously rubbed dry. The men left the cleaning up to Mrs. Burket ("Oh, Lor' bless us all," she said in dismay) and took Billy upstairs to ferret out some suitable clothes.

"He should be in some sort of livery," Rob pronounced, looking at the shivering, sheet-wrapped figure. "What can we invent in a hurry?"

"I had first thought to dress him as a blackamoor," said Geordie, "but now that he's clean . . ."

"Why did I not save some of my childhood finery?" Rob mourned. "But it would be in Dorset if I had. Damn."

"That sheet . . ." said Geordie. "Is Mrs. Burket handy with a needle?"

"Who do you think mends your shirts? Of course she is."

"Then," said Geordie, "you shall have a tiger that'll be the talk of the *ton* for years to come. Picture it, your lordship. A tiger attired in a white Grecian toga! The way everything's goin' back to ancient Greece these days, the buildin's with their fancy columns, the ladies' gowns—you'll be settin' a style they'll all want to copy."

"No!" said Billy.

"Yes," said Rob. "Geordie, you get to clean up the bath mess after all. I have other duties for Mrs. Burket."

Despite her own and her mother's indecision, Bets was dressed, ready to go driving, a good hour before Lord Burlingham was due. She had gone through her small stock of gowns in hopes something new and fashionable would magically appear, and then finally settled on a deep ivory challis designed in Empire style. Because of its short, puffed sleeves and low neckline, Lady Stanbourne insisted she should add a tippet to keep warm, but Bets' best tippet, of dark green velvet, would clash with her pale blue bonnet and gloves. Lady Stanbourne offered to lend her own brown fur tippet, but Bets demurred. It would be too warm on a fine spring day, she insisted. After some rather heated argument, Bets, torn between clashing colors and overwarm fur, gave in. Should it prove too warm she could cast off the fur, she decided.

She had an hour to calm herself. Or, more accurately, she had an hour to become even more agitated and unsure. Never, she realized, had she been so bent on making a good impression on a gentleman. Her mother, who reminded her over and over that Burlingham might be her last chance and she should make the most of it, only added to her anxiety. By half after four she was ready to flee to her chamber, bury her head under her pillow, and never come out.

"Tea," said Lady Stanbourne, who was heartily weary

of Bets' constant pacing the length of the sitting room, the smoothing of the gown, the repeated donning and doffing of the gloves. "Tea will steady your nerves." She reached for the bellpull, then remembered and went out into the hall to call to Molly.

By the time Molly arrived with the tea service it lacked only ten minutes to five. Let him be late, Bets prayed. Let him be very late. Let him not come at all.

But promptly at five of the clock, she heard the rap of the lion's-head knocker. Her death knell, she was certain. Her legs refused to support her as she tried to rise, ready to greet her guest. She sank down again and sipped her tea, her eyes intent on her cup, as she heard Molly admit his lordship and escort him to the sitting room.

Molly had forgotten to change her apron.

That was her first thought as the maid opened the sitting room door and stood squarely in front of the opening. " 'E's 'ere," said Molly, finally moving aside to let Burlingham enter.

"Thank you, Molly," said Lady Stanbourne, frowning slightly. "Would you bring brandy for his lordship?"

"Yes'm," said Molly, but Burlingham held up his hand. "Thank you, no," he demurred. "It is such a glorious day, I believe we should waste no time. Are you ready, Lady Elizabeth?"

Bets dragged her glance away from Molly's apron long enough to observe the Earl of Burlingham in all his finery. No fop, this, but still a gentleman of the first stare, his trim body dressed in biscuit pantaloons, a coat of dark blue superfine over a paler blue waistcoat, a neatly tied but not extreme cravat, and shiny black Hessians. He held in his hand a beaver hat that was not, she was pleased to notice, the battered one of the day before. His black hair was neatly combed but one errant lock had fallen in his face. Again she wished to smooth it back.

He smiled. She saw that lapped tooth, the one thing that marred his physical perfection. He was human and flawed, just as she was. She smiled and rose to join him.

Outside, all was not going so well. Five urchins of assorted sizes were standing around the toga-clad Billy, hooting and going into paroxysms of laughter as they pointed at the embarrassed young tiger. Billy, holding the horses as he tried to fend off his tormentors, communicated his unease to the pair, which were stamping and snorting.

"Off with you!" Rob shouted, seizing the whip from its socket in the curricle. He brandished it over the urchins' heads. Two of the smaller ones ran off, but the largest, a boy of about Billy's own age of fourteen, stopped a few feet away and stuck out his tongue at Rob. The other two stood behind him.

"Do you wish to go before the magistrate and explain why you are annoying the Earl of Burlingham?" Rob roared. "You there"—he indicated the largest boy—"you should just fit in beside me; I will take you with me."

The boy looked sullen but did not move.

"I have it!" Rob continued, smiling evilly. "You shall appear before the House of Lords. Perhaps before the Prince Regent himself. You can explain to His Royal Highness why you believe a Grecian toga is not appropriate attire for an aristocrat's tiger. I have no doubt His Royal Highness owns a toga himself."

The boys backed away in alarm. "That there's a toga?" the oldest said in wonder before he gathered his companions and first walked, then broke into a run.

Rob laughed.

"Does the Prince Regent really have a toga?" Bets inquired, looking in concern at the embarrassed Billy.

"I have no idea," said Rob. He nodded at his tiger, helped Bets into the curricle, and walked around the front of his rig, speaking soothing words to his horses before climbing into place. Billy got on behind and they set out for the park.

Bets smiled to herself. Her trepidation at driving out with this notorious gentleman faded away. Take those ragamuffins before the Prince Regent indeed! But the lads had believed him, or given him the benefit of the doubt. She glanced back at Billy, now looking every inch the aristocrat's tiger.

"You know, of course, that togas are Roman, not Greek," she said, "but the idea is excessively clever. I have not seen others dressed so; this is a new fashion, I take it?"

"Yes, very new," Rob said seriously. "You mean to tell me the Greeks did not wear togas? I shall have to track down those young lads again and correct my mistake?" He made as if to turn the horses but the street was too crowded. "Tell me, madam, how you come to know the sartorial habits of the ancient Greeks."

Bets laughed. "One has only to look at the antiquities in the British Museum," she said. "Paintings on vases, carvings, statues—have you never visited the museum, your lordship? 'Tis a fascinating place."

"A friend dragged me there once," he said. "It was about a wager—well, never mind. I confess I did not give my full attention to the Greek costumes or lack of them. Though I do remember a few instances of a marked dearth of covering on some of those statues. Or were they Roman? Scandalous!" He watched her face for her reaction.

Bets grew pink. She could just imagine how a libertine like Burlingham would greet those unclothed statues. He probably found them amusing. She remembered how uncomfortable she had felt on first seeing the statues herself, for some of the male statues lacked even fig leaves! Best to change the subject immediately.

"You are from Dorset, I believe?" she asked. "Tell me of Dorset."

"Ah, Dorset," he said, smoothly guiding his horses into Hyde Park. "What did you wish to know?"

"Where is your home?"

"Dors Court is west of Dorchester, near a village called Steepleton. Have you heard of Maiden Castle? We are not so far from Maiden Castle."

"Oh, yes!" she said, her voice full of excitement. "I have read of Maiden Castle. I remember finding mention of it in a book of my brother's—Godfrey's, that is. I was so disappointed at first to learn it is not a castle at all, but an earthworks. I had visions of a lovely old stone fortress with turrets and arrow slits."

"England has many old stone fortresses with turrets and arrow slits," he said gently, "but nothing like Maiden Castle. I went there often as a boy and tried to imagine what it must have been like when it was built— thousands of years ago, they say. It is near two miles around! Are you interested in such things? I do not mean to prose on about it."

Bets looked up at him, her eyes shining. "To think you have seen it yourself!" she said in awe.

"Many times," he said. "I would like to take you there."

Bets could not say a word. He wanted to take her to Dorset! And they had become acquainted only yesterday! She pulled her mother's fur tippet more closely around her shoulders, for a breeze had sprung up. They were tooling through the park but she barely noticed the spring bulbs in a riot of blooms or heard the song thrushes and blackbirds caroling in the shrubbery. Her mind was absorbed in her companion. What a delightful gentleman he could be when he chose.

Numerous other rigs were out in the park, enjoying the day. Rob greeted several gentlemen and couples. He looked straight ahead, however, and seemed not to see the tulip of fashion who hailed him jovially as he drew near.

"Burlingham!" the tulip, dressed to the nines and driving a spanking new cabriolet, called again. "Missed you last night."

Grim-faced, Rob pretended not to hear. Then it occurred to him that there was no reason to demonstrate his dislike of this man in front of Lady Elizabeth. Rob managed a smile and said, "Sorry, old chap. Was it a good party? I was out of curl."

"You are better now?" asked the tulip, all sympathy.

"We must get together soon. Are you not going to introduce your charming companion?"

Rob seethed inwardly. He looked down at Bets, who appeared interested, if puzzled. "Lady Elizabeth, this is my cousin, George Purtwee. George, may I present Lady Elizabeth Fortescue."

"Charmed," said George. "Fortescue, eh? Are you one of the Devonshire Fortescues, by any chance?" He smiled ingratiatingly.

"They are related only distantly," she said. "My father was Earl of Stanbourne, and we are from Suffolk."

"So happy to make your acquaintance," said George. He caught Rob glowering at him and drove on.

Both occupants of the curricle were silent for a few moments after George's departure. Finally Bets ventured, "I gather you and Mr. Purtwee are not the closest of friends."

Rob set the horses on their way again. "You have the right of it," he said. "Known him all my life and never could come to like him. We are only third cousins. Why should one keep up with third cousins? No doubt I have dozens of third cousins I never even heard of. And hope I never do." He frowned, seemingly lost in thought.

Bets wondered why Burlingham would dislike his cousin so. The man seemed friendly and affable. He had been solicitous over Burlingham's ill health of the night before (most likely a result of Burlingham's overimbibing before visiting Almack's, she thought. Served him right!) George Purtwee, while not classically handsome, was a well-set-up young man, impeccably turned out (perhaps a bit fussy, she had to admit) and apparent owner of a glorious new cabriolet. Perhaps Burlingham did not like him but *she* was pleased to have met him.

"How is it that you and George have not met before?" Rob asked suddenly. He greeted the driver of another carriage, then turned to her, an intent look on his face. "You have, I believe, had several seasons? George is a devoted member of the *ton*. Surely your paths must have crossed."

Bets sought madly for an appropriate answer. She would not tell this aristocratic gentleman that she was in the midst of her fourth season without taking. She dared not explain how comparatively few invitations she and her mother received. Her mother's old friends, those who had known her when the gregarious, popular Earl of Stanbourne was alive, had been generous with their hospitality—to a point. Because Lady Stanbourne rarely entertained in return, the invitations grew fewer.

Lady Stanbourne occasionally murmured apologies—in a small house, she explained, one simply cannot have a proper ball—and hoped that excuse would suffice, but Bets knew otherwise. She had been privy to several conversations in which words such as "clutch-fisted" and "cheeseparing" were mentioned. Others with longer memories recalled that Lady Stanbourne's father had been in trade; it was obvious she did not know how to go on. No one, it seemed, had any idea of their poverty. The Earl of Stanbourne had been wealthy.

"I do not know why we never met," Bets said now. "I may have seen him; I do not remember. I do remember seeing you, however." She smiled, hoping the subject of George Purtwee was closed. It was.

"You remember seeing me?" Rob asked eagerly.

"Oh, yes. Did I not mention it yesterday? You were usually disappearing into someone's card room, or emerging from someone's card room. I do not recall seeing you dance, or even visit the refreshment table. I never saw you at a musicale or at the opera, however. I assume your tastes do not run to music."

"No, they do not . . . Lady Elizabeth, I am flattered that you have watched me so carefully from afar. Surely someone you knew could have introduced us. To think, we might have met ages ago and have become old and dear friends by now! Did I seem such a dreadful fellow? Is that why you forbore to seek an introduction?" He looked disappointed.

Bets laughed and with unaccustomed boldness patted the hand that held the reins so effortlessly. "Was I to fol-

low you into the card room?" she demanded. "Or wait
until you came out, if you ever did? I cannot see you
leaving your game to be hauled out by some acquaintance in order to meet *me*."

Rob looked down at his hands. She had just patted
one. No lady had ever patted his hand before. That
friendly gesture was not at all the kind of touching he
was accustomed to from his mistress of the moment, but
he liked it. What graceful hands Miss Fortescue had,
covered by stylish pale blue gloves. He grasped the hand
nearest him and placed it again over his.

"If you had patted my hand I would have come running," he said. He deftly moved the reins to his other
hand and tucked the hand lying on his into the crook of
his arm, hugging it against his body.

"We shall have to make up for lost time," he announced. "I had no idea what I was missing, spending all
my time in a beastly card room."

The two occupants of the curricle were startled to hear
an odd noise behind them. They had almost forgotten
Billy's presence. He was trying to stifle his merriment.

Chapter Five

Bets and her mother were to be otherwise engaged on Saturday, and Rob shied in horror from trying to see Bets on Sunday for fear he should be invited to attend church services with her. He had no desire to hear an enumeration of man's sins, most of which were his.

Before he left Knightsbridge Terrace he had Bets' acceptance of his request to call on her Monday, and a single small glass of brandy from Lady Stanbourne's stock.

"Yer lordship," Billy asked hesitantly as they drew away, "kin I wear something warmer next time? Who's to know what I got on underneath? A sheet ain't enough!"

"A toga, you mean," said Rob sternly. "Never, never refer to your livery as a sheet, young man, or it will go the worse with you. I shall have to warn you that we are to put forth the impression that we are in funds, plump in the pocket. My future—and yours, too, you jackanapes—depends on winning a wealthy lady such as Miss Elizabeth. What fine lady would have me—me, with my notorious reputation, which as you know is utterly false—if it were known that I live in dun territory?"

"Yes sir, yer lordship," said the tiger, chastened. He brightened. His lordship rarely minded a bit of chaffing. "False, is it, yer lordship? The reputation, I mean. If you say so, sir." He grinned.

"Speak to me like that again and you will wear that toga all next winter *with nothing under it,*" Rob growled. *"Barefoot!"*

That evening Rob was restless. He had not heard a

word from Tom Hazleton. He would have liked to join a
game at White's but he had so many things on his mind
he feared he could not concentrate on the cards, and he
dared not take the chance. Finally, after a meal during
which Mrs. Burket reminded him that the larder was
nearly bare, he met with Geordie to take stock.

When no outsider was present he treated Geordie as
an equal. He had to confide in someone, and while Tom
Hazleton was a close friend, Tom had no money worries
and Rob did not wish to burden his friend with his.
Geordie was a canny Scot who knew the value of a
penny.

"I believe I am gaining Lady Elizabeth's confidence,"
Rob said when he and the servant had settled at the
kitchen table. The cookstove still gave off some heat,
and Rob had decided it would be wasteful to light a fire
elsewhere. Mrs. Burket was putting the kitchen to rights
and listened with half an ear.

"Congratulations, sir," said Geordie, "but that's a long
way from a wedding. What to do meanwhile? You got
enough to last us?"

Rob jumped up and went to the library to find his accounts book. This took some doing, as its customary
hiding place was behind some of the old leather-bound
volumes in his bookcase. It was nearly dark and the
room was dim. Some of the old books fell out as he tried
to reach behind them, landing with a thud and a puff of
dust on the carpet. He noted the back had come off one
of them. He left them where they lay for Mrs. Burket to
rescue another time.

He returned to the kitchen and opened the accounts
books, peering at the entries written in minuscule script.
Another way to save money; the accounts book would
hold more if the writing was small. Still it was hard to
read his own handwriting.

"What do you make of this?" he asked, shoving the
book under Geordie's nose. "There." He pointed to an
entry. "I think that reads four hundred sixty-three

pounds. Seems to be more than enough to live in the lap of luxury for years, does it not?"

Geordie opened his eyes wide in surprise. "Four hundred sixty-three pounds it is, sir," he agreed. "Why, sir, we're in clover!"

"Hardly," said Rob. "Hire of the stable, due in—ah—four days. Feed for the horses. Food for me and the three of you. Candles! Mrs. Burket, how is our candle supply?"

"Low, and you know it. I told you so Tuesday," she said.

"Sorry, slipped my mind. You had best get tallow this time. We will return to beeswax when our fortunes pick up. I fear we shall have to get some clothes for Billy. He complained of the cold in his toga, and of course he cannot wear that sheet thing around here! Though I must say it was a complete success. Now what else—?"

"Coal."

"Firewood."

"Soap, and a new scrub brush."

Amid this recitation Rob felt a furry presence on his foot. Caterine Purr was trying to get a word in.

"She wants us to know she's not best pleased with fish 'eads," Mrs. Burket said fondly. "Nasty things! The bones could get stuck in her throat. A nice bit of meat for the cat now and then wouldn't come amiss."

"True," Rob agreed. "If we are to have a cat we must be prepared to feed her."

"By all means," said Geordie. "We may starve, but Miss Purr must have her dainties." He grimaced.

"Now, Geordie," Rob remonstrated. He knew Geordie only tolerated the creature.

"Another thing—the spout come off the china teapot," Mrs. Burket reported. "They say you can 'ave 'em mended so's you can 'ardly tell. I don't know, myself. What do you think, sir?"

"Find out," said Rob. "I do not expect to be serving tea to the *ton*. We can live with it. What else?"

"Your neckcloths, sir," said Geordie. "You have plenty, but they're getting a wee bit frayed."

"Let me see them," Rob directed. "Perhaps they can be turned. And what about that hat I sat on? Is it hopeless? Thank God it was not my best hat."

"Hopeless, sir," Geordie reported morosely. "All cock-a-hoop. Bad grass stains."

"Give it to Billy," said Rob. "He can set another new fashion."

"That'll keep his feet warm," Geordie mumbled under his breath.

"What did you say? His feet? Lord, we shall have to get him some shoes, I suppose, as well as breeches and a shirt. And stockings! Have you no old stockings you could pass on, Geordie?"

"You seen my stockings lately, sir? Holes so big, my feet go right through 'em."

Rob slapped the accounts book closed and looked at his two servants. It is a wonder they elect to stay, he thought.

"You see where a large part of that four hundred sixty-three pounds must go," he said. "Heaven knows how long we can go on. I must get my hands on some money! Damn. I did not even take into account what I already owe the tradesmen. Or that fool McNally at the Friend at Hand. They shall have to wait."

"Nothing to be had from your father?" Geordie inquired.

"You know better than that!"

"Sorry, sir. I hoped . . ."

"Are you prepared to live on bread and cabbage? We may come to it." Rob slumped in his chair.

"Oh, sir!" Mrs. Burket spoke up. "Did I tell you bread has gone up again? Gettin' terrible dear, it is. Reminds me of '95; you remember, sir? That were the year the price of bread doubled."

"No," said Rob in a tired voice. "Then I was too young to care."

* * *

The Fortescue ladies were to go to dinner at the Welborns' Saturday evening, with a musical performance
promised afterward. Bets planned to spend much of the
day altering the trimmings on a dress of the year before
in hopes of making it look new. She was in a day gown,
plying her needle and wishing she were driving out with
the Earl of Burlingham instead of going to the Welborns'
when Molly announced that she had callers, not one but
two!

"Two gentlemen, they be," Molly reported as she
stood in the doorway of Bets' chamber. She eyed the
pale yellow muslin lying in Bets' lap. "Oh, miss! You're
takin' off them rosebuds? Kin I 'ave 'em? They'd be a
treat on me bonnet."

"Perhaps," said Bets, annoyed. "Who are the gentlemen? Surely they presented cards? Oh, dear, I must
change gowns. I was not expecting anyone."

"They 'ad cards all right. Left 'em in the tray, I did,
just like you told me to."

"No! Cards go in the tray if we are not home! Mama
has told you and told you, Molly. I suppose I must receive them even if I have no idea who they are. Where is
Mama?"

"Out in the back garden, lookin' for weeds."

"Is she dressed?"

"O' course! I never seen her ladyship 'less she was
dressed! Why, think of the scandal."

Bets groaned, told Molly to show the gentlemen into
the sitting room, dumped the yellow gown unceremoni-
ously on her bed, and changed quickly into a three-year-
old green gown that was now too loose. A glance at the
looking glass and she frowned at her hair, untidy after
her change of gown. Hardly time to take it down and put
it up again, so she smoothed it as well as she could and
went down to the sitting room.

Her callers were Arthur Percival and George Purtwee.
Together? What did this mean?

Percival lost no time in explaining. After the customary greetings had been exchanged and the visitors invited to sit, Percival mentioned that they had not come together, but had arrived at the same time by happenstance.

"I must apologize for the accident the other day," he said. "Oh, Lady Elizabeth, I vow I shall never drive a phaeton again! You could have been badly hurt! Or killed! The horses could have run off! The phaeton could have been damaged, and my brother would have had my head! Even with him so poorly, he still takes an interest in his horses. Why, I will never forget how he—"

"Stop! Stop!" Bets held up her hands. Evidently Mr. Percival could talk—and talk and talk—about subjects other than the weather when he was rattled. "I was not injured, only shaken, as you must have known when you saw me depart on my own two feet. You are forgiven, Mr. Percival, but I do not believe I should go driving with you again."

George Purtwee listened to this exchange with interest. He had not said a word since greeting Bets.

"I do not blame you, dear lady," said Percival. "In any case, the opportunity is not likely to arise again. My brother has decreed . . . Let us say he is not in charity with me at the moment. I wished to come and offer my apologies earlier, but he . . ."

"I am sure he did," said Bets, stifling a giggle. "Let us say no more about it."

Percival seemed glad to stop. He sat back and looked at Purtwee as if willing him to pick up the conversation.

Purtwee sat quietly and smiled.

"Where are my manners?" Bets said into the silence. "Will you gentlemen take some refreshment?"

Both protested halfheartedly, but were easily overruled. Bets excused herself and left the room to find Molly. When she returned she found the two visitors looking at each other uneasily.

"I am happy to see you, Mr. Purtwee," she said. "I was mentioning you to my mother only last night. Such a handsome cabriolet you drive!"

That did not sit well with Arthur Percival. He seemed touchy on the subject of carriages.

"Thank you," Purtwee replied graciously. "I do enjoy a good rig. Perhaps you would go driving with me one day."

The wretch! Bets looked from one gentleman to the other. Percival looked forlorn and Purtwee, superior.

"Perhaps," she said. "Ah, here are the refreshments. Would you take a glass of wine?" She sighed in relief.

Arthur downed his wine in one gulp and announced he must be off. Bets firmly ushered him out before he had a chance to arrange another outing, with or without horses. She returned to the sitting room, where Purtwee waited.

"I did not wish to discuss it with that jinglebrains in the room, but might I ask just what happened in this 'accident' he spoke of?" he said. He turned a warm smile toward her and leaned forward for her answer.

Bets gave him the barest outline of the accident, assuring him she had not been injured. She made light of the entire incident.

"Do you mean to say he *left you to walk home alone* while he picked himself up and caught his horses?" Purtwee demanded in amazement. "The utter bounder! The unmitigated cad! I cannot believe it."

"Ah—no." Should she bring in Burlingham's name? Did she want this man whom Burlingham disliked to know how she and Burlingham had met? "A friend happened by," she said lamely.

"How very fortunate. Just happened by, did he? Or she? I trust you were driven home in a less dangerous vehicle than Percival's? His brother is a dab hand with the ribbons, I happen to know, but Arthur—you found out how he drives, did you not?"

"I did indeed. I understand the brother is ill. Do you know whether it is serious?"

"Why not ask Arthur? How should I know? You are avoiding the question, my lady. How did you get home?"

It was none of Purtwee's business. Why was he so curious? Bets resolved she would not be intimidated. "I was escorted safely," she said.

"Surely not by my esteemed cousin Burlingham?" he persisted.

Bets hesitated.

Purtwee hitched his chair closer and tried to look her in the eye, but her head was down as she stared at her lap. "It must have been Burlingham!" he said gleefully. "I thought so! You two looked thick as thieves when I met you in the park yesterday. Please do not tell me you have a *tendre* for him. Please do not say you are accepting his addresses and no others. If that were the case I should not be able to persuade you to drive out with me in the cabriolet you admire. Now that you have freed yourself of Percival you need not consider his feelings any longer." He looked beseechingly at Bets, who finally raised her head.

"I believe I should be able to go for a drive with you," she said. She had not confirmed Purtwee's guess about Burlingham's escorting her home. She was sorry he had guessed, but what, really, did it matter? Resolutely she fixed her thoughts on that spanking new cabriolet.

"I am delighted," said Purtwee, reaching for her hand and kissing its back. She snatched it away. "Perhaps Monday?"

At this point Lady Stanbourne arrived, out of breath and showing signs of having dressed too hurriedly.

"Molly said we had guests?" she said, looking around in perplexity for a gentleman other than the one who bounded to his feet to greet her.

"It was only Mr. Percival," her daughter reported. "He has gone. Mama, may I present Mr. George Purtwee? Mr. Purtwee, this is my mother, Dowager Countess of Stanbourne."

"Charmed," said Purtwee, bowing over her hand. "How fortunate I am to meet two such lovely ladies in one visit!" He looked appreciatively at Lady Stanbourne. Did he notice that the two top buttons of her bodice were

in the wrong buttonholes? Bets hoped not. To her the resulting puckers stood out like signal flags.

"I was just inviting Lady Elizabeth to drive out with
me on Monday," said Purtwee with a smile. Bets noted
that his teeth were straight, though small and somewhat
far apart. She decided she preferred lapped teeth.

Lady Stanbourne did not give her daughter time to answer. "How kind of you!" she said. "I am sure Bets
would be delighted." She turned to Bets, waiting for her
agreement.

"No!" said Bets. "I mean, I regret I have a previous
engagement. Perhaps later in the week?"

"Tuesday?" Purtwee asked.

"Tuesday it shall be."

Purtwee drained his wineglass, thanked his hostesses,
and departed. The door had hardly shut behind him before Lady Stanbourne pushed Bets back into the sitting
room to answer all her questions.

"Why did you refuse to drive out with him on Monday? Do you think he is truly interested in you? What
was Arthur Percival here for? Did they come together?
Why would they come together? Did Mr. Percival apologize for that dreadful accident? Do you think he would
have recompensed you for the damage to your gown,
had you asked? That gown is beyond hope, I fear."

When her mother eventually paused for breath, Bets
undertook to explain the two gentlemen's visit. She also
reminded Lady Stanbourne that she had already agreed
to see the Earl of Burlingham on Monday.

"Oh, yes, Burlingham . . ." said Lady Stanbourne.
"Yes, I suppose you must honor your commitment. But
Bets, dear! This George Purtwee—his father is a wealthy
baron! He is next in line! Had I only thought of him earlier . . . His reputation, so far as I know, is excellent. He
is said to do nothing to excess—not gambling, or wenching, or drinking . . . Look at this." She indicated the wine
bottle on the tray nearby. "He must have taken but one
glass! Not like Burlingham, who bid fair to finish a bot-

tle at a single sitting. My dear, you would do well to en-
courage Mr. Purtwee."

"He is Burlingham's cousin, you know," said Bets, ir-
ritated at this about-face on her mother's part. "They are
not on the best of terms."

"So?" said her mother.

As soon as she could, Bets returned to her chamber to
finish the alterations on her yellow gown. Having
mended a torn seam and carefully snipped off all the silk
rosebuds, she sat staring into space.

From having no gentleman admirers worthy of the
name (she refused to consider Arthur Percival), within
the space of a few days she now had two she believed
worth considering. Her lips curved into a smile as she
savored that. The fact that they disliked each other—or
was it one-sided, with only Burlingham disliking
Purtwee?—could prove amusing if she handled the situation adroitly. Not that she had any experience pitting
one man against another! She rather favored Burlingham, but as her mother had pointed out, Purtwee was no
wild young buck bent on breaking every accepted stan-
dard of behavior. Purtwee was an exquisite in his fine
clothes and drove a spanking cabriolet. On the other
hand, Burlingham's curricle was perfectly acceptable.
She remembered with a warm rush how he had evidently
thought ahead of her comfort and draped a tartan shawl
over the seat for extra softness and warmth. How
thoughtful he was! And how original, to have his tiger
dressed in a toga!

She realized, however, that she did not yet know
Purtwee well enough to know how thoughtful or original
he might be. He might well put Burlingham in the shade
in that and many other facets of his nature. Time would
tell.

Bets gathered up the silk rosebuds and stored them in
a drawer of the highboy for some future use, if she did
not give them to Molly. She began measuring and cut-
ting lengths of pale green riband to fashion into knots for

trimming the sleeves and neckline of her yellow gown. She rather liked the effect; it seemed springlike.

It proved an acceptable costume for dinner at the Welborns'; at least no one looked at it askance. Neither of her two gentlemen admirers was present, and she considered it a wasted evening except for the excellent meal.

Chapter Six

Gad! This pursuit of an heiress certainly played havoc with one's drinking and carousing, Rob decided glumly on Monday morning. His need to keep up a pretense of wealth ruled out long sessions at the gaming tables. Should he lose, as he did oftener than he liked, he would incur debts of honor that would have to be paid. He knew well how to cheat but it would never do to run the risk of discovery; his reputation would sink lower than it was already. Other creditors could be stalled indefinitely; they would not sue a member of the nobility. Even so, he did not wish to be known as a gentleman deep in dun territory. The mamas and papas of the young ladies on the marriage mart might learn the true state of his financial affairs, and would not, he knew, look kindly on the prospect of having to pay off his debts. That certainly included the family of Bets Fortescue. He wondered just who held the reins on her wealth. Her mother? He thought it unlikely. Probably that older half brother of hers, who was now the Earl of Stanbourne. Stanbourne kept to his estate in Suffolk and little was known of him in London.

Rob stared out the window of his tiny bedchamber. The sun had not been up more than an hour or two; what an ungodly hour for a gentleman to rise from his bed! Today it could not be helped. He opened his chamber door and yelled into the passage.

"Geordie! Tea! And send up Mrs. Burket, would you?"

He heard no reply. The house was silent.

He walked barefoot to the head of the stairs. "Geordie!" he roared.

Eventually Mrs. Burket, not Geordie, appeared, pushing her gray hair back from her face as she smoothed her apron with the other hand. "Oh, sir, Geordie's down at the stable for Billy," she said. "Wants to send him after the coal merchant to deliver us a load. What was it you wanted, sir?"

"Tea," said Rob, lowering his voice. "Then I wanted to talk to you about some clothes for Billy. Would you take him along and outfit him? You would know where to go."

"Beggin' your pardon, sir, but the lad'd feel better if he went with Geordie," said Mrs. Burket. "He's fourteen, sir! He don't want a woman to be choosin' his bits and pieces. 'Sides, I got a stew started for dinner and I must be 'ere to put in the vegetables. You think Geordie'd know about vegetables? Ha!"

"Very well. Send Geordie up when he comes in. Tea, Mrs. Burket! Is there tea?"

"Right away, sir." Mrs. Burket disappeared toward the kitchen and soon returned with a cup. Rob went down the stairs to accept it and carried it back to his chamber, spilling only a very little and scalding his fingers only minimally. He cursed more heartily than the occasion called for.

By the time Rob had conferred with Geordie and Billy had returned from the coal merchant's, the morning was well advanced. Rob immediately sent the man and boy out with a few coins and instructions to outfit the boy as quickly and cheaply as possible; he needed Billy to act as tiger when he called on Miss Fortescue.

"I don't 'ave to wear that toga thing, then?" Billy asked, pleased.

"It will go over your new clothes," Rob explained. "You said you wished something warm underneath, remember?"

"Yessir," said Billy. His face fell, but he went off with

Geordie without demur. The prospect of new clothes of his very own obviously excited him.

Rob fidgeted until their return. Should he take Lady Elizabeth out driving again, or merely call at her home? What other entertainments could he offer her that would not cost money? Damn, everything cost money. He repaired to his library to go over the invitations at hand. A musicale. A rout. Why would anyone bother to invite him to such affairs? He never went. The only ball was that of Lady Donaldson's for her daughter Faith, more than a week away. Would Lady Elizabeth be there? He would have to ask her. These invitations had arrived before the incident at Almack's. Nothing had come since. Word obviously had got around.

Rob had himself dressed, his neckcloth nicely tied though without the intricacies Geordie could accomplish, by early afternoon. Geordie and Billy had not returned. Always impatient, Rob cursed as he paced his library. The horses must be harnessed and put to the curricle; he dared not risk soiling his good clothes to do it himself. He was certain to be woefully late for his call on Lady Elizabeth.

A drink! He would have a drink and calm himself.

He had the glass out and the decanter in hand, ready to pour, when he stopped. It occurred to him that should he have one, he would want two. If Geordie and Billy did not return, he would be tempted to have three. He would enter the little house in Knightsbridge Terrace late, smelling of brandy, and what effect would that create? Certainly not the one he wished. He recalled the slight frown on Lady Stanbourne's face when she entered her sitting room to find the level in the brandy bottle the maid had brought him suspiciously low. It would seem Lady Stanbourne disapproved of drink, or at least an excess of drink.

He decided the brandy would have to wait.

In another hour Geordie and Billy returned, cheerful and full of a tale of going from one stall to the next of secondhand clothes sellers. Finding items that did not hang loosely on Billy's slight frame had been an adventure, Geordie reported. He showed off their finds on the proud Billy: a rusty black coat over a multicolor striped shirt, fawn breeches that had once been good quality but were now darned at the knees, black stockings, and a pair of badly scuffed boots.

"Had to buy stockings new," Geordie reported. "Sorry, sir."

Billy smiled a huge, satisfied smile. "Never 'ad no stockins before," he admitted. "Just look at 'em!" He thrust out a scrawny leg.

"You are bang up to the mark, my boy," said Rob, amused. "Now cover that finery with your toga and you, Geordie, help him hitch up the curricle. I am late! Must not keep Lady Elizabeth waiting! Time is wasting!" He swept the pair out of the room and vaulted up the stairs to check his appearance in the looking glass. His hair, as usual, was disheveled. He tried to comb an unruly lock out of his face and gave up. He would have to do. He ran down the stairs again, whistling.

The Earl of Burlingham had not named the precise hour when he expected to call, so Bets was prepared to receive him long before he arrived. No nervous tremors assailed her today. Her mood swung between impatience and eagerness. Molly had been thoroughly drilled on proper behavior. Water for tea was simmering on the back of the stove, should the earl accept tea rather than brandy (vain hope, she was sure); the brandy bottle had been dusted off and put ready to hand, with a glass; biscuits were artfully arranged (to appear more plentiful than they were) on a plate bedecked with greenery; Bets herself was attired in a becoming pale green carriage gown. She made numerous trips to the sitting room window to keep abreast of any changes in the weather so she would know whether a tippet or cloak was called for. She had just decided on a cloak when her caller arrived.

Not trusting Molly, she opened the door herself to his knock.

"Please come in," she said at the same time he said, "Sorry to be so late." They both laughed in confusion as he made a slight bow. Molly, in a clean apron, hurried to take his hat, and Bets led him into the sitting room, where Lady Stanbourne sat reading.

"Good afternoon, your lordship," Lady Stanbourne greeted him and laid her book aside. "May I offer you some refreshment?"

"Not at the moment," Rob answered, sinking into a chair next to Lady Stanbourne. "May I know what you are reading? I do not wish to interrupt your story."

Lady Stanbourne blushed a delicate pink as she held up the volume. "Thucydides," she said. "Greek, you know, but in English translation. All the ladies' fashions are Grecian these days, and I thought I might get some ideas for new gowns. I own I have not found anything useful yet." She moved to set the book down again on the table next to her when something slipped out. Rob quickly bent to retrieve it.

Lady Stanbourne's blush deepened to dark red. "Oh, dear me," she gasped.

Rob glanced at the slim volume that had been hidden inside the larger book. *Agatha, A Sad Tale*, by A Lady, it said on the flyleaf. He passed it to Lady Stanbourne without comment.

"I just could not stomach another page of Thucydides," she admitted in embarrassment. "Not that I am not trying. Please believe me! But do you know, he neglects ladies' fashions quite shamefully. I find I must rise for air now and then."

"I give you full credit even for trying, my lady," Rob said, and smiled at her in friendly fashion. "I fear I did not take to old Thucydides myself in university." He turned to Bets. "Would you care to go for a drive, Lady Elizabeth? It is a bright day if somewhat chill. Should you wrap up warmly I am certain you would be comfortable."

"Oh, yes, that would be lovely," Bets agreed. She was struck anew at the earl's thoughtfulness. He had smoothed over her mother's embarrassment and given her time to recover by turning his attention to Bets. "Would you not take some refreshment before we leave?"

"Perhaps when we return," he said. "Shall we go?"

Bets fetched her cloak and bonnet, Rob picked up his hat in the hall where Molly had left it, and they repaired to his curricle. Bets greeted Billy and told him what a splendid figure he made, bringing wide grins from the tiger as he adjusted his toga.

Once they were headed toward Hyde Park, Rob confided his surprise that Lady Stanbourne would be trying to read Thucydides.

"Surely she would not expect to find a treatise on ladies' fashions in that book!" he said. "The old historians paid no attention to such things."

"I know," she said.

"You do?"

"Of course."

"Do not tell me *you* have read Thucydides?" He frowned.

"Some."

"In *Greek?*"

"Alas, no. Only in English. In fact, in that very book."

"My God," said Rob. He was silent for the space of a minute.

"It was Papa's book," she explained after settling herself more comfortably against the plaid shawl on the curricle seat. "I like to read. Do you not like to read? I have read most of Papa's books. It is so much more convenient to pull a book off the library shelf than to make a journey to the circulating library." And cheaper, too, she thought.

"My God," he said again. "Do I like to read? I hardly know. I never seem to have time. I do not believe I have opened a book since I left Cambridge."

"Oh, but you are missing so much!" Bets grew quite excited. "Then you will never know the heart-wrenching tale of Romeo and Juliet, or laugh at Puck, or . . ."

"Or weep over the sad tale of Agatha?"

"*That* was not among Papa's books," she said indignantly. "Sir, you are joshing me."

"I meant no offense," he said. "You have every right to weep over Agatha if you wish. One must leaven one's Shakespeare with a bit of fluff now and then, I am sure. Please forgive me."

She smiled, suddenly cheerful again. "Shall I tell you what happened to Agatha?" she asked impishly. "It seems there was this devilish duke . . ."

"Spare me," he implored, rolling his eyes heavenward.

"I could lend it to you once Mama has finished, if you like. It is very easy to read—large type, too—if you would wish to work gradually into Shakespeare and Jonson and Plato and the others." She looked at him appealingly.

"Thank you, no. Perhaps some other time," he said. She was afraid he would laugh at her, but his face was sober. "And here we are in the park. Would you care to walk for a bit? Billy can watch the curricle."

"Splendid," she said. "One needs the exercise."

He helped her down, his gloved hands grasping hers. She almost wished he would never let go. Then he tucked her arm into his and she found it as pleasant as she had the day he had escorted her home after the accident—was it only last week?

They had strolled a few yards away from the carriage path when a loud hail from behind stopped them. Rob turned, his arm still firmly holding Bets' arm, only to see George Purtwee in his shiny new cabriolet. He was alone. George waved madly and beckoned them over.

"Damn," said Rob under his breath.

"Thought I saw you ahead of me," George said in evident satisfaction. "Your rig break down? Poor old cattle too weary to go any farther? I would take you up but I have seat space for only one other. Lady Elizabeth, may I come to your rescue?"

Bets laughed. "I have no need of rescue," she said.

"Please do not jump to such a ridiculous conclusion. As you can see, his lordship's curricle is right as rain." She nodded toward Billy, who was standing by the horses, his toga billowing in the breeze despite his frantic efforts to hold it down. "We are merely going for a walk. Getting healthful exercise."

George frowned. Burlingham, she noted, was just short of frothing at the mouth. What was it with these two? She was not at all pleased with the unconscionable remarks Mr. Purtwee had made to the earl, obviously expecting to anger him.

"Dear me, my mistake," said George, his voice dripping with honey. "I am so sorry. Nice rig you have there, cousin. Is that tiger a female? Her gown is quite up to the mark, is it not?"

"We will bid you adieu before I forget myself and plant you one," said Rob, holding himself under tight control. He turned abruptly and led Bets away from George and his taunts.

Bets could feel his rage. He held her arm so tightly it ached, and his jaw was clenched. He stared straight ahead and pulled her along as if he were a soldier marching with a reluctant captive.

"I confess I do not understand," she ventured when they had marched in a straight line over grass, through flower beds, and almost into a clump of bushes. She halted him with difficulty by a giant oak. "Do stop, sir! We are far away from Mr. Purtwee."

Rob seemed to come out of a trance. He rubbed his head and looked at her as if he had never seen her before.

"Why cannot that blasted creature leave me alone? What have I done to deserve this?" he demanded.

"I have no idea," she answered. "Does this happen often?"

Rob looked down, lost in thought again. When he raised his head to look at her, she saw pain and determination in his eyes. He placed his hands gently on her shoulders.

"I have not fought with George since we were children," he said slowly, "but recently he seems to have taken me in strong dislike. I have no idea why. May I tell you about it? I would prefer that it not get out, but . . ."

"Please do!" said Bets. "Shall we walk again? But more slowly, please."

"Of course," he said, and placed her arm once again in his. They ambled now, skirting the flower beds and shrubs.

"Perhaps you have heard of my supposed faux pas of last week at Almack's," he began. "Drat!"

"I—I did hear something of it," she admitted. "I could not believe it of you."

"Thank you! But we had not met then. If you are at all acquainted with my reputation I am surprised you could not believe it. Everyone else seems to take it as fact." He studied her face.

"I mean, once we had met I could not believe it," she amended.

"Why not?"

What could she say? That he was charming, and polite, and gentle, and thoughtful, and she did not think it would be at all difficult to fall in love with him? Instead she said, "You did not seem to be the kind of gentleman who would do such a thing."

"I thank you," he said gravely. "In truth I remember none of it. I recall having a drink at the Friend at Hand and getting into my curricle to drive to Almack's, where I was to meet a good friend. The next I knew it was the morning after and I was in my bed at home.

"I have a strong suspicion that I was drugged and coerced. Led? Pushed? to the presence of Mrs. Drummond Burrell, where I collapsed. My friend is helping me ferret out the truth, but I am beginning to believe George Purtwee is behind it. He is the only person I can think of who has taken me in acute dislike recently. Damn the man! What have I ever done to him?"

Bets regretted that she had agreed to go driving with George Purtwee the next day. After Burlingham's tale

how could she be civil to Mr. Purtwee? Then she saw
what she must do.

"I am to drive out with Mr. Purtwee tomorrow," she
said. At Rob's gasp, she added quickly, "Perhaps I can
learn something useful. Will you allow me to help you?"

"You must not think of it," he said immediately. "If he
believes you and I are—are close friends, shall we say, it
could go the worse for you. He certainly would not tell
you anything."

Bets pulled her arm from his and stopped dead. She
turned to face him, her stance full of purpose, her brown
eyes looking into his.

"I have not lived through four seasons for nothing,"
she said firmly. "It is well known throughout the *ton* that
I *have* no 'close friends' of the opposite sex. The few
that would have me, I would not have. I tell you this in
all truth. It is an admission I do not like to make, but I
wish you to understand. If I cannot lull Mr. Purtwee into
the belief that you are merely one more soon-to-be-rejected suitor, I vow I will go happily on the shelf and become a nursemaid to my half brother's brood of
children."

Rob's expression mirrored his amazement. He said
softly, "Am I?"

"Are you what?"

"Am I one more soon-to-be-rejected suitor?"

Bets' face turned scarlet. "Not quite yet," she said.

"Very well," said Rob, all businesslike now. "I will
trust you to go driving with George. Promise to take
care."

Bets nodded and glanced around to see how far they
had come. The curricle was nowhere in sight.

"Had we not best return to your carriage?" she asked.
"I fear it is growing late."

"Of course. Come along." On their way back Rob remembered to ask whether she expected to attend Lady
Donaldson's ball the following week, and learned that
she did. He offered to escort her and her mother, and she
accepted.

"I hope to see you again before that," he said. "It is a week away!"

"But if we are seen too much together, word will reach your cousin and he will refuse to believe that—that—"

"That I am a soon-to-be-rejected suitor," he finished for her and laughed. "Perhaps you are right. If I am to get to the bottom of this Almack's incident I have much to do and had best go to ground for a few days, anyhow. If we do not meet in the meantime, then, I will see you the night of the Donaldsons' ball."

When the curricle had carried them back to Knightsbridge Terrace, Rob agreed to come in for a few minutes. He wished to pick Lady Stanbourne's brains.

"Tea will do nicely," he told his hostess when she offered him a choice. When it came, carried by a careful and self-conscious Molly, he accepted it and dug into the plate of biscuits with evident enjoyment. Lady Stanbourne and her daughter watched the biscuits disappear one by one. Each lady took one for herself before it was too late.

"It is plain that you have heard the tale of my supposed conduct at Almack's last week," Rob said without preamble, reaching for another biscuit. "I have no knowledge of what happened, but I cannot believe I would have made the remark to Mrs. Drummond Burrell that was attributed to me. Why, I have only the slightest acquaintance with the lady! I doubt I have ever said anything more than 'Good evening' to her. Were you there, ma'am?" He looked at Lady Stanbourne. "Or where did you hear of it? Not fourth or fifth hand, I hope."

It was clear Lady Stanbourne was happy to hear that there might be some doubt about Burlingham's guilt. She brightened, and set down her teacup.

"No, I was not there; I got the story from a friend," she said. "The friend saw it—you—but said she was too far away to hear. She got the report of what you said from her husband, who got it from—let me see. Who was it, Bets?"

"You did not tell me," said Bets. "Think, Mama!"

"I am trying to!" her mother said, distraught. "You know how the very thing you want is on the tip of your tongue, but it refuses to come out? I must be getting old. I know I am getting old! Oh, dear. Oh, dear!" She rubbed her forehead as if that would force her brain to release the name she wanted.

"You are not getting old, Mama," Bets hastened to reassure her. "We will enjoy our tea and perhaps it will come to you."

"I know!" said Lady Stanbourne, brightening. "I shall make it a point to ask Lady Staf— . . . to ask my friend. She will tell me. Should I go now?" She started to rise as if to rush off that instant.

"Oh, no, my lady," said Rob. "Your friend would wonder at your sudden interest. I do not wish to create a stir. Perhaps next time you happen to meet her you could mention it in passing. Meanwhile the name may come to you. If I just had a name . . . Then I would have to learn who told that person, and who told *that* person . . . This investigation will take some time."

"I can see that, my boy," Lady Stanbourne agreed. "Such a shame. Believe me, I shall think on it!"

The teapot now empty, the biscuit plate reduced to a border of greenery and a few crumbs, Rob took his leave.

Bets was having a particularly pleasant dream—she was riding in a shiny new cabriolet, but her companion was the Earl of Burlingham, who told her repeatedly that he refused to become a soon-to-be-rejected suitor— when her name was called.

"Wha-a-at?" she said groggily. Her mother's face loomed above her in the light of a single candle. "Is it morning already?"

"Mercy, no! Were you asleep? It is hardly eleven. I was just preparing for bed when I thought of it! I thought of it!" Her mother's joyous voice rang out in the night-time silence. "Bets, it came to me at last!"

"What did?" Bets roused and rubbed her eyes. The lovely dream was all but gone, vanished in the mists.

"What Amelia said. Remember, I told you she got it from Rupert, and you made an unkind remark about Rupert. Why, I do not know; Rupert has always been most courteous to us both."

Bets was wide awake now. She sat bolt upright and pulled her mother down beside her on the bed.

"It was not Rupert," she said decisively. "I remember about Rupert. He heard it from someone else. Mama! Please stop prosing on about Rupert and tell me before you forget again. *Where did Rupert hear it?*"

"Amelia said . . . Let me think. She said something to the effect that Rupert heard it from Lord Purtwee, or it might have been from his son George. One or the other, or perhaps both of them, happened to be standing near Mrs. Drummond Burrell and heard the entire thing. So there! And now, my dear, I fear we must think carefully about believing Burlingham's innocence. I have every confidence in Lord Purtwee's integrity. He would never invent such a tale out of whole cloth! And do not forget, Amelia saw Burlingham fall in a drunken heap with her own eyes."

Bets dismissed her mother's defense of Lord Purtwee as not worth considering. "I knew it!" she cried. "I knew it! George Purtwee, of course! That snake!"

Lady Stanbourne was taken aback. "Snake? But I thought you were to go driving with him tomorrow. He is a most exemplary gentleman. You have no cause to call him a snake! Better call Burlingham a snake! I do not trust him, Bets. He should at least have the courage to admit his grievous mistake at Almack's and try to atone, rather than this pretense of knowing nothing about it. Ha! Drunken fool, that is what he was." She sniffed.

Bets decided against thrashing out the pros and cons of Burlingham versus George Purtwee at such an hour. She announced she was going back to sleep and they could sort it out in the morning.

She hoped her pleasant dream would resume but it did not.

Chapter Seven

"So what did you learn from Tessie?" Rob asked Tom Hazleton. They were seated in Rob's library sharing a decanter of brandy from the next-to-the-last cask of Rob's supply.

"Clever creature, that Tessie," said Hazleton. "She makes you pay for every word from that over-wide mouth of hers. I have spent near two pounds on her and learned precious little."

"Are you sure you are not prolonging this—this investigation so you may spend more time in the Friend at Hand with a comely wench?"

Rob knew Hazleton's habits. They were much like his own—or rather, like his own had been before he set out in search of a wealthy wife. He poured himself another tot of brandy. It was a hard life when one had to forgo the brandy in public, and he disliked drinking alone. Thank heaven Tom had arrived.

Hazleton laughed. "Perhaps in other circumstances," he said. "Now I am engaged in a serious endeavor for a friend wrongly accused. You still believe you were wrongly accused?"

"Damn you," said Rob. "You doubt me? Come on, tell me what Tessie had to say for your two pounds."

Tom crossed his legs and stared at the toes of his boots. "I have had to guess at what she meant," he said slowly. "It was not easy, having a conversation with her. McNally keeps her busy, you know. She was constantly having to leap up and get another beer for some lowlife. For God's sake, man, whatever possessed you to frequent that place? I swear, the most genteel of the customers was a sweep just come out of somebody's chimney! Aside from myself, of course."

"Yes, yes," said Rob impatiently. "What did you learn?"

Hazleton recrossed his legs and sipped his brandy. "After much sweet talk on my part," he said with a leer, "I learned that the paltry amount I was spending on her was nothing to what she had earned 'not long back'— that is what she said, 'not long back'—when a swell whose name she did not reveal paid her to 'help him out with a little matter.' 'A little matter?' I asked her nicely, and she bridled. I had to give her another shilling 'to buy yourself something pretty—you deserve something pretty,' I said—to find out what the 'little matter' could be. All I found out was that she had helped the swell get back at someone who had pigeoned the swell out of something. Is that any help?"

Rob groaned. "Not much," he said. "Did she give you any hint of who the swell might be?"

"Said she did not know," Tom reported. "I gave her a hum about how he might be a friend of mine and I would like to help him, but I am not sure she bought it. She said she had never seen him before."

Rob rose and absentmindedly straightened the row of books on an upper shelf of his bookcase. "Did she describe him?"

"I asked what he looked like and she said he was 'a reg'lar gentleman.' Whatever that means. Then I asked whether he had indicated he wanted to use her services again. She said no. So then I asked whether she was acquainted with the 'someone' who had cheated the swell. 'Oh, yes!' she said. 'He comes in here reg'lar.' I asked his name. She refused to give it to me. I asked whether he was in the Friend at Hand at the moment. She looked around and said he had not been in, to her knowledge, since 'the night we dru . . .' She stopped herself, but I do believe she was about to say 'drugged.' Does that help?"

"Damn!" said Rob. "I knew it, I knew it! You have

done well indeed, my friend. How many evenings did this require?"

"Three," said Hazleton casually. "Or was it four? One loses count when one is enjoying oneself. Of course I was forced to consume several pints of ale each evening. That, plus what I laid out for Tessie's confidence, means you owe me—let me see—say four pounds?"

"You shall have it the moment my ship comes in," Rob promised, slapping his friend on the back. "Meanwhile, drink up. I would not like to see this brandy spoil."

"Nor would I. Tell me, how is the pursuit of your 'ship'? Has she mothered you to death?"

Rob forgot the Almack's incident for a moment to turn his thoughts to Lady Elizabeth. He was beginning to feel an utter cad for the game he was playing with her. He knew he was a cad; had never worried about it, but he rather liked Lady Elizabeth. She did not deserve such treatment.

And it was true. He had been drugged, as he had suspected. If only Tessie had at least described the 'swell.' He had nothing to prove George Purtwee was involved. Perhaps Lady Elizabeth would be more successful, but he had no real hope. George was no fool, and was hardly likely to confide such skulduggery to a young lady he took for a drive.

Rob and Tom grew more morose as the level in the brandy decanter sank lower and lower.

Bets believed in preparation. On the Tuesday she was promised to drive with George Purtwee, she rehearsed herself in imagined dialogues where she could—oh, so subtly—learn whether Mr. Purtwee was behind the Almack's incident, and why. She would be entirely noncommittal about any relationship with the Earl of Burlingham; she might even make a few disparaging remarks. She did not like to bend the truth, but it was all in a good cause. . . . She grinned to herself. The afternoon promised to be most enjoyable.

* * *

As it turned out, the drive was like none of her imaginings.

Purtwee was prompt, polite to Lady Stanbourne, solicitous of Bets' comfort. He handed her into the shiny cabriolet as if she were a queen and asked frequently if she was comfortable, warm enough, had enough room, had any preferred destination in mind. The solicitude was at first flattering but grew wearing. Hyde Park was the obvious destination, being so close to Knightsbridge Terrace, and Bets could think of nowhere else.

"If you do not mind, we will drive by way of an interesting street that I know, and then turn toward the park," Purtwee said. He seemed inordinately cheerful about it. He smiled and smoothed the sleeve of his coat. If that was intended to draw Bets' interest in his attire, it worked. Purtwee was dressed in perfectly fitted garb that was of highest quality but lacked ostentation: black pantaloons and boots, a deep wine waistcoat with a narrow navy stripe and plain wine coat. Having taken those in, Bets stared at the gaps in his teeth before she caught herself. What was this preoccupation with teeth? she wondered.

"Very well." she answered. "What is of interest in the street you mention?"

Purtwee's grin widened. "You shall see," he said, and urged his horse onward.

In a few minutes they were in Belgravia, where Purtwee turned into a minor street he told Bets was Grosvenor Row. Bets observed it carefully while Purtwee negotiated the traffic, but could find nothing whatever notable about it. It contained a row of identical brick houses, closely packed together. Only one, a corner house, differed. Larger, it had more land around it and appeared to have stables at the back.

"There," said Purtwee triumphantly. He pulled up his horse in front of one of the houses.

"Why are we stopping?" Bets asked. Were they to call on some friend of Mr. Purtwee's? She had expected him to stop at the single large house, but he had paused next door.

"That—*that* is where your friend, my cousin, lives," said Purtwee with a sneer. "I wager he never told you, did he? Let you believe he lived in Mount Street, did he? You see what he has come to. Squandered all his blunt on gaming, and drink, and women—monstrous, I tell you!" His countenance reeked of righteous indignation.

Shock seemed to paralyze Bets' vocal cords. She stared at the little brick house as if hoping it would change before her eyes. She had guessed it to be the home of some tradesman.

"Had enough?" George asked, and when she did not reply, he clucked to his horse. They traveled in silence toward Hyde Park.

"I feared my cousin might be attempting to pull the wool over your eyes," said Purtwee sometime later. "He is deep in dun territory, you know. Has not a feather to fly with. Along with his violent nature—he has shot two men; did you know that?—and his shocking habits, he has little to recommend him. I believed it my duty as a gentleman to warn you, Lady Elizabeth. You are much too fine a lady, too gently reared, to let your name become linked with his."

Purtwee looked down at her, smiling. He was the picture of sincerity.

Bets struggled to think. All the brilliant and subtle strategies she had devised earlier in the day sank into black oblivion.

Bets hardly heard George Purtwee's rambling conversation as he drove toward the park. She was dimly aware that it seemed to be a thorough listing of every fault Burlingham had shown, every mistake he had made since the age of two. So he had tried to run away from his nanny when he was four, had he? She caught that in the midst of her misery. What child had not tried to run away from a nanny? Finally George, by now tooling through Hyde Park, reached Burlingham's twenties in his chronological recital and repeated the accusation that Burlingham had shot two men. Bets mentally shook herself and interrupted Purtwee's monologue.

"Shot two men?" she inquired sharply. "Why? How did that come about?"

"Duels," said George portentously. "Duels! Over two females not worthy for you to wipe your feet on."

"He was the challenger in both cases?" she asked.

"Ah—well—no, actually," George confessed. "Not that it mattered. The man is rotten to the core. Very unpleasant situations, both of them. Burlingham quite ruined Andrew Digby's right wrist; his penmanship has been abominable ever since. Sent a ball clean through it."

"Clean through his penmanship?"

George looked annoyed. "Through his wrist, of course," he said.

Bets persisted. "And the other situation?"

"I—ah—disremember all the details," he hedged.

"Surely if you recall his running away from his nanny, you can recall the duel. You seem to recall every event of Burlingham's life from birth as if you were reading from a journal," she said. She could not disguise her asperity.

"I did not know him from birth," Purtwee announced. He grasped the reins tightly and looked straight ahead. "I am a year younger than he."

"What a pity he lived an entire year before he had you to chronicle his every move," she said. "You still have not told me of the second duel."

"It is too dreadful for your tender ears," said Purtwee. Evidently deciding he had exhausted the topic of the Earl of Burlingham, he turned to Bets and smiled. "Do you go to the Donaldsons' ball next week? You must save a dance for me."

Thoroughly upset at all she had heard, Bets was torn. She laid much of it to spite, but there must be some truth in the recital, for it bore out what she had heard elsewhere of Burlingham, and Purtwee *had* known the earl most of his life. Did she wish to continue a friendship with the odious cousin of Burlingham's? Or was he odious? If what he said was true, and he was doing his best to warn her off a thoroughly despicable character, she could not fault him.

"Yes indeed, we go to the Donaldsons' ball," she said. "I would be happy to save you a dance."

"Delightful!" He gave her a warm smile. "Perhaps if I do not step on your feet you will even grant me two dances."

"We shall see," she said. "Should we not be returning? We usually have tea about this time and we would be happy to have you join us."

"Delighted," he said. He drove her directly home, with no more side excursions to Grosvenor Row.

Bets could not avoid contrasting his visit with Burlingham's of the day before. Another plate of carefully arranged small cakes appeared with the tea, and George Purtwee accepted only one. Several times he tried to press more cake on his hostesses. He looked comfortable and relaxed, as if he were enjoying himself. He admired the tall clock on the mantelshelf and said he placed its date somewhere in the seventeenth century; was that right? And surely it was of English make? Lady Stanbourne beamed on him. Admitting he had always had an interest in clocks, he engaged Lady Stanbourne in a spirited discussion that had her eyes sparkling and her voice full of enthusiasm.

Bets looked on, her thoughts in a jumble. Her mind was not on clocks. As if from a great distance, she examined George Purtwee and tried to figure him out. If he had falsely maligned Burlingham she would never forgive him. She remembered Purtwee's gibes at Burlingham's curricle and his tiger, which she had considered malicious and uncalled for. But if Burlingham was as despicable as Purtwee said, did he not deserve such remarks?

Then the worst blow of all hit her dulled brain. Burlingham had no money. He was penniless and in debt. He was courting her in the mistaken belief that she was wealthy. The easy friendship—she refused to call it anything more—they were developing was all a sham as he put on his best behavior merely to ensnare her. Oh! How that hurt!

The murmur of her mother's and George Purtwee's voices, the delicate clink of teacups, faded away as she laughed mirthlessly. How could she fault Burlingham for wanting her supposed wealth? She was equally at fault, wanting his riches. They were two of a kind, mere fortune hunters.

Pleading a sudden headache, Bets hurriedly excused herself and fled to her chamber.

Bets was lying facedown on her bed, the bed curtains drawn, so she was hidden in a gloomy cocoon that suited her mood perfectly. She paid no heed to the knock on her chamber door. Probably Molly with some inane announcement, she thought.

The knock came again, followed by her mother's voice. "Bets? Are you there?"

Deliberately she rose, pushed back the bed curtains, and opened the door. Her hair was askew and her gown rumpled. "Yes, Mama?"

Lady Stanbourne's expression changed from polite inquiry to consternation. "What—whatever is the matter?" she demanded, looking Bets up and down. "Are you ill?"

"In a manner of speaking," Bets replied. "Sit down, please, Mama. This may take some time."

When her mother was comfortably settled in a faded blue velvet chair, Bets returned to the mussed bed and leaned against one of its posts.

"I fear all the dreadful things you heard about Lord Burlingham are only too true, and do not begin to cover the half of it," she began. She repeated what she could remember of the long list of Burlingham's faults and mistakes George Purtwee had told her, from the nanny episode to the duels. When Lady Stanbourne tried to interrupt, Bets hushed her and went on, until she came to the worst part of all.

"He has no money, Mama!" she cried. "He is as deep in dun territory as we are! Mr. Purtwee says he has debts he will never be able to pay! Oh, Mama, what will I do? His lordship has been so kind to me—so thoughtful—Mama, he is not the despicable rogue Mr. Purtwee makes him out to be, is he? Tell me he is not. But he has not a rag to his name, Mr. Purtwee says, and he surely would know. Evidently Lord Burlingham believes we are plump in the pocket or he would not be so attentive, would he? And here I thought—I thought he had some affection for me." Bets grasped the counterpane and wiped her eyes with it.

"Get yourself a handkerchief," Lady Stanbourne said automatically. She rose and walked over to her daughter, putting her hands on Bets' shoulders and looking into her face.

"The answer is simple," said Lady Stanbourne. "I own I made a mistake, but it is not too late. We merely transfer our attentions to George Purtwee."

Startled, Bets was silent for a moment while she absorbed the idea. "You mean I should never see Lord Burlingham again?" she asked. "What would he think? And do not forget, he is to escort us to the Donaldsons' ball. I cannot see how we are to get out of that if we are to attend the ball at all. Could I not just—slowly—taper it off? But, Mama, he is so pleasant to be with. Oh, dear." Bets heaved a sigh.

"Is not Mr. Purtwee pleasant to be with, as well?" Lady Stanbourne feared she had her work cut out for her. "Bets, there is no question at all that Mr. Purtwee is in funds. His manners are impeccable and his reputation is spotless. He is interested in you. He is knowledgeable on many subjects. I declare, I never met anyone so well informed on the subject of old clocks! To think that he knew immediately the period of Papa's old clock there on the mantelpiece!"

"Probably read the writing on the back when you were not looking," Bets muttered.

"Bets!" Lady Stanbourne was scandalized. "I fear we shall have to permit Lord Burlingham to escort us to the Donaldsons', but I believe I should be cool toward him from now on. He will soon get the message."

"The soon-to-be-rejected suitor," Bets mumbled.

"Pardon? What did you say?"

"Never mind, Mama. I was thinking aloud. Oh, dear. I really do not like Mr. Purtwee very much."

"You hardly know him. Give it time."

"Yes, Mama." That was what she needed. Time. Time to worm her way into Mr. Purtwee's confidence and learn, if possible, whether he was behind Burlingham's contretemps at Almack's. Time to enjoy a few more drives with Burlingham and his incredible little tiger. Time to sort out her feelings about both these gentlemen, so different, so at odds with one another.

Chapter Eight

Despite the slurs George Purtwee had cast upon him recently, Rob could not really believe George was behind the Almack's incident, as he preferred to call it. Perhaps "incident" was too mild a word, but the euphemism took away some of the horror that struck Rob whenever he thought about what it could do to his already regrettable reputation—his entire future, in fact. Why had he suspected George? His cousin had nothing to gain by such treatment. He was not in line for Rob's title, and Rob could think of no reason why George disliked him so.

Somehow he believed Lady Elizabeth could arrive at the truth of Purtwee's involvement, if anyone could. She was persistent and seemed sensible and intelligent. Could it be true that she had managed to live through four seasons without losing her dignity and self-respect? And, he supposed, her hope? Considering her undoubted fortune, it was a miracle she had not found a gentleman to whom she could give her heart and hand. Thank heaven she had not. Rob intended to be that gentleman. He believed he could manage to live a blameless life until the parson said the words, so long as the wait was not interminable. Then, his debts settled, coins once again jingling in his pocket, he could resume the gaming and the races and the drinking. . . . He might even stay home on an occasional evening if he could persuade Lady Elizabeth, who would of course by then be the Countess of Burlingham, to learn to play cards.

Having decided to leave George to Lady Elizabeth's

tender mercies for the nonce, Rob considered what other of his acquaintances might wish him harm. Someone to whom he owed money? These were legion, but they were tradesmen who surely would not have access to Almack's or even recognize Mrs. Drummond Burrell and what she stood for. Rob was certain whoever had plotted this incident would have wanted to be there and watch his downfall. In fact, the more he thought about it, the more certain he became that the culprit would have steered Rob in Mrs. Drummond Burrell's direction; otherwise he could not believe he would have sought her out. He knew the lady's starchy reputation and never purposely went near her.

Lolling in front of his library fire with a very small tot of brandy in his hand—heaven knew how long the brandy would last—he realized he must consult again with Tom Hazleton. He wrote a note and summoned Geordie to have Billy deliver it, then settled back with another, somewhat larger tot of brandy to wait.

Hazleton, fortunately, was at home and came immediately, giving the exultant Billy a ride back in his curricle. When Hazleton, looking quizzical, had been settled by the fire, Rob asked Geordie to join them as well.

"I have asked you here to help me list all my enemies," Rob addressed the puzzled faces. "I must get to the bottom of this! Obviously someone believes he has a score to settle with me, though I cannot imagine why. Tom, what have you heard?"

"Nothing! Good God, man, I sat in the Friend at Hand drinking indifferent ale night after night, just for you. Is that not enough? Why have you not followed up on the information I got out of Tessie? You are not asking me to go there again, surely? If so, I refuse. I refuse, I tell you!" Hazleton sprang to his feet and paced the library, then stopped to add a stick to the dying fire. "At least you got some firewood," he muttered.

"Tom!" Rob cried. "Old friend, do not take me amiss. You need never darken the Friend at Hand's door again. I only want to know whether anyone has taken a sudden dislike to me for any reason at all. Of course that could happen and you would never learn of it, but I thought perhaps—someone might mention something to you . . ."

Hazleton, appeased, thought it over. "No," he said at last. "Aside from all the gossip about your evening at Almack's, which I assure you is still on everyone's lips even though it is now last week's news, no one has mentioned your name. Which reminds me, last night I heard that you struck Mrs. Drummond Burrell—a slap on the face, it was said—before you went down. Did you?"

"My God," said Rob, his head in his hands. "Of course not. Or at least, I think not. Surely not! Where were you, Tom? You were there! Say I did not do it!"

"As I have been at pains to point out, I was *there* but not on the spot," said Tom. "We were to meet, remember? But we had not yet met. Only when I heard the commotion did I arrive at the spot and find you."

Rob looked morose and ran his fingers through his hair, which stood up in every direction with one lock in his eye. "Damn," he said. "Have a brandy, Tom. You too, Geordie?"

"No, sir," said Geordie. "I shall inquire of Mrs. Burket for tea, sir." He ducked out of the room.

"Treats me like a four-year-old," Rob grumbled. "Worse than my father."

"Someone must do it," said Tom agreeably. "Would that your father were here."

"Stow it," Rob ordered. "Poor father. He must be frantic, rusticating with my mother in Dorset. He was never meant to rusticate. Likes a good game, a fine bit of horseflesh, as much as I do. Last I heard, he was planning to try his hand at keeping the accounts at Dors Court. Keep the accounts! This will never happen. I doubt he knows the difference between a debit and a credit."

Rob rubbed his arms as if he had taken a chill and looked longingly at the nearly empty brandy decanter. Geordie gave him a stern look as he appeared with a tray of tea things and a plate of biscuits. "Here, your lordship. Tea will warm you up," said Geordie.

Rob settled for tea.

"Now, back to my enemies," he said when they had restored themselves with tea laced with plenty of sugar. "Geordie?"

"I been thinkin'," said Geordie. "Last enemy, if you can call it that, would be that Winterfield you dueled with. He never forgave you for puttin' a ball so near his—er—um—"

"I did *not* unman him," Rob protested.

"P'raps not, but it was a near thing. Probably left a scar that disfigured his hum—hum—manly beauty." Geordie snickered.

"And completely put off his adored Olivia," said Rob, grinning. "Serves her right. Why he would challenge me over that hussy I will never understand. Could I help it if she was trying to crawl all over me that night? I was merely minding my own business, if you will recall, Geordie. Perhaps I had had a cup too much, but I was hardly floored. I was trying to leave the George and Dragon to get in a game, you remember, when she—"

"Yes, yes, I know," Geordie cut him off. He had heard the tale many times.

"But that was more than two years ago! Why would Winterfield want revenge now?"

"That is what we must find out," said Geordie.

Rob looked at Tom. Then he looked at Geordie. "Tom?" he said.

"No!"

"Tom, you know Winterfield. You can have dinner with him at your club or something. If he bears me a grudge he should be glad to tell you all about it. Geordie cannot do that. It is up to you, Tom."

Tom sighed. "The sacrifices I make," he said lugubriously. "I will add the cost of said dinner to your bill. Four pounds you owe me already, remember." His face broke into a quick smile and he rose to clap Rob on the back. "For you, I sacrifice."

* * *

Once Hazleton had departed and Rob had finished the decanter of brandy, Rob sat down once again over his accounts book. Its scrawled figures had not improved. He had hoped Geordie would come up with some miracle—was he not a Scot, a race known to be tight-fisted? But Geordie had lived in England since the age of seven, and had even lost much of his accent. Perhaps he had lost his canniness as well. Considering the coal, wood, and foodstuffs recently purchased, as well as Billy's clothing, the funds at hand had shrunk alarmingly.

Rob slammed the accounts book shut and removed some of the volumes in his bookcase to place the accounts book behind them. Why was he hiding the accounts book? Out of sight, out of mind, perhaps. Casually he glanced at the spines of several leather-bound volumes he had brought from Dors Court to fill his case. Other than the one whose cover had come loose when he dropped it a few days before, most seemed to be in good condition. Someday he would read them. He flipped several open to look at the title pages. Pope. Dryden. Shakespeare. Bacon. Familiar names from his days at Harrow and Cambridge. He supposed he should have studied them more assiduously, for he remembered little of their contents. Other things had been on his mind in those halcyon days at Cambridge—playing jokes on his tutors. Drinking. Gaming. Wenching. Getting into trouble with Tom Hazleton. Ah, what fun they had had.

A sudden tingle enveloped Rob as he stared at the volume of Shakespeare, which was bound in such a way that it seemed to be a number of pamphlets put together. He could see that the paper was old, very old, and the printing somewhat imperfect. Perhaps it was valuable. Perhaps several were! In a frenzy of excitement he tore more books from his shelves, spread them out on a table and examined them one by one. Publication dates, where he could find them, reached back into what Rob considered dim antiquity.

"Geordie!" he yelled, his voice full of joy, and hope, and enthusiasm. "Geordie! Come bundle these up for me. I must go out. Immediately!" When Geordie popped his head in, Rob indicated seven or eight books he had put in a pile.

"Goin' to take 'em back to the circulatin' library, are you? I don't remember you borrowin' 'em," said Geordie.

"No!" said Rob, grasping Geordie's shoulders and smiling at him in delight. "I shall seek a bookseller. I do believe some of these are worth a goodly sum. Blunt, Geordie! We may have a gold mine here!"

"Them old things? Who'd want 'em?" Geordie looked at his master as if Rob had lost his mind. "I thought they was just to fill up the shelves."

"We shall see. Hurry, man! I must seek out a bookseller." Rob dashed upstairs to make himself presentable. Look prosperous, he told himself. Pretend you are doing the bookseller a favor. It would never do to go begging, hat in hand, or the price he would get would be paltry.

While Geordie attended to wrapping and tying the books, Rob raced to the stable behind the next house and helped Billy put the horses to his curricle. Billy, crestfallen, was instructed to don his toga over his clothes, but he revived when he noted Rob's air of suppressed excitement. Maybe they were to take Lady Elizabeth for a drive. He hoped so.

But no. Rob turned the curricle toward Piccadilly, not toward Knightsbridge Terrace. Piccadilly was crowded with carriages, and Rob cursed under his breath as he jockeyed for a stopping place. Finally a spot opened and he maneuvered his pair into it, jumped down, gave the reins to Billy, and dashed with his bundle into Hatchard's.

He wanted to shout, to call out what valuables he was deigning to offer to Hatchard's. The quiet, refined atmosphere, the clerks attending graciously to the patrons, came as a shock. He dropped his bundle on a counter and drummed his fingers.

"May I be of assistance, sir?" said a thin, bald, middle-aged man wearing spectacles.

"I believe I have volumes of some importance, which

I am prepared to let you have," said Rob, summoning his haughtiest air. He worked at the knot Geordie had set in the string around his bundle. Damn Geordie. Sometimes he was too efficient.

"Let me help you," the clerk said mildly. He produced a penknife and cut the string. Opening the volume of Shakespeare, which lay on top, he glanced through the first few pages. He turned to Rob, his eyes wide.

"Sir! Where did you get these?" he asked in a hushed voice.

"They have been in the family for years," Rob said casually. "I dislike having to part with them, of course, but I have been called to a mission abroad and must divest myself of—of many things. Have to give up my house, of course. No—no family to leave them with, alas. Might Hatchard's be interested?" He tried to look unconcerned.

"I shall have to ask," said the clerk. "May I take these with me? I shall return as quickly as possible." Gazing reverently at the books, he cradled the pile in his arms and disappeared to the back of the shop.

He was gone not more than fifteen minutes, but to Rob it seemed like hours. He dared not move from his spot for fear the clerk might not find him again. He stared, unseeing, at the patrons browsing among the bookshelves. None seemed concerned. Could they not tell how important his visit was?

Finally the clerk returned, without the books, and invited him to step back to the office. Rob followed, his heart in his mouth.

"You realize you have a fortune in early editions," said a tall, imposing, gray-haired man whom Rob took to be the manager. "Of course, we cannot offer you a fortune for them." He smiled deprecatingly. "We may have to hold them for years before we find buyers. The rare book market is volatile. We could lose money just as easily as we could make money."

"I understand," said Rob, quaking inside.

The man launched into a long sermon on the pitfalls

of the rare book trade. Rob only half heard him. His eyes were fixed on the pile of books, which the man flipped through as he pontificated.

At last his sermon came to an end, and he looked hard at Rob. "Two hundred pounds for the lot?" he asked.

Rob thought fast. What did he know of the value of rare books? But a bit of bargaining would not come amiss.

"I believe they are worth at least four hundred," he said firmly. "You will note their leather bindings. Worthy of the finest library, aside from their age and rarity."

"Perhaps if you were to sell them to collectors yourself," said the man. "Would you prefer to do that? If so, I wish you a good day."

"Three hundred fifty?" Rob asked hopefully.

"Two hundred fifty," said the man.

"Three hundred twenty-five?"

"Two seventy-five."

"I will let you have them for three hundred pounds, and that is final," said Rob, making as if to gather up the books and leave. "I have more, sir. These are only a sampling. If I cannot get a fair price from you, I shall have to go elsewhere."

The man's eyes gleamed for a moment before he once more showed an impassive face.

"Very well," he said. "Three hundred pounds. When may I expect you with more?"

Inwardly gleeful, Rob adopted a bored look. "In a few days," he said carelessly. "I have so much to do—packing, you know, and arranging places for my servants—I will try to make another visit soon."

"Very well," said the man. He moved behind his desk and drew out a cash box from a drawer. As he counted out three hundred pounds, he asked, "Might I have your name, sir?"

"Robert Francis Frederick Farnsworth," said Rob. "Earl of Burlingham."

"Ah," said the man. "Pleased to do business with you, your lordship."

Rob stuffed the bank notes into a pocket and walked out. He almost missed the remark the manager made to the clerk.

"Burlingham," mused the manager. "Was he not the one who . . .?"

Oh, God, Rob said to himself as he climbed into his curricle. Did even the help at Hatchard's know of the incident at Almack's?

Once safely back to Grosvenor Row, Rob lost no time in storing the three hundred pounds in his wall safe so he would not be tempted to spend it immediately. Then he yelled for Geordie to help him empty the library bookcase, giving full attention to the title and publication date of each volume. What did Rob know about the value of old books? Precious little. Geordie, although willing, knew even less. Rob had a sinking feeling that the books he had left at Hatchard's were worth far more than three hundred pounds, but he could think of no way to make himself an expert overnight.

" 'Twould be easy to visit other booksellers and inquire the price of some of their old books," Geordie suggested.

"True, but that would take time, and I have no time," said Rob, flipping through an ancient treatise written in Latin. Latin was one language that had appealed to him. He started to translate and then gave it up. He must not form an attachment to any of these volumes.

"Why no time?"

"I am busy, man. Do you not understand? Busy! I must get to the bottom of the Almack's affair—I must court Lady Elizabeth—I have not had a decent game of cards in a fortnight . . ."

"Sir! When did you become a sniveling coward?"

"I could sack you for that." Rob looked threatening, his black brows drawn down, his fists up. "Put up your dukes!"

"Oho!" Geordie grinned in delight. "Time for a sparrin' match, eh? I was beginnin' to wonder was you goin' to let yourself get lazy and run to fat. We ain't had a good kickup in months."

Geordie began raining punches on Rob, who quickly retaliated. The library soon looked as if Napoleon's army had marched through it, tables overturned, books scattered on the floor, a chair knocked dangerously close to the fire. When Rob saw his accounts book fly through the air, hit a chair arm, and slide to the floor, its pages crumpled, he called a halt. The two men looked at each other ruefully. Both wore bruises and Rob's cheek was bloody.

"Damn! You near darkened my daylights," said Rob. Gingerly he felt the skin around his left eye. "And here I thought I could belt the Great Geordie. How old are you now, Geordie?"

Geordie, breathing hard, admitted to three-and-forty. "Been twenty years since I was fightin' as the Great Geordie," he said, examining his skinned knuckles. "Well, maybe fifteen years. Last mill I won was in '98. 'Twas the drink did me in. I ain't what I used to be or you'd be out cold on the floor." He dusted himself off, then looked critically at his master. "You've ruined another neckcloth, your lordship," he said, once again the concerned servant. "Let's get you cleaned up. Then you can play with your books."

The books! In the heat of the moment Rob had forgotten them. Sorrowfully he noted a cover torn off, a cracked spine.

"Another match in the back garden tomorrow," he told Geordie. "Must get back into shape. May have to scuttle a few nobs when I find who is after me. Meanwhile I suppose you have the right of it. I shall have to visit a few booksellers. A monstrous bore, let me tell you."

With great care he picked up the fallen books, dusted them off as best he could with his coat sleeve, and set them reverently into piles. Then he and Geordie climbed to his chamber to repair his battered appearance.

* * *

The next days were spent with sparring each morning and visits to booksellers all over London each afternoon. Rob was so weary by evening that he found himself dozing by the fire soon after supper. He was horrified. What would his cronies think of him now! He, whose life was dedicated to the never-ending pursuit of pleasure, a life that invariably kept him up and out until the wee hours. He wondered how many times he had watched the sun rise through bleary eyes as he wound his way home. Under his new schedule he was waking early, and someday he might see the sun rise at the beginning of the day rather than the end, heaven forbid. At least this situation was temporary, he assured himself. Once he had possession of Lady Elizabeth and her fortune, he could revert to his old habits.

Ah, yes, Lady Elizabeth. Tonight he was to escort her and her mother to the Donaldsons' ball.

Bets' moods varied from defiance to miserable acceptance in the days after her eye-opening drive with George Purtwee. She thought about Lord Burlingham's town house, not that she had seen much of it; it was small, true, but seemed quite handsome. As a bachelor with no one else in residence but servants, obviously he did not need a large house. She and her mother lived in a small house as well, and had no reason to apologize (except for being unable to entertain large groups, she had to admit). Burlingham drove a well-kept curricle pulled by a pair of prime goers, or so he had referred to them. She saw no evidence of poverty, whatever George Purtwee might say.

Her thoughts shifted to the reported duels and again she sank into misery. Duels were frowned upon. She was certain Lord Burlingham knew that. She feared he was the kind of man who would not care. Probably loved the danger of it, the fool! But he might have been killed! He must have suffered no ill effects or Mr. Purtwee would have dwelt upon them. At least Mr. Purtwee had admitted that Burlingham had been the instigator of neither one. Both had been over women. Did that not tell her something? And what was so dreadful about the second one, that Mr. Purtwee could not repeat the details? She resolved to ask Burlingham next time she saw him.

The list of Burlingham's faults, shortcomings, and bad habits reported by Mr. Purtwee had had little effect. Mr. Purtwee had overdone it. His dislike must have festered for a long time; why else bring up imperfections dating back to infancy? Mr. Purtwee was so near perfect himself, or so Lady Stanbourne reported, that he would tend to exaggerate another's faults, she was sure. Especially when it was his disliked cousin.

Bets dreaded her next meeting with Lord Burlingham. It would be so difficult to be cool toward him! On the other hand, she could not wait to see him and learn how much of Mr. Purtwee's report was true. She believed she would be able to sense the answer without resorting to embarrassing questions.

Meanwhile, there was Mr. Purtwee. He became a faithful caller. With her mother's blessing he took her for drives in his splendid cabriolet, escorted her to the opera and a rout, and when she suggested it, took her for a visit to the British Museum. He no longer prosed on about Lord Burlingham, but set about making himself pleasant. He paid her compliments on her appearance, on her appreciation of opera, on her interest in the museum's antiquities.

She could find no fault with his behavior. If he seemed overeager to instruct her in the subject on which he deemed himself an expert, which was clocks, she forgave him. He did seem to be well read and intelligent. But she could not warm to him.

Bets racked her brain in an effort to devise a way to learn whether he might be the one behind Burlingham's Almack's incident. Because they no longer mentioned Burlingham, she was at a loss as to how to bring it up.

They were rolling along Rotten Row in Hyde Park, the cabriolet's top down so they could enjoy the exquisite weather—and so Mr. Purtwee could see and be seen, she was sure—when she decided not to beat around the bush. She knew every tree, every shrub, every blade of grass along the drive by now and found little in the way of scenery to catch her interest. Even the flower beds looked just as they had yesterday.

"Were you present when Lord Burlingham insulted Mrs. Drummond Burrell at Almack's?" she asked, looking sweetly up at her companion.

Purtwee frowned. "What makes you ask that?" he said. She had interrupted his learned discourse on pocket watches.

"Mama heard—I disremember from whom—that you were there, or was it your father? Of course one knows how gossip grows. I was only curious. Did Lord Burlingham really fall down at Mrs. Drummond Burrell's feet? And did he really insult her? Do tell me." Bets affected an expression of avid curiosity. "I should enjoy receiving a report from the horse's mouth, as it were," she added. "I could live on the tale for a week around the tea tables."

His reservations lulled and his self-esteem puffed, Purtwee relaxed. "Indeed, I was there, and indeed, Burlingham did exactly as you said," he told her. "Despicable! He was despicable! Poor Mrs. Drummond Burrell. I had to help her to a chair afterward, she was so overcome."

Bets laid a hesitant hand on Purtwee's sleeve of deep green superfine. She looked into his eyes with what she hoped was an expression of moral outrage.

"Monstrous," she said. "Tell me every detail."

Purtwee hemmed and hawed for a moment. She wondered whether he was inventing a few new details.

"He appeared out of nowhere," he said. Purtwee did not look at Bets, but at his horse, trotting decorously. "I just happened to be standing near Mrs. Drummond Burrell at the time. We had exchanged greetings and I was about to seek out a friend. Then along comes Burlingham, strutting like a cock. He bowed to Mrs. Drummond Burrell, rather sketchily I might add, and said, ah, um,

'Good evening, my dear, what a dreadful gown.' Then he collapsed at her feet. Naturally my first thought was for Mrs. Drummond Burrell. She looked to be ready to faint. I helped her to a chair, as I said, and fanned her a little with someone's fan. By the time she had recovered, Burlingham had been removed."

"You heard every word he said?"

"Oh, indeed."

"Did Mrs. Drummond Burrell hear as well?"

"But of course. How could she help it? He stood immediately in front of her."

"You believe Burlingham to have been drunk?"

"No doubt about it. He has been overindulging for years. Everyone knows it."

"Yet if he was so foxed that he collapsed immediately, how do you explain that he strutted in like a cock? I should have thought he would stumble, or shamble, or lurch."

Bets, watching his face like a hawk, caught the sudden frown. Immediately Purtwee smoothed his expression. "You are well acquainted with the habits of tosspots, are you? I believe Burlingham is said to be able to navigate even when corned, pickled, and salted. I do not know from observation; we do not go about together. He must do so or how else could he reach home again after one of his—his sojourns with the devil?" Purtwee looked fiercely righteous.

"Ah. Now I understand," said Bets. "However much he drinks, he stays on his feet. Am I correct? Then how did he come to collapse in front of Mrs. Drummond Burrell?"

"How should I know?" Purtwee shot back angrily. "I am not his keeper. Why are you quizzing me? Do you not believe what I have told you? It is God's truth. Ask Mrs. Drummond Burrell if you do not believe me." Affronted, he glared at Bets.

"Oh, assuredly," said Bets with irony. "We are bosom bows, Mrs. Drummond Burrell and I."

Purtwee did not catch the irony. "You are?" he asked with some trepidation. "I had not realized."

Bets had overlooked the slight discrepancies in Purtwee's recital. He had undoubtedly told the tale so often that he no longer remembered which was fact and which was embroidery. But his reaction when she said she and Mrs. Drummond Burrell were close friends . . . As if he feared she would hear a different version from the lady herself. Bets immediately decided she would have to inquire of Mrs. Drummond Burrell, if that could be arranged. How? She would have to think on it.

All smiles again, she put herself out to be charming and polite. "Thank you for telling me," she said sweetly. "A vastly diverting tale. I can see why you and your cousin are not close. Mercy! What a scandalous creature."

"You are not seeing him any longer, are you?" Purtwee inquired.

"I have not seen him since that day we met in the park," she assured him. "Nor have I any plans to. Oh, pardon. Mama and I did agree to let him escort us to the Donaldsons' ball. I intend to be very cool toward him. Nothing is planned beyond that." Bets adopted a yearning look intended to convey to Purtwee that he, Purtwee, was now the object of her hopes.

Purtwee was jubilant. He stopped the cabriolet just short of the park exit and kissed her hand. Then he clucked to his horse and drove her home.

"How well do we know Mrs. Drummond Burrell?" Bets demanded of her mother once George Purtwee had departed.

"Dear Clementina?" Lady Stanbourne made a moue of distaste. "Who knows her well? Who would wish to? Why do you ask? You must be aware of the answer already."

"It is as I feared." Bets sighed. "Do you believe she

might receive me if I were to call? Or must I seek her out at Almack's? Have we a voucher?"

"Whatever for?" her mother countered. "Surely you can have no reason to wish to . . ." A thought struck her. "It has something to do with Lord Burlingham, does it not? Oh, my dear, can you not let the matter rest? It is none of our affair. Let that presumptuous puppy wage his own battles. As for vouchers, I have sought none this season. You must agree that Almack's is sadly flat, and the cost—it did seem a waste, considering our situation—"

"You could approach Lady Sefton again, could you not?" Bets stood behind her mother's chair and wound her arms around her mother's neck. "Please, dear Mama. If you are so determined to put me in the way of some gentleman's fortune, I must meet more gentlemen. You have dismissed Lord Burlingham, and I have no fondness for Mr. Purtwee." She gently stroked her mother's hair.

"You need not try any of your wiles on me," said Lady Stanbourne, laughing. "Oh, very well. I will bestir myself, I suppose, and seek out Lady Sefton. Dear Maria. She is truly a gem of the first water."

"Oh, thank you, Mama!" Bets hugged her parent before sitting down across from her and pouring herself a cup of tea. "Do you think that Mrs. Drummond Burrell attends every Wednesday? I should dislike it exceedingly should I get so caught up in flirting with a host of wealthy gentlemen that I overlooked her."

"Ha!" said Lady Stanbourne. "Do not try to pull the wool over my eyes. In the first place, it is difficult to overlook dear Clementina, and in the second place, your purpose in visiting Almack's is *to make yourself known to young gentlemen*. Do I make myself clear? I will not have you embarrassing us by trying to quiz Mrs. Drummond Burrell. That is what you have in mind, is it not? Believe me, she will not take kindly to it. I repeat, Lord Burlingham's little incident is his own affair." Lady

Stanbourne frowned. "Promise me, Bets. Promise you will not raise a dustup. I will not have it."

"No dustups, Mama. I promise to try to avoid any dustups. Now, when should we expect to go to Almack's? Perhaps next week? That should allow you time to ask Lady Sefton. This week is the Donaldsons' ball, and I must add some new trimming on my peach gown. I believe I shall start on it after supper. Do come up with me. I should like your approval."

Chapter Nine

Rob was able to hire a respectable town coach to transport the ladies to the Donaldsons' ball. He made sure the squabs were whole and clean, and personally led his own pair, Myrtle and Box, to the livery to be hitched. Once home again he set Billy to sweeping and shining the well-used vehicle as the horses fidgeted. Meanwhile he put himself into Geordie's hands. His appearance must be above reproach.

Did Lady Elizabeth favor Corinthians? Rob had never aspired to be an exquisite, but he remembered his cousin George's attire the day he had been forced to introduce George and Lady Elizabeth. Had she admired his cousin's splendid waistcoat? He had not noticed, really, but he was under the impression Lady Elizabeth had been more taken with George's shiny cabriolet than with the clothing of the man who drove it.

Deftly Geordie got Rob into handsome fawn pantaloons, a frilled white shirt, pale blue waistcoat with a fine white stripe, black coat, and black shoes. His neckcloth knot was so simple Beau Brummel would have sniffed at it. His watch chain bore only a single gold fob. Evidence of the bruises suffered in sparring matches was hidden as much as possible with salves and ointments Geordie produced. An errant lock of black hair was permitted to fall over a purpling forehead bruise. Rob ran a finger over unruly black brows as he glanced into his looking glass, and decided he was acceptable. He whistled as he ran down the stairs.

Feeling more cheerful than he had in weeks, eager to

see the wealthy Lady Elizabeth again, Rob made the journey to Knightsbridge Terrace in record time. The maid Molly opened the door to his knock and without a word ushered him into the sitting room, where Lady Elizabeth and her mother awaited him. He was pleased to note that they seemed ready to go; he would not have to cool his heels as the ladies took interminable time dressing.

"He's here, ma'am," said Molly, filling the doorway with her hand on the jamb. Rob waited quietly until Molly realized she was blocking the way and stepped aside.

Rob smiled, and Bets smiled back before she thought. She was so glad to see him! She had not realized how she had missed him. He looked so handsome! She wanted to run to him and hug him, brush his stray lock off his forehead, and put her arm in his.

Instead she looked at her mother, who was greeting him, politely but without warmth. Lady Stanbourne turned toward Bets then, with an almost imperceptible frown and shake of the head. Bets' smile faded.

All her apprehension at the evening's prospects came rushing back. She had no hard facts, only suspicions, of George Purtwee's involvement in the Almack's affair. She doubted there would be much opportunity for confidences in any case; Lady Stanbourne, who had dismissed Lord Burlingham as a prospective suitor, would stick like a burr. George Purtwee was to attend the ball also. That surely would complicate matters, for she must not show any interest in Burlingham in front of Mr. Purtwee.

Until the very moment Burlingham's knock was heard, Lady Stanbourne had been issuing admonitions. Be polite but distant, she said. Act the lady, but let him know discreetly that he is not truly welcome. Do not chatter. Maintain a genteel silence except when spoken to. Avoid being near him when partners are chosen for each dance. Plead a headache should he wish to bring you refreshments, and then disappear for a time. And for heaven's sake, *do not* agree to walk in the garden with him!

At least Burlingham's arrival had put a stop to her mother's harangue. Bets resolved to get through the evening as best she could. Just seeing Burlingham again was a joy, whatever that odious George Purtwee said about the earl's true reason for pursuing her. See, she thought happily as they descended the steps toward the coach, he cannot be in dun territory, for he has a coach as well as a curricle! There were his two horses, a chestnut and a chestnut roan, which she remembered well. And Billy. Billy in his toga, waiting. Billy grinned at her.

The drive to the Donaldsons' provided no opportunity for conversation, for to the ladies' surprise Burlingham sat upon the box and drove himself. Lady Stanbourne was incensed. "Where is his coachman?" she demanded of Bets. "Where is his groom? This is not *the thing*, Bets."

"No need to be overset," Bets tried to soothe her mother. "He must be a member of the Four-in-Hand Club; they make a point of driving their own coaches, though he drives but two horses. At least you note he *has* a coach. No man with pockets to let has both a coach and curricle, never mind two such fine horses." She figured that took care of that.

"Did you see a coat of arms on the door?" Lady Stanbourne asked ominously. "I did not."

"It was getting dark." Bets wrapped her shawl more tightly about her shoulders and turned away from her mother. "I did not notice. I do not recall a coat of arms on his curricle either. Do you?"

Lady Stanbourne had to admit she could not remember.

Rob wished he could eavesdrop on the ladies' conversation as they drove. Something was havey-cavey here; he could not put his finger on it, but Lady Elizabeth and her mother seemed distant and withdrawn. He could have sworn Lady Elizabeth was glad to see him when he appeared, though her mother apparently was not. What had he done? He was not foxed; his dress was faultless; the coach was in good repair; his steeds were the best. He would ask Lady Elizabeth point-blank as soon as he could get her alone.

By some happenstance he was never able to get her alone. The ball was a monstrous crush. After greeting the Donaldsons and their daughter, Faith, at the top of the broad flight of stairs, Rob turned to ask Lady Elizabeth for the first dance, only to discover she and her mother had disappeared into the crowd. He spent fruitless time looking for them—Lady Elizabeth's vastly becoming peach-colored gown was distinctive and would not be difficult to spot—and finally retired to the sidelines of the ballroom to watch in case she danced by with another partner.

It was there he saw her mincing gracefully in the minuet with George Purtwee.

Rob was furious. Not Purtwee! He had been pleased and flattered when she had volunteered to learn what she could of Purtwee's plotting, if any, but . . . What could she learn during a dance, for God's sake? There was precious little time for conversation. And to give Purtwee the first dance! He, Rob, her escort, should have had that privilege. He ran his fingers through his carefully arranged hair and inadvertently brushed the bruise on his forehead. It hurt. He swore.

Rob tried to keep Lady Elizabeth and Purtwee in sight in the vast ballroom, intending to ask her for the next dance, but once again he was thwarted. When next he spotted Purtwee, that fribble, dressed to the nines, was dancing with a blond beauty Rob had never seen before. Purtwee caught Rob's eye and gave him a knowing smile. Rob gave no sign he had noticed.

Eventually he spied Lady Elizabeth again. She was smiling into the face of Arthur Percival. That looby! That nincompoop! Percival seemed as inept on the dance floor as he was driving a phaeton, but one never would have known it from Lady Elizabeth's expression. Fawning, she was, he thought fiercely. What had come over her? Was he, in truth, the soon-to-be-rejected suitor who had now been rejected? God's blood, that she should choose to dance with Arthur Percival, when she had made it clear that he had already been rejected! There was no accounting for women, he knew that, but somehow Lady Elizabeth had seemed different. . . .

She is not worth it, he told himself. There were other fish in the sea, wealthier catches. Now that he had sold some books and had a few guineas to call his own, he would look elsewhere. Still, a thread of disappointment ran through his thoughts as he gave up and headed for the card room. Soon caught up in a game, he gave the Fortescue ladies hardly a thought. He was lucky. He won and lost and won again, and considered himself fortunate to come out ten pounds better than he had started. By then the crowd was thinning and he had no difficulty finding the ladies.

Bets and her mother were standing together, talking quietly, trying not to look apprehensive. Had their escort deserted them? Bets would not have blamed him. With her mother hovering near, she had not danced even a single dance with Burlingham. George Purtwee had claimed two dances, and even that utter jinglebrains, Arthur Pervical, had sought her out. Bets had been aware of Lord Burlingham's presence, staring fixedly at her, several times during the evening. He had looked like a thundercloud. Evidently they were no longer friends.

"It is time to depart," Rob told them as he joined them. "I will summon the coach while you get your wraps." His face was grim.

That accomplished, he escorted them into the coach, climbed onto the box, and drove them home. When they reached Knightsbridge Terrace, he helped them out, escorted them to the door, said a stiff "Good night," and departed without another word.

Bets was certain she would never see him again.

"Did I perform to suit you, Mama?" she cried once they were in the house. "Are you satisfied?"

She ran up to her room without waiting for an answer.

That night she spent sleepless hours pounding her pillow.

Rob drove away so wrapped in his thoughts that Billy had to remind him to head for the livery, not the house in Grosvenor Row.

"They'd ask extra if you was to keep the coach till tomorrer, and where'd we keep it anyways?" Billy remarked. He sat on the box next to his employer, feeling important. Never mind that at this hour there were few to see.

"The coach was a waste of money," Rob said despondently. "Make sure I remember that when next I try to impress a lady."

"Oh, she were impressed, sir." Billy bounced up and down on the hard seat to emphasize his point. "Saw 'er lookin' at it when you three come out of 'er 'ouse. Eyes as big as saucers, they were."

"Truly?"

"Oh, yes, sir."

Rob felt a little better until it occurred to him that the well-worn coach beneath him hardly merited any kind of reaction. A wealthy man with several vehicles at his disposal would not expect anyone to go into transports of delight at being conveyed in a coach. Of course not. His brief surge of pleasure subsided.

The man at the livery wanted four shillings above the agreed-upon hire price because of late return. Grudgingly Rob counted out the coins, then he and Billy each led a horse home through the silent streets. Rob was dead tired, but he helped Billy give his animals a rubdown, water, and feed. His horses, he reflected, were the only things of value he owned.

Chapter Ten

Twice more in that unhappy week, George Purtwee paid calls on the Fortescue household. It was as if, Bets decided, he was determined to woo Lady Stanbourne rather than herself. He hung onto every word Lady Stanbourne uttered, and kept her fascinated with his learned discourse on clocks.

During his second visit he became immersed in an explanation of how the clock balance wheel had replaced the foliot in the late Middle Ages. Warming to his subject, he was exhilarated and almost handsome except for the gaps in his teeth. Which goes to show, looks are not everything, Bets thought snidely. His talk of verge escarpments and foliots and horizontal pin barrels had her itching to escape, even if it meant one more drive along the too-familiar paths of Hyde Park.

Purtwee stopped for breath and pulled his chair closer to that of Lady Stanbourne, who occupied the chair with the split silk seat. Her skirts hid the splits nicely. "You are one in a thousand, my lady," he said, a look of awe on his face. "Never have I had a listener who so appreciated the brilliance of the men who have improved, little by little, the timepieces that we now tend to take for granted. I vow, when I have completed my treatise I shall dedicate it to you. 'To the lady who listened, and was as enchanted as I.'"

"You are writing a treatise on clocks?" Bets asked. It was the first time she had entered the conversation for what seemed hours. Not that she had been listening. Her mind was elsewhere as she stared at a dangling thread in the embroidered band around the hem of her gown.

"I am indeed," said Purtwee proudly. "I fancy I have learned as much as any man on the subject, and it would indeed be a pity should all my study go for naught. I wish to share it with the world, and those who come after."

Conceited puppy, Bets thought. Her mother, however, looked at Purtwee with shining eyes.

"Dear Mr. Purtwee," she said, holding out a dainty hand to put it over his, which was holding his teacup. "I should be immensely flattered, to be sure, to receive your dedication, but I have done nothing to deserve it. Oh, my! To think you will be published! What do you plan to call your treatise?"

"*Clocks*," said Purtwee. "But, dear madam, it is not yet complete. Perhaps by early next year."

"Clocks," Lady Stanbourne repeated softly to herself. She poured herself a fresh cup of tea and nibbled a biscuit. "Clocks," she murmured again.

While Lady Stanbourne went off into her dreamworld of having a learned treatise dedicated to her, Bets fixed George Purtwee with a stern eye.

"Mr. Purtwee," she said, "while I cannot but be impressed with your learning, your undoubted knowledge of timepieces, I wonder if we might discuss something else. Or was your visit meant only for my mother's edification? If so, then pray excuse me. I had best be about my—my duties. Molly still requires a firm hand, you see. She has not been with us long." She glowered at Purtwee.

Purtwee gave himself a little shake and moved his chair away from Lady Stanbourne but nearer Bets' chair. "Forgive me!" he begged, chastened. "I do tend to get carried away. Of course I came to see you, Lady Elizabeth. I had not realized you were not—not as eager to open your mind to the fascination of man's efforts to divide the days into hours and minutes—it all began with sundials, and hourglasses, and . . ."

Bets' eyes were glazing over. "Spare me," she begged.

"I see I have upset you," he said stiffly. "Perhaps I should leave now; it is growing late. I believe we had agreed I would call again on Friday? Until Friday, then. Your humble horologist goes to his lonely study to write. I am about to describe Thomas Tompion's Great Clock, made for the Royal Observatory at Greenwich in 1675. It wants winding only once a year! The pendulum is thirteen feet long!"

"Yes, Mr. Purtwee," Bets said wearily. "Until Friday, then."

"Surely, Mama, you can see why I cannot like Mr. Purtwee," Bets said as the two of them cleared away the tea things. "His pea-size brain admits of only two subjects, clocks and the vices of his cousin Burlingham. Going trains! Balance wheels! Reversed fusees! Why in heaven's name does he think we care? I was never so bored in my life. And you—you ate it up. If he so much as mentions the word 'clock' on Friday I shall throw that monstrous thing on the mantelpiece at his head. I believe I shall throw it anyhow. It was *that*—I do not wish to say the word—that started it all, when he admired it on his first visit." Bets clamped shut her lips before she could express more pointedly how she felt.

Lady Stanbourne was almost tearful. "But he plans to dedicate his treatise to me," she said plaintively.

"Do you wish to wager on it?"

"Bets! I am certain he is a man of honor!"

"Mama. Stop and think." Arms akimbo, Bets stood before her mother, her back to the hated timepiece on the mantel. "He said, and I believe I quote him exactly, 'To the lady who listened, and was as enchanted as I.' That could be anyone. No one could know he meant you. Your name would not be mentioned. Mama, can you not understand?"

Lady Stanbourne clasped her hands and looked up at the ceiling. A beatific smile lit her face. "But I would know," she said.

Bets groaned. "Yes, Mama," she said.

* * *

Lord Burlingham tried to make sense out of the snubs accorded him by the Fortescue ladies, but they were only one of the things on his mind. He had allowed his muscles to become slack; surely the drinking and whoring and time spent at the game tables could not be at fault? Whatever the reason, he faithfully engaged in a sparring match with Geordie each morning, then bathed, to the distress of both Geordie and Mrs. Burket. To them fell the onerous job of heating and carrying buckets of water upstairs, then disposing of the used bathwater afterward. Geordie finally put it to him plain. Take your blasted bath in the kitchen or the scullery or your servants will mutiny, he threatened. Somewhat abashed, Rob had his tub brought down and made do in the scullery. At least he had privacy, he thought in disgust as he searched for the soap in the dim little room. It had but one tiny window.

Afternoons, refreshed, he visited London's bookstores. Posing as a prospective buyer, he bargained and argued with booksellers of every stripe over old, rare, and unusual books, but never bought. He soon saw that he should have been more thoroughly prepared when he visited Hatchard's, for even taking into account the bookseller's profit, he should have received more than three hundred pounds for the lot he had sold them.

Finally he took eleven more books, the best of a mixed lot, back to Hatchard's. Fixing the manager with a gimlet eye, he offered the package for seven hundred pounds.

The manager raised his eyebrows and pointed out a slight stain on the leather cover of one volume. He made an offer of three hundred pounds.

Rob in turn raised his eyebrows and pointed to the title of the book, "*Des Erasmi Roterod. Concionator.*"

"So?" said the manager.

"Look across the bottom," Rob suggested.

At the base of the intricately tooled front cover were the words IO GROLIERII ET AMICORUM.

"Grolier," Rob pointed out happily. "Jean Grolier. I defy you to tell me that this is not one of the most valuable books ever offered you. And look at this—*Pilgrim's Progress,* first edition! I see I shall have to go to another bookseller."

Rob lowered his eyebrows, gathered up his bundle, and prepared to walk out. The manager called him back.

After some spirited bargaining, during which Rob indicated complete disdain for the entire transaction, he received seven hundred pounds. His investigations had paid off.

The remaining books in his library were, he could see, so much dross, worth filling a bookcase for effect and not much else. His source of funds seemed to have run out, but with a thousand pounds stowed in his safe, he need not worry for the time being. He would have to draw on his hoard soon, for his original funds were nearly exhausted.

Tom Hazleton appeared the evening of his last visit to Hatchard's, congratulated him on his newfound wealth, and helped him dispose of a decanter of brandy. Hazleton had learned that Winterfield was out of town, called to Somerset by the illness of a relative, so Tom had been unable to learn whether Winterfield held a grudge against the Earl of Burlingham. He promised to try again.

Rob told Tom of the cool reception he had received from the Fortescue ladies the night of the Donaldsons' ball, which Tom had not attended. The more he thought about it, the more it rankled.

"Just as well," said Tom, unperturbed. "Plenty more fish in the sea."

"That is what I told myself," Rob admitted, "but I would like to know *why.* It cannot be the incident at Almack's. They know all about that and Lady Elizabeth, at least, assured me she does not believe me at fault. What is more, she offered to sound out that bastard Purtwee to see if she could learn whether he was behind it! Instead, there she is, dancing with Purtwee at the ball and giving me the cut direct." Rob frowned as he refilled his brandy glass.

"Perhaps she is still worming her way into your cousin's confidence and does not dare let him know that you and she are—shall we say—friendly?" Tom offered. "Assuming you are—friendly?" He grinned.

"I have no idea what we are," said Rob, frowning again.

"You looby! When did you become such a poor specimen? Are you planning to sit here and weep into your brandy for fear the fair lady has lost interest? Good God, Rob, that is not like you. I cannot believe it. Of course, you have to decide whether she is worth it."

"You know, Tom, I rather like her," Rob mused. "If I have to get leg-shackled, she seems as good a candidate as any. Not to mention that lovely fortune."

"Very well, then, do something about it." Tom topped up his brandy glass and looked keenly at his friend. "Now that you are in funds, spend some on her. If you win her, it will come back with interest. Which reminds me, about those four pounds you owe me . . . ?"

"Yessir. Right away, sir." Rob counted out four pounds into his friend's hand. "I shall follow your advice. But do you know, I feel some guilt. Surely I am not about to acquire a conscience? I believe Lady Elizabeth deserves someone better than I. She is certain to fly up into the boughs when she learns how deep in dun territory I am—after we are wed, of course. I rather dislike having to do that to her."

Tom broke into a fit of coughing to cover his laughter. "Is it truly the Earl of Burlingham I see before me?" he demanded, "Cheer up, my friend. It is done all the time. The ladies expect it, you may be sure. Else why do we all cluster around every chit with a rich father? 'Tis human nature. You are just lucky that Lady Elizabeth's cluster seems to be a very small one. Which tells me something. Let me warn you again about her 'mothering' habit, not to mention a certain tendency toward becoming a bluestocking. Which reminds me. Someone told me she reads Shakespeare *for enjoyment!* Now, I ask you . . ." Hazleton's face betrayed his consternation.

"Egad! What next?" Rob smote his forehead in feigned horror. "But I believe I could live with that. She may read all of King Othello—no, it was King Hamlet, was it not? Or Lear? Or Richard? I can never remember—to keep herself amused while I am playing at White's. Best she have something to occupy her time while I am out."

"True," said Tom. "There is that."

Rob took some money from his wall safe and sent Geordie out to purchase a dozen neckcloths. He set Billy to polishing the curricle within an inch of its life while he curried Myrtle and Box himself. It was still early, much too early in the morning for a social call, but with his usual impatience he could not wait. He had decided to call on Lady Elizabeth without warning. Should he send a note he might be rebuffed. He could not imagine Molly having the ability to say, "Not at home," if in fact the Fortescue ladies were at home but not receiving.

Soon after ten of the clock he set out for Knightsbridge Terrace. He was arrayed in his best, with a new, and unusually stiff, neckcloth tied just so. His forehead bruise had faded, and he had canceled the morning's sparring match to avoid any further signs of injuries. The mark under his left eye was well hidden by one of Geordie's ointments. Billy's toga had been freshly laundered.

A sharp rap on the lion's head doorknocker soon brought Molly, who looked frightened the moment she saw who stood at the door.

"Oooh," she said. She glanced behind her. "Was you expected?"

"Not precisely," Rob answered. "Are the ladies at home? I hope I am not too early."

Molly seemed to be having trouble with her answer. She pondered a moment and finally said, "Well, yes—I mean they ain't gone out, but they ain't in 'ere neither."

She looked at him expectantly, as if waiting for him to puzzle that out.

"And where exactly might they be?" he inquired.

"Grubbin' in the back garden," said Molly. "Both of 'em." She stood solidly in the doorway, making no move to usher him inside.

"Might I come in?" Rob was ready to push past her.

"Your lordship! You can come in, but they ain't 'ere! They're out back in the garden!" She moved aside reluctantly, looking worried.

"Very well," said Rob. "I will wait. Please tell them I am here." He headed for the familiar sitting room as Molly scuttled to the back of the house.

His long wait was punctuated by various murmurs and exclamations and moans heard from a distance. Stirred them up proper, he chuckled to himself, imagining the panic his unannounced visit was causing. He passed the time with a close examination of the clock on the mantelpiece. Probably worth as much as all his books put together, he thought. Why had not someone in his family thought to buy such a clock? It would pay for oats for his horses for several lifetimes.

Moving the heavy clock an inch or two, he was craning his neck to see what, if anything, was marked on the back when he heard a pleasant "Good morning" behind him. He turned to see Bets staring at him.

Bets' welcoming smile turned into a look of utter dismay when she saw what he was doing. Surely not another clock fiend! Did it run in his family? She was not prepared for a droning recitation of balance wheels from this man. She should have made sure the clock was moved to a location where she and any visitors would never have to see it—her mother's bedchamber, perhaps.

Completely misconstruing Bets' expression, Rob could feel his heart sink into his boots. This visit was not going to go well. He knew it immediately.

"Good morning," he said, turning the clock back to its original position. Disconcerted by his reception, he wondered what to say next. Stick to safe subjects, he told himself.

"I have been admiring this magnificent clock," he said brightly. "I have seen it on earlier visits, true, but never took the time to examine it closely. You must be very proud of it."

"Ugh," said Bets.

"I beg your pardon?"

"It may be Mama's pride and joy but it is not mine. Are you interested in clocks?" Bets narrowed her eyes as she drew closer to Rob.

"Only as a means of keeping myself on time. I confess I know little about their workings. Are they a particular interest of yours?" Rob wished he knew what caused Lady Elizabeth's unhappy expression. What had he done now?

"No!" she said vehemently. She calmed somewhat and said, "No, I feel about them much as you do." Suddenly she beamed a delighted smile. "Will you have some refreshment? Tea? Coffee?"

"Tea would be welcome," he said, returning her smile.

Bets hurried out to notify Mrs. Arkwright, their cook who came in by the day, and Molly while Rob pondered what could have caused Lady Elizabeth's sudden change. Obviously something about clocks. He turned a chair away from the fireplace, where it had faced the mantel clock, and sat down. He felt better—until Lady Stanbourne bustled in, looking harried and stern.

"Good morning, your lordship," she said coldly. "What brings you here so early?"

It was imperative that he get Lady Elizabeth away from her mother for the moment. He did not hesitate.

"I have been neglecting you ladies, I fear," he said with a determined smile. "We have not met since the Donaldsons' ball and I have missed your pleasant company. This morning when I realized how long it had been, I determined to drive to Knightsbridge Terrace without delay, and here I am!"

"So I see," said Lady Stanbourne. She did not seem

overjoyed. "Would you care for tea? Or brandy perhaps?" Rob could tell it was costing her to offer him brandy.

"Lady Elizabeth has just gone after tea," he said. "I wonder you did not meet her as you came in."

"Oh," said her ladyship. She seemed relieved that brandy was not mentioned. "Yes." She seemed rattled. "Of course. Will you sit, my lord?"

"Thank you," he said gravely. He sat in the nearest chair. As he settled himself, something caught on his pantaloons. He rose again and looked at the seat. Worn blue silk with a number of splits; its warp threads had coalesced into a rope that had caught the fabric of his garment. Quickly he smoothed the silk and sat once again. He did not wish to embarrass Lady Stanbourne, who must be unaware of the state of that particular chair. Why did they not give up on Molly? he wondered. Surely she or whatever other servants they employed should have called it to Lady Stanbourne's attention long since and sent it out to be repaired.

Rob understood how such a small thing as a ripped chair seat could be misconstrued. While he was certain it was a matter of carelessness on the part of servants, some might believe the Fortescues had pockets to let. That was not a good impression for them to leave, he knew; if Lady Elizabeth hoped to attract a suitable husband she should make sure the Fortescue fortune was displayed and unquestioned. He considered himself a case in point. Always neat in public, his curricle in good repair, his house looking its best when viewed from the street. No one could know from appearances that he was in dun territory. And no one should be permitted to make that mistake about the Fortescue ladies. He decided he would try to drop a hint in Lady Elizabeth's ear if he could word it so as not to offend.

"Your tea, my lord," said Lady Stanbourne, startling him from his reverie. Molly had brought in the tea things. Lady Elizabeth was still missing, but soon appeared bearing a plate of biscuits. A wreath of green leaves twined around the edge of the plate and tiny sprigs of bluebells were stuck here and there among the leaves. Rob was delighted. He recalled her greens-be-decked plate from another tea. Here was a lady with an artistic touch who would bring her talents to the entertaining they would do when they were married. Lady Elizabeth appealed to him more and more.

"Could I interest you in a drive, Lady Elizabeth?" he asked once he had eaten a single biscuit and drunk his tea. "My curricle awaits, and it has been some time since we have driven out together." He gave her his warmest smile.

"I should enjoy that," said Bets as Lady Stanbourne waved her hands wildly, seeking to interrupt.

"But, Bets," she cried, "you must remember you . . ."

Bets knew immediately. She had agreed to discourage the earl's attentions. But she was eager to tell the earl of her conversation with George Purtwee, and that required privacy; she had no intention of confiding in her mother, who was bemused by the hateful Mr. Purtwee. Bets glanced at the earl, who was waiting expectantly. Was he as debt-ridden as Mr. Purtwee claimed? He showed no evidence of it. If it came to a choice of believing the earl or Mr. Purtwee, she decided to choose the earl.

"I must get my tippet—and bonnet—I will be down in a trice," she said and hurried up the stairs. Lady Stanbourne stared after her, her mouth open.

"I know it is long before the fashionable hour," Rob told Lady Stanbourne, "but the day is so fine, I am eager to take advantage of it." He smiled. "I shall have her back by nuncheon. I hope that is satisfactory?"

Remembering her manners, Lady Stanbourne composed her startled face. "Would you care to share nuncheon with us?" she asked.

Rob detected the lack of eagerness in her tone, but he believed another hour or so with Lady Elizabeth was worth it. "I should be delighted," he said.

Chapter Eleven

Bets fingered the plaid shawl draped so comfortingly over the seat of the Earl of Burlingham's curricle. Such a thoughtful man he was, never forgetting the little extra touches a lady appreciated. She approved of his friendly relationship with his tiger, as well. They had greeted each other in comradely fashion when she and the earl had left her mother's house for their drive. The scrawny boy in his spotless toga seemed to worship his employer but was not above teasing him a little.

"How long has Billy been your tiger?" she asked. That should keep his attention for a few minutes. She could not bring herself to blurt out Mr. Purtwee's sordid tale of the state of the earl's finances, much as she wished to know the truth. What if Mr. Purtwee had told the truth? It was too monstrous to contemplate. She would have to give the earl the cut direct if he were penniless. Somehow, somewhere, she had to find a suitor with money. . . .

"Not above eight months," said Rob.

"I beg pardon?"

"Not above eight months, I said," Rob repeated. "I do not believe you were attending." He looked down at the brown eyes fastened on his neckcloth. "Is something bothering you?"

"I—I must tell you of my conversation with your cousin," she said. She continued to finger the plaid shawl.

"That bad, was it?" He chuckled. "I opposed this plan from the beginning, you know. Did he let go with any useful information, or did he spend all his time assuring you of what a rotten bounder I am?"

"Yes—no—I did learn something," Bets said with a sigh. Maybe she could concentrate on Mr. Purtwee's account of the Almack's incident and leave the question of the earl's fortune or lack of it for another time.

"Yes? Are you going to tell me?" Rob placed his hand over the smaller hand clutching the plaid shawl. "Is it so very dreadful that you cannot speak of it?"

"Oh, no, not at all!" Bets brightened. "Mr. Purtwee told me he was *there* and saw it all, but, your lordship, there were holes in his story. He—"

"Not your lordship," Rob said firmly. "Rob, if you please. Or at least Robert. Please continue."

Bets smiled. "Then you must call me Bets," she said. "To go on, Mr. Purtwee was persuaded that you were badly foxed, yet he indicated you walked into Almack's on your own two feet without stumbling, then suddenly collapsed at Mrs. Drummond Burrell's feet."

Rob grimaced. "I believe I have been known to do that," he said.

"Oh?" Bets was crestfallen. "I did not realize. I thought—my brother—"

"Ah, the estimable Godfrey? He has a fondness for the bottle?"

"No, no, I mean my other brother, William. Half brother, I should say. I have seen him—but never mind. It is possible I am wrong, but I would wager a groat that in quoting what you are supposed to have said to Mrs. Drummond Burrell, Mr. Purtwee was making it up as he went along! No one but he—and Mrs. Drummond Burrell of course—seems to have been within earshot. I propose to ask Mrs. Drummond Burrell myself, if I can arrange to see her."

"But she is the veriest dragon! You would do that for me?" Rob's grip tightened on her hand.

"Do watch out!" Bets cried. Rob's attention had strayed from his horses and they were about to drive past the park entrance.

Rob removed his hand and turned his pair into the park. "Of course," he said. "Thank you."

Now how was she to draw that warm, strong hand back upon her own?

"Tell me what else he had to say," Rob continued. "Not that one can trust him. I am curious to hear his version. I have had it third hand, but never before from anyone who thought to question him on it."

Rob's hand came back upon hers. It was if she had been starved, given a meal, had it suddenly removed, then had it returned to her again. Bets felt warm all over. And somehow comforted. Cosseted. She looked down at his hand with its strong, long fingers, lightly holding hers. Other gentlemen had held her hand on occasion and she had thought it merely presumptuous. Not so today. She was becoming much too fond of this exciting man, whatever his reputation, whatever his fortune. She could not bear to learn he was penniless, so resolutely she turned her thoughts away from the subject.

"I became most suspicious when I mentioned that Mrs. Drummond Burrell and I are bosom bows and Mr. Purtwee seemed taken aback," she said. "It was as if he feared I would find out the truth from her, and it would not agree with his story. That is why I am determined to quiz her, if I can arrange it."

"You? You and that battle-ax are bosom bows? I would never have thought it!"

"Oh, you ninny! I was speaking in jest! I have never even engaged the lady in conversation. Lady Sefton, who is my mama's friend, sponsored us at Almack's. I have persuaded Mama to see her and seek a voucher for Wednesday next in hopes Mrs. Drummond Burrell will be present as well. That seemed simpler than calling at her home, where I might not be received. Do you not think so?" Bets looked at him appealingly. The idea of bearding the dragon had her quaking inside, but she was determined to go through with it.

"As you wish," he said. His hand tightened on hers and it was all she could do not to return the pressure. "I am still overwhelmed that you should wish to do this for me. I would go myself were I not certain the dragon lady would have her butler throw me out the door. But you—I cannot see her denying you admittance."

"I shall try to see her at Almack's first," said Bets with finality. "If that fails, I shall try a visit to her home."

At this early hour the couple had the park almost to themselves. Only a few solitary horsemen traveled its paths and paid them no attention. What a glorious day for a walk, Bets thought suddenly, and suggested it to her companion.

"I agree," he said, and pulled up. "Billy, we shall not be gone long. To the Serpentine, my lady?" He motioned toward the water, where two small boys were sailing their toy boats under the watchful eyes of a nursemaid.

Rob helped her down and they strolled decorously toward the Serpentine, Bets' hand on his arm.

"Now will you tell me?" he asked, stopping their progress. He turned to face her and took her hands gently in his. "Why did you avoid me at the Donaldsons' ball? Had I done something wrong? Or is it that you do not wish to be seen in public with me? Must we meet only in the privacy of your home, or in a near-deserted park early in the morning? I believe I deserve to know."

Bets saw the hurt look on his face and turned away. How could she explain that she *had* to find a wealthy suitor or she and her mother would soon be reduced to poverty? Oh, it was done all the time, she knew that, but it seemed so heartless. Besides, she and Lady Stanbourne were determined not to admit near-poverty until the wealthy suitor was firmly in hand and the banns read.

"I—I was not avoiding you," she said finally. "It—it just happened that way."

Rob dropped her left hand and turned her face toward him. "Look at me," he said. "That is not true, and you know it. Look me in the eye and tell me."

"Perhaps—perhaps you are another about-to-be-dismissed suitor?" she said hesitantly.

Rob's eyes narrowed. "Then why are you preparing to beard the lady dragon for me?" he demanded. "That will not fadge, Lady Elizabeth—I mean Lady Bets. Is it that you believe I truly did do the unpardonable at Almack's, and you only await Mrs. Drummond Burrell's confirmation to consign me to the nether regions?"

"No!" An agitated Bets pulled away from Rob and hid her face in her hands. "That is not so!"

"Then . . . ?" He reached for her hands again, but she clasped them behind her back.

"You must not ask!" she cried. "Please do not ask!"

"Aha," he said. "Some devilish plot is afoot here. No doubt my fine cousin has sweet-talked his way into your confidence and is pursuing you himself. That sounds like him. No doubt he has filled your pretty ears with scandalous tales about me while making himself out to be a knight on a white charger. Be assured that once he has captured your regard and relegated me to the devil, he will parade you on his arm in my presence—and later drop you like a hot coal. Believe me."

Bets looked at him, wonder in her gaze. He had read her mind—all but the part about Burlingham's being in dun territory. "I believe you," she said. "That is exactly what he has tried to do."

"I have faults—God knows too many faults—but lying to a lady is not one of them," said Rob. He felt a pang of guilt at his pretense of wealth—but had he ever actually said he was wealthy? No. He had never mentioned the subject.

"Am I to hope that a fascination with horology is not one of them either?" Bets asked, smiling now.

"Heaven forbid! What would make you think so? Was it that clock on your mother's mantel?"

"You had me worried for a moment," she confessed. "You are aware, surely, that your cousin considers himself an expert horologist? And bores us—me—to tears raving on about—about whatever those things are, linch pins I think they are. Some part of a clock." As Rob burst into laughter, she looked affronted. "Why do you laugh?"

"Linch pins, my dear Lady Elizabeth, are what hold the wheels on the axles of a carriage. I will be glad to show you when we return to my curricle." He laughed again. "I can see Cousin George has not made the impression he hoped."

"No, he did not," Bets agreed. She laughed. "And we have not even reached the Serpentine. Shall we go on?"

Rob tucked her arm in his and they walked sedately to the Serpentine.

Rob believed he had reestablished some kind of rapport with Lady Elizabeth but he was in a quandary as to how to proceed. It was evident that the damnable George Purtwee as well as Lady Elizabeth's mother were doing their utmost to discredit him, as if his reputation were not dismal enough already. He remained silent, thinking, as he drove slowly back toward Knightsbridge Terrace. Damn. He was growing fond of this chit; she would make an admirable wife. He could do much worse than spend the rest of his life with her. His heart leaped as he realized anew that she had offered to face Mrs. Drummond Burrell. He turned to his companion, smiled, and put his hand over hers.

"A drive in the park and a walk to the Serpentine have never been so pleasant before," he said. "May I look forward to your company again soon?"

"I should like that," she said. She started to draw her hand away and then thought better of it. She blushed.

Rob gave no indication that he had noticed. "Perhaps I could interest you in a visit to Astley's," he said. "Drives in the park are all very well, but possibly you would enjoy something more exciting."

"Oh! Astley's!" Bets grinned and her eyes sparkled. Without thinking she turned her hand to grasp his in a firm grip. "I have always wished to go there and see the horses perform! Mama has always held that Astley's was not a genteel place for a lady to visit, and no one before has seen fit to invite me there. Oh, I should love to visit Astley's."

"Then you shall," he said. "It is perfectly respectable, I assure you. Many of the *ton* go there. Of course, one must rub elbows with the common folk, but I do not believe that would bother you."

"No indeed," she said. "Of course not." She squeezed his hand, then suddenly realized what she was doing. How could she be so forward! In confusion she looked down at the strong gloved fingers held in her own, covered in delicate kidskin. She released her grip and instead clasped the edge of the seat. What he must think of her!

"I would like to hold your hand more often, you know," he said softly.

More than three seasons had left Bets with plenty of experience politely fending off the advances of other gentlemen. Never before had she wished *not* to discourage one. She looked down at her lap as she tried to think of a suitable response. "Oh," she said finally.

"Does that dismay you?"

"You are forward, sir."

"Sir? I believed we were beyond 'sir.' The name is Rob."

"Rob," she said in a small voice. She still could not look at him.

"Please bear it in mind," he said. He returned his hand to the reins. "When might you be free to go to Astley's?"

"I hope to see Mrs. Drummond Burrell at Almack's on Wednesday. Perhaps Thursday? By then I might have something to report."

"Thursday it is," he said as he drew up before her home. He helped her alight and walked with her to the door.

"You are coming to nuncheon, are you not?" she asked as she opened the door.

"Certainly. Just tell me where your stable is so Billy

can put away the horses. How does one reach the stable? Go around the corner?"

Bets blushed crimson. "We—we have no stable," she admitted.

"No horses? No carriage? How do you ladies get where you wish to go?"

"We—we hire," she said. "We really do not need a carriage—the shops are all so close—it seemed a useless extravagance for two ladies. I am sorry, sir." She bowed her head.

"Rob, not 'sir,' " he said absently. "Is there a livery nearby? If you would be so kind as to tell Billy the direction."

"Yes," she murmured. They returned to the curricle and she explained to Billy how to reach the livery on the next street. Then they went in to nuncheon.

Lady Stanbourne was chillingly polite toward their guest. Bets, afraid that their lack of a stable told the earl more than they wished him to know of their circumstances, said little. Rob tried to make small talk with his hostesses and found it hard-going. Bets noticed his frequent glances around the dining room. Was he measuring the worth of their furnishings? Did their straitened circumstances show? The food was unexceptionable, served by an awkward Molly. Molly's apron was clean; perhaps Mrs. Arkwright in the kitchen had seen to that. The darn in the damask tablecloth was hardly noticeable. Still Bets could not relax.

Rob did not linger after nuncheon. He was stiffly formal as he accepted his hat and prepared to leave.

"Until Thursday, then," he said as he departed. He did not smile.

The Earl of Burlingham felt oddly dejected as he guided his curricle toward home. The Fortescue ladies had no stable. They did not even have their own horses, which could have been boarded at a livery, or their own carriage. They seemed to have but one visible servant, the poorly trained Molly, though he supposed someone else had to be in the kitchen; Molly certainly had had no time both to cook and serve. Suddenly he remembered the split seat of the chair. He recalled other telltale signs—had that been a darn in the tablecloth? It was so inconspicuous he would not have noticed had he not been studying the dining room so carefully. He had heard the front door groan as he departed, which must mean no one had oiled the hinges. So many little things, and he began to fear they added up to a pair of ladies trying to put on a good front while short of funds.

Just as he was doing himself.

The Earl of Burlingham groaned more loudly than the Fortescue door. Could it be true? Was he trying to court a lady for her fortune when there was no fortune? And then a horrible thought struck him. Was she, by any chance, only after *his* fortune?

He tried to think calmly as he reached his own home and strode up the steps, leaving Billy to take care of the horses and carriage. Inside he found Geordie laboriously polishing the stair rail.

"Leave it and bring brandy into the library," he ordered.

"Sir? This is a mite overdue," said Geordie. "We just got the polish, if you remember, and Mrs. Burket, she asked me to help while she works upstairs." He continued to rub a rag over the smooth oak.

"You do not take orders from Mrs. Burket," Rob reminded him sternly. "Brandy. Library. NOW."

"Aye, sir. Right away, sir." Geordie left the rag draped over the rail and scurried off.

Rob dropped his hat on the hall table, ran his fingers through his hair, and repaired to the library, where he sat fuming until Geordie appeared with brandy.

"A mite early in the day for brandy, if I may venture to say so," Geordie chided him.

"You may not," his employer said sternly. "We have a new problem. It requires brandy."

"And what might that be, your lordship?"

"I fear me that Lady Elizabeth lacks the ready. She

has no brass. She is in dun territory. In other words, the fortune I have been chasing does not exist. How can that be, when it was well known that her father oozed money from every pore? He would not have left her penniless. Yet the more I see of the Fortescues, the more evident it becomes that they are watching every farthing and have none to spare. How can that be? Do you think they could have spent it all since her father died?"

Rob poured himself a liberal helping of brandy and drank it down. He frowned at Geordie.

"When did the late earl die?" Geordie asked.

"Five or six years ago, I believe."

"They could ha' spent it all," Geordie mused. "Aye, they could ha'. You said Lady Elizabeth's been through three or four seasons? That would account for plenty of blunt. Why not ask your friend Hazleton? He's known her for years."

"Perhaps," said Rob. He poured himself another drink. "Maybe I should call on him this evening." He downed the brandy and stared at the decanter. "I shall need more of this. Have we more?"

"Oh, yes, sir. Now that you're no longer rolled up, we have plenty."

"Bring it."

Rob did not visit Tom Hazleton that evening. Geordie found him snoring gently in his chair when he went to summon him to supper. Awakened, Rob protested volubly and fought all attempts to get him on his feet. Finally Geordie went after Billy, and with some help from Mrs. Burket, they got Rob upstairs and on his bed. Geordie removed his boots, draped the coverlet over him, and left him.

" 'E ain't done that in weeks," Mrs. Burket said regretfully as the three servants went downstairs. "I'd 'oped 'e'd turned a new leaf."

"Poor lad," said Geordie. He frowned.

"Might as well eat," Mrs. Burket remarked. "Plenty of it, with 'is lordship missin' 'is supper."

Among them they cleaned up every bite of oxtail

soup, a leg of veal, plaice, vegetables, and various savories. Rob slept on, unknowing.

"My lord. My lord? Are you awake? Your friend Hazleton is here. Should I show him in?"

"Go away, Geordie. Come back tomorrow. Good God, what happened to my head?" The Earl of Burlingham opened his eyes and snorted. He found himself lying fully dressed on his bed, his lower half wrapped in a tangle of coverlet. He closed his eyes again.

"You're out of practice," said Geordie. "Shall I tell Mr. Hazleton—excuse me, sir, here he is." The servant stepped aside to admit an exasperated Tom Hazleton, who was attired in a new green coat.

"My God, Rob, have you come to this?" Hazleton demanded. "Where were you last night? Out with some young bucks and you did not call me? Or have you started to drink alone? You are a disgrace to the bloods of London. For shame! Geordie, what happened?"

"The master overdid it a mite," said Geordie, straight-faced.

"I can see that. Bring us some tea, would you? And perhaps some toast? If our fine fellow here can keep it down. I will endeavor to rouse him while you are gone."

So saying, Hazleton heaved roughly at Rob's shoulders until Rob was half sitting, half lying. When Tom let him go for a moment, Rob sank down again on his pillow and groaned.

"Geordie told me you had planned to visit me last evening," Tom reported. "Changed your mind, did you? Went elsewhere and got foully floored? What did you want of me?"

"Tea," Rob said weakly. "Where is that blasted Geordie and the tea?"

"Coming soon. Now sit up and tell me what this is all about."

"I fear I am hoist by my own petard," Rob mumbled as he pushed himself up and gingerly put his stocking feet to the floor. "Ooh! Where are my damned slippers?"

"A pox on your slippers. There are your boots; put them on. I know nothing of your slippers. Do you plan to tell me what this is all about? Hoist by your own petard? Ha!"

Mrs. Burket must have had tea waiting, for Geordie entered with a steaming cup.

"Shall I hold it for you, your lordship?" he asked. "Your hands don't seem too steady."

Rob scowled at him and took the cup. A sip told him it was not too hot, and he drank several drafts. His hands shook ever so slightly despite his best efforts.

He rubbed his eyes and sat up straighter. "Could Lady Elizabeth have run through a fortune in five or six years?" he demanded.

"Ah, it is Lady Elizabeth, is it?"

"It is her fortune I am asking about," Rob corrected him. He looked with irritation at Geordie, standing ready to take his cup. "More tea, you scoundrel, and where is the toast?"

"Aye, your lordship," said Geordie. "Right away, sir." He waited until Rob had drained the cup, then took it and hurried away.

"It has come to my attention that Lady Elizabeth pinches her pennies," Rob said. He sighed. "No stables. Chair covers in rags. No decent servants. Other signs of near-poverty, but that will suffice. Yet we know her father the esteemed earl was rolling in the ready. A regular Croesus, by all accounts. Where has it gone? Could her mother have spent it all on her seasons? I cannot court a penniless wench. Damn it all, just as I was getting rather fond of the girl. What have you heard?"

Tom stared at his friend in amusement. "I have heard nothing," he said. "I warned you! You cannot want such a forward creature in any case. She will be mothering you to death, mark my words. Try someone else. Plenty of fish in the sea, as I have been at pains to remind you."

"And consider all the time and attention—and even some money!—I have spent on her as wasted? Not on your life! I tell you, I am halfway there. She likes me.

She is prepared to face Mrs. Drummond Burrell on my account. D'you hear that? Face Mrs. Drummond Burrell! I do not see you doing that for me." Rob rubbed his unshaven jaw and glared at his friend.

"Perhaps she angered her father somehow and was cut off with a shilling," Tom offered. "I have no idea. If you like, I could nose around . . . I believe my older sister's husband's brother had some dealings with the old earl once or twice. He might know something."

"Would you? Where is this brother?"

"Hampshire, but he comes often to London."

"Very well. Ask him, will you? And what about Winterfield? Were you ever able to see him?"

"Ah. That came to naught. Had dinner with him at m'club, all right and tight, and brought up your name. 'That bastard,' he said. 'Heard he had to go back to Dorset, tail between his legs. Serves him right.' 'Have you seen him recently?' I asked, and he said, 'Hell, no, not since our duel, and if I ever see him again it will be too soon.' I turned the talk to other things, and learned he was in Scotland when the Almack's incident happened. I do not think very highly of Winterfield, but I have never known him to lie."

"Did he marry his adored Olivia?"

"He is not married. That is all I know."

Rob heaved a great sigh. "Nothing is going right," he mourned. "Where is Geordie? I need more tea. Will you have a cup, if he ever gets here?"

Tom turned from perusing the ominous gray clouds visible out the window. "Thank you, no," he said. "I must get home before the rain starts. Open carriage, you know. Get a hold of yourself, old man. You are a sorry sight. I will see you when you are feeling better. Now eat some toast, and count your blessings." He turned to go.

"Blessings? Ha! I would not recognize one if it hit me in the face."

"Here is your tea, sir," said Geordie. He carried a tray to the bedside, where Rob still sat. "A fresh lot, sir, and toast. The toast is still warm! Eat up, sir, before it gets cold!" He handed Rob a napkin.

Rob bit into his toast. Warm, nicely buttered, spread with blackberry jam . . . He felt better.

Chapter Twelve

Wednesday. Time for Bets' visit to Almack's in hopes of getting a private word with Mrs. Drummond Burrell. Lady Stanbourne had obtained a voucher from Lady Sefton. Lady Stanbourne was against the entire plan, Bets knew. She had told her daughter that she did not plan to jeopardize Lady Sefton's friendship for such a nonsensical notion.

It was important that Bets look her best. For days she and her mother had labored over the gown she had worn for her presentation at court—well over three years ago now!—which had not been worn since. Much too fussy for ordinary wear, it looked to be exactly what it was: a white court dress with huge skirt looped over a petticoat bedecked with acres of lace. The plumes she had worn in her hair had been dyed long since and one now adorned her riding hat. The dress, though, had hung untouched in her wardrobe. Bets had snipped the bodice from the skirt, and together she and Lady Stanbourne decided the skirt alone would provide enough fabric for an entire gown if they cut it in the popular slim, straight Grecian style.

Lady Stanbourne was even now pressing its creases as Molly looked on in awe. Molly was not to be trusted with such an important gown. Bets meanwhile was pacing her bedchamber in agitation, recalling herself at intervals to gather shoes, stockings, gloves, fan, reticule, and all the other necessities. How was she to gain Mrs. Drummond Burrell's ear? What if that supercilious patroness dismissed her out of hand? A gentleman's reputation—nay, his very future—might depend on her and what she hoped to learn.

She thought of her last parting from the Earl of Burlingham. He had been stiff and cool during nuncheon at the house in Knightsbridge Terrace and had not lingered. What had she done? She could think of nothing. Perhaps he believed that her offer to try to talk to Mrs. Drummond Burrell was made in jest. Well, she would show him. They had an engagement on the morrow. Bets squared her shoulders and was donning her stockings when her mother walked in, carrying the dress.

It was a triumph. Cut low, with brief sleeves (to save fabric), it was white silk crepe de chine, unadorned (there had been no time for embroidery or other trimming); it fit her slim figure perfectly. Her mother's pearls, which had last appeared at the court presentation, were the finishing touch. Between them they got Bets' hair in order, and Lady Stanbourne produced a few more pearls to twine through the topknot she created laboriously on Bets' head.

"Why it should take so much effort to dress one's hair so that it looks effortless, I shall never understand," Lady Stanbourne complained as she drove in another hairpin. She stood aside to admire the effect. "I do believe you will do. Now remember, speak nicely to the young gentlemen, but do not let any one of them monopolize you."

"Yes, Mama." Bets' mind was far away, intent on her evening's assignment.

"What time is it? Oh, dear, I must get dressed myself. Do go and sit quietly somewhere so your gown is not mussed. I shall be ready shortly."

Almack's was abuzz with conversation when they arrived in a hired hackney. Several heads looked up in appreciation as Bets, quaking inside but regal and assured outside, entered with her mother at her side. She knew she looked her best, which gave her a measure of confidence.

Where was Mrs. Drummond Burrell? Best get it over

as soon as possible. Bets scanned the crowd but did not see the patroness anywhere.

Lady Sefton walked up to them, smiling, and greeted them warmly. "You are truly in looks tonight," she said, eyeing Bets' gown. "I wonder that some gentleman did not steal you away the moment you walked in the door."

Bets blushed. This was an accolade indeed, from a patroness of Almack's! That gave her the courage to ask Lady Sefton whether Mrs. Drummond Burrell was in attendance.

"I believe I saw her earlier," Lady Sefton replied, her eyes still on Bets' gown. "You must tell me the name of your dressmaker."

Bets and her mother exchanged glances. "Oh, your ladyship, she only sews when she feels like it," Bets hastened to say. "She is—ah—retiring, and this may be the last gown we shall have from her. I am so sorry, your ladyship."

"Should she change her mind, you will let me know," said Lady Sefton as she turned to go. She waved at a friend and left them.

"So Mrs. Drummond Burrell is here," Bets said softly. "I must go in search of her."

"You must not! This gentleman"—Lady Stanbourne indicated a blond man resplendent in military uniform—"is about to ask you to dance. I am sure of it!" She turned to smile at the gentleman.

"Lady Elizabeth! Is it really you?" said the blond gentleman. He stood before her, looking intently into her face. "Surely you remember me, John Cravenshaw?"

One of her admirers from her first season! He had not been in the army then. She recalled him as a foppish dandy with little to say. "Of course I remember you, Mr. Cravenshaw," she answered.

"*Captain* Cravenshaw," he corrected her. "I have the honor to be serving in His Majesty's forces to put Bonaparte where he belongs." He smoothed his red coat. "I go to the Continent in a fortnight. I am in no hurry, frankly. Deuced difficult to keep one's self tidy in a war, I am told."

"I wish you Godspeed," said Bets. She grasped her mother's arm and said brightly, "Oh, there is dear Minerva! I have been wishing to speak to her for this age." She tugged a surprised Lady Stanbourne toward a distant knot of people.

"Bets!" said Lady Stanbourne, following reluctantly. "Who is Minerva?"

Bets did not answer.

As they drew closer, Bets was able to separate the cluster of women in a variety of fashionable gowns into individuals. Holding the attention of the group was none other than Mrs. Drummond Burrell.

Bets steered her still-protesting mother to the edge of the group. Evidently Mrs. Drummond Burrell was incensed at the behavior of someone. She waved her arms and gasped. Could it be the Earl of Burlingham she was castigating?

"I was never so shocked," said the lady, looking shocked. "A pea green gown! Pea green, mind you! And him dead not six months! He would turn over in his grave. At least she could have gone to the trouble of having it dyed if she had no proper mourning. I shall cut her dead should I ever have the misfortune to meet her again." She sniffed.

The group of women waited eagerly for more details, but Mrs. Drummond Burrell apparently had none. Some of the gathering began to drift away. Bets waited until only one remained, an elderly soul with thin white hair. She was dressed entirely in rusty black.

"What did you say, Clementina?" the old lady asked. "Speak up! A body cannot hear with all the chatter."

Mrs. Drummond Burrell looked sternly at the old lady. "Where is your ear trumpet?" she demanded. "I was merely reporting on Lady Forrester's gown. I shall not repeat it. I have told it twice." She seemed to notice Bets and Lady Stanbourne for the first time. Dismissing the old lady with a wave, she looked critically at Bets. "You wished to speak to me?"

"Oh, yes, please, madam," said Bets. She closed her fingers around her fan in a death grip. "I would have your tale of the collapse of the Earl of Burlingham here recently from your own lips." There, she thought. I have said it.

Mrs. Drummond Burrell's face grew red with rage. "That obnoxious poltroon!" she spat. "That—that harebrained, beef-witted bumble! Is he a friend of yours?"

"We are acquainted," Bets acknowledged. "That is why I wished to hear the tale from your own lips. I cannot believe it of him, but of course you know best." She looked modestly at her feet.

Lady Stanbourne seemed about to join the conversation. Knowing how she had come to feel about the Earl of Burlingham, Bets wanted anything but that. She put a restraining hand on her mother's arm and gave her a telling look. Lady Stanbourne subsided.

Mrs. Drummond Burrell's wrath had not cooled. "Does he admit he impugned my gown?" she demanded. "Does he admit he fell at my feet in a drunken heap? I have never been so insulted in my life!"

"Just what did he say?" Bets persisted.

"He had the nerve—the nerve!—to—to call my gown unbecoming," she said. "My blue one with the Brandenburgs! Oh!" The memory obviously rankled.

"You heard him say this?"

Mrs. Drummond Burrell stopped short as if a memory had just struck her. She paused for several moments, thinking hard.

"Now that you mention it, I am not certain that I did," she said in a more normal voice. "It was noisy—the din here can be something terrible, as I have pointed out to the other patronesses many times, you may be sure—and his remark came out in more of a mumble than anything else. But he said it! He did! None other than—who was it? The young Purtwee? I believe it was he—was standing near, and such a gentleman! He helped me to a chair—naturally I was overcome—and repeated what he had heard Burlingham say. I have no reason to doubt it. Why should he make up a tale from whole cloth? He is a most exemplary young man. But indeed, I can assure you that the drunken Burlingham did fall in a heap and had to be carried out. Such behavior! At Almack's!" Her temper looked to be rising again.

"Oh, madam, it must have been monstrous," Bets said sympathetically. "I am so grateful for your side of the story. How kind of you to tell me, when I am sure the memory is so unpleasant for you."

Mrs. Drummond Burrell preened a little, then looked sharply at Bets.

"I know you, do I not?" she asked. "You are . . ."

"Lady Elizabeth Fortescue," said Bets. "And my mother, the dowager Countess of Stanbourne." Lady Stanbourne smiled.

"Of course," said Mrs. Drummond Burrell, cheerful now. "I remember your husband the earl. Such a fine man. Of course I was but a child when he passed on."

"Yes, he was a fine man," Lady Stanbourne agreed. "Thank you."

A few more pleasantries and Bets was able to steer her mother away, though Lady Stanbourne seemed willing to discuss her late husband as long as Mrs. Drummond Burrell was willing to listen.

Bets was jubilant. "You see?" she asked gleefully. It was all she could do to keep her voice down. "She did *not* actually hear Burlingham say those dreadful things! She relied on what that toad George Purtwee told her! I vow, I knew it all the time. Burlingham never would have insulted her so. That is not at all his way. You know that, Mama—has he ever spoken out of turn in your hearing? Of course not!"

"But he was foxed," Lady Stanbourne remonstrated. "You must know how a gentleman can forget his manners when he is foxed." She gave her daughter a telling look. They both were only too aware of the drinking habits and resulting behavior of the late Earl of Stanbourne's younger son, Godfrey's brother William.

Incensed, Bets forgot herself. "Burlingham is nothing like William!" she declared, only to blush fiery red when she saw heads begin to turn toward her. This was no place to be bandying the Earl of Burlingham's name about. Too many people were aware of his supposed transgression and felt no sympathy toward him.

"I must fix my hair," Bets muttered, and pulled her mother toward the ladies' withdrawing room. "Like William indeed," she said under her breath. "Ha!"

Once calmed down, Bets returned to the crush. Her animated face, radiating good cheer now that she had accomplished her mission, and her vastly becoming gown drew the glances of more than one gentleman—now that she wished only to go home and ponder how to let the Earl of Burlingham know the good news at the earliest possible moment. When she suggested to Lady Stanbourne that they leave, that lady was horrified.

"Just as you are beginning to take!" said Lady Stanbourne. "That is why we are here, if you will search your memory. Do look! Is that not the Marquess of Mackworth's son approaching? And I see Viscount Praed looking at you! We shall remain." She frowned at her daughter, then turned and broke into a smile aimed at the Marquess of Mackworth's son.

Bets heaved a small sigh and tried to look pleased at the advent of the gentleman, whose gait, she was certain, was learned from a duck.

They remained until near eleven of the clock. Bets danced, was treated to stale cake and orgeat, and danced some more. Lady Stanbourne beamed at her from the sidelines. Young Lord Fidminster insisted on taking them home in his carriage when he learned they had no escort, and held Bets' hand overlong when he helped her alight.

"A vastly successful evening!" Lady Stanbourne crowed once they were inside their own home again. She removed her turban and fluffed her hair before the look-

ing glass in the entrance hall. "Was it not so? You look
tired, dear. Not accustomed to so much dancing, I fear."

"Probably," said Bets. Her mind was elsewhere. Tomorrow! Tomorrow she would see him, and tell him
George Purtwee had made up the insult to Mrs. Drummond Burrell out of whole cloth. He would be ecstatic.
He would take her hands in his and look into her eyes as
he loomed closer—and closer—and . . .

But what future was there for them? What if Mr.
Purtwee's revelations regarding Burlingham's penury
were true?

She had already caught Mr. Purtwee in one lie, she assured herself. No doubt he had also lied when he insisted
Burlingham had not a farthing to his name.

Having convinced herself, she begged off the detailed
recall of the evening her mother was eager for, and went
up to bed. She fell asleep almost at once.

The next day, Thursday, was a miserable, gloomy,
drippy day. Fog alternated with periods of drizzle, and it
was so dark Lady Stanbourne called for candles to light
their breakfast. The atmosphere seemed to put a damper
on the entire household except for Bets. Lady Stanbourne looked unhappily at her soft-boiled egg, her mind
far away, and Molly slammed dishes around as if they
were her enemies. Bets' cheerful countenance seemed
out of place.

"Why so gay this morning?" her mother asked once
she had come out of her daydream and noticed Bets'
face. "I declare, I had expected all manner of posies and
notes and invitations this morning, after such a successful evening at Almack's. I thought at least young Lord
Fidminster would . . . I mean, he did have the courtesy to
bring us home, and . . . but nothing and nobody have arrived. Ah, well, perhaps later . . ." She heaved a theatri-
cal sigh.

"But, Mama! Burlingham is to call today! How could
you forget? I am heartily relieved that no one else has
appeared, or I should have to leave them for you to en-

tertain while I go driving with the earl." Bets smiled in anticipation.

"Driving? Today? In this weather? What can you be thinking of? Of course you will not go driving. I doubt that the earl will even suggest it, should he appear, which I also doubt. In any case I will not permit you to go out and catch your death. Look at you! That thin muslin would not keep a flea warm. Whatever are you thinking of?" Lady Stanbourne lapsed into a series of "Tut-tuts" as she tackled her egg, which had grown quite cold.

"I shall wear my cloak, of course, and a hat, and take an umbrella," Bets replied. She sat down and took a swallow of tea. It was lukewarm. "Would you get me some fresh tea, Molly?" she addressed the hovering maid. "This has grown cold."

"It were hot when I brought it in," Molly mumbled. "Them as is late to meals . . ." She went off toward the kitchen, carrying the teapot. Bets could hear a loud exchange with the cook, and soon Molly, looking belligerent, returned with the teapot.

"Here," said Molly. "Cook wants to know, how much more of her 'ot water are you goin' to need?"

"*Her* hot water?" Lady Stanbourne was scandalized. "Molly, will you ask Cook what she means by that?" She rose hurriedly, pushing her cold egg away in disgust. "I shall have to speak to her myself, I suppose . . . or would you do it, Bets? You were the one who complained about the tea." She sat down again and contemplated her egg.

Molly hid a malicious grin as Bets reluctantly headed for the kitchen. Bets' cheerful mood was evaporating fast. Their two servants were at odds again. Lady Stanbourne was bemoaning the lack of day-after attention from the gentlemen Bets had met at Almack's. None of them had made the slightest impression on her. And Burlingham—would he expect her to go driving on such a miserable day? In his open curricle? But how else was she to get him alone to tell him about her meeting with

Mrs. Drummond Burrell? Were they not to go to Astley's?

She was attempting to placate the cook when the door knocker sounded. Molly, her hands full of breakfast dishes, was on her way to the kitchen when Bets stepped into the passage, intending to open the front door herself. It seemed inevitable. She and Molly ducked to one side—the same side—as they met, then ducked the other way, but to no avail. They clashed, and Molly dropped Lady Stanbourne's plate, the half-eaten egg leaving its cup and landing squarely on the hall carpet. Molly screamed.

Bets stood stock-still for a moment, her fists clenched. She looked at Molly.

"Clean it up," she ordered. "I will go to the door."

"Yes'm," said Molly, abashed. She was attempting to pick up the remnants of the egg with her fingers when Bets brushed past her to reach the front door.

"Good morning!" said Rob brightly.

Bets looked beyond him to the curricle. Billy was holding the horses while doing what seemed to be a rough dance. His toga was soaked, plastered to his thin frame, and there seemed to be very little beneath it.

Rob noticed her glance. "He is trying to keep himself warm," he explained. "Nasty day out there. May I come in?"

"Of course," she said, remembering her manners. "But what about Billy?"

"What about him?"

"You cannot leave him in the cold and rain! He will catch his death!" She drew Burlingham inside, but held the door open to watch Billy.

"He is used to it. Besides, I do not plan to stay long. Will you come driving with me? I thought we might visit the British Museum, considering it is no day to remain outside." He smiled down at her as he removed his dripping hat. At the British Museum they could talk without interruption—if they ever got there. Astley's could be put off to another day.

All of a sudden she wanted to drive to the British Museum with him more than anything else in the world. Hang the weather.

"I would love to," she told him, and returned his smile. "Do come in and dry off by the fire while I get my cloak." She led him to the sitting room and motioned him to a chair by the fire.

Rob rose once she had gone and stood as close to the fire as he deemed safe. Ah, a fire! How glorious it would be to be wealthy enough to have a fire at this time of year without a worry! He had decreed that the season for fires at his house was over for the summer, and he and his household had only the kitchen cook stove to provide warmth. He turned slowly, toasting himself on every side as he waited. He began to feel almost human again, except for the feet. They were wet, and felt like cold lumps of lead.

Bets entered the sitting room in a rush. "I am ready," she said breathlessly. She had on her cloak, a serviceable black hat, and black gloves, these left from mourning wear for her father, and she carried an umbrella. "Shall we go?"

"I should wish to make myself known to your mother," he said quietly. He hated to leave the fire.

"Oh, certainly," said Bets. "I shall fetch her." She dropped her umbrella and reticule in an empty chair and left to find Lady Stanbourne.

Lady Stanbourne entered with a glint in her eye. "You are not expecting to take my gel out driving in this weather, surely?" she said as she greeted him.

"Only for a short trip," said Rob. "To the British Museum. Will you join us?"

"Heavens, no!" said Lady Stanbourne. "And I do not like it above half that you two plan to go out. You will catch your death, mark my words! You look half frozen as it is, your lordship." She looked pointedly at his feet, which he had been stamping to restore circulation.

Rob had the grace to blush. "Foot went to sleep," he lied. "I was just trying to wake it up."

"Ha!" said Lady Stanbourne.

The three looked at each other. No one said anything for long moments. Finally Rob broke the silence.

"If you are sure you do not wish to go with us?" He looked genially at Lady Stanbourne. When she shook her head, he went on, "Then let us leave, Lady Elizabeth. Billy has endured the rain long enough." He handed Bets her reticule, put her umbrella under his arm, and escorted her out to his curricle.

"Does—does it not have a top?" she asked in dismay. The seat was covered with an old blanket, but the blanket looked as wet as the rest of the carriage. Rob flipped the blanket aside in a grand gesture and showed her the plaid shawl beneath it.

"I believe it is dry beneath the blanket," he said. "Yes, the curricle has a top, but somehow it refuses to arise. A recalcitrant top, that is what it is. Billy and I fought with it before we came, but we lost. That meant either we come for you topless, or we do not come at all. Will you forgive me? Let me open your umbrella for you." He snapped open the umbrella and handed it to Billy while he helped her into the curricle; then he put the umbrella handle in her hand. "There now." He smiled uncertainly. "Will that do?"

"I—I think so," she said.

Rob quickly rounded the carriage, climbed into his place, and noted that Billy was on tight behind. They set out. Bets had to tilt the umbrella slightly to keep its ribs from gouging her companion, and had to head it forward to keep the wind from catching it. It was awkward in the extreme, and several times she felt rivulets of water running down the back of her neck. But she was away from home, away from her mother, away from her problems. She was with the gentleman she most wanted to be with of anyone in the world. She laughed in pure happiness.

Damn and blast! Rob had left home in anger at the state of his curricle. Of all things, its disrepair was a signal to the world that he was either on his uppers or had grown monstrous careless.

He and Geordie had spent the better part of two days trying to apportion his funds from the book sales where they would do the most good—meaning preserve his facade of wealth—while keeping enough by to live on, if frugally. It might be months before he could lay his hands on Lady Elizabeth's fortune, if there was one, and he was beginning to doubt there was. They had set aside a sum toward reupholstering the curricle, but it had never occurred to them that the hood needed work as well. Today, at the last minute, he and Billy had learned that the catch that held the top, once it was raised, had quite disappeared. That is, it had disappeared on one side; on the opposite side it remained, but looked as if someone had taken a maul to it. An accident? A result of age and neglect? Rob thought not. It looked like vandalism to him, but it was too late to do anything about it. Seething with anger and full of regret that he had not thought to check it earlier, he had set out for Knightsbridge Terrace anyhow. The need to learn whether Lady Elizabeth had been able to gain an audience with Mrs. Drummond Burrell was paramount.

The ride toward the British Museum was not conducive to confidences. The pervasive drizzle had given way once more to fog, and Rob had to keep his mind on his driving as he attempted to penetrate the blank whiteness surrounding them. At intervals Lady Elizabeth tried to shield his head with her umbrella, but it was not large enough to cover them both. Once the drizzle stopped it did not matter. He was wet all over anyhow.

"Have you eaten?" he asked suddenly. "This driving is damn—I mean dreadful—and I know of a coffeehouse just up the way."

"Oh, that would be most welcome," Bets replied. She remembered the few sips of lukewarm tea that had constituted her breakfast. "I believe Billy needs something too."

"Always worried about Billy, are you not?" he asked

in amusement. "He is a sturdy lad, never fear, though I confess he hardly looks it. He has put up with much worse."

"Is that any reason he should suffer?" she demanded. "Unless you promise to let Billy out of the rain I refuse to stop."

"But who is to hold the horses? Tell me that."

"Then we must stop at an inn that has a stable." Bets gave her escort a quelling look. "I shall not be able to tell you of my meeting with Mrs. Drummond Burrell until I know Billy has been warmed and fed."

Rob nearly let his curricle collide with a dray in his excitement. "You saw her! You talked to her! Tell me!"

"Just as soon as we are settled—and Billy is cared for," she said calmly.

Despite the dense fog Rob knew roughly where they were. With Bets helping by calling out landmarks, he guided them to an inn in Great Russell Street not far from the British Museum and thankfully turned his curricle over to a stableboy. He sent Billy to the kitchen and escorted Bets to the inn. It was not busy at this time of midmorning, and he was able to bespeak a private parlor and a hearty breakfast for two.

Bets was bursting to tell Burlingham every word of her conversation with Mrs. Drummond Burrell, but whenever she began, he interrupted with some remark about the food, urging her to have more tea, eat her ham, have a piece of toast. When she looked mulish he laughed and said, "You refused to tell me until Billy was taken care of. Now I refuse to listen until I see that you are well fed. I can be as stubborn as you are."

"So I observe," she said dryly. She caught his eye and looked down in confusion. Then the humor struck her and she broke into laughter herself. "I fear we are two of a kind," she said. "And now I believe I have eaten my fill. Will you listen, or must we blunder on to the museum first?"

"I am all ears," he said gravely. He reached across the

table for her hand and examined the fingers, one by one. "I am so afraid I will not wish to hear what you have to say that I have been putting it off. Now I have stiffened my spine and am ready for the worst." His brow was knit with worry.

"But you are wrong!" she said excitedly, rising and facing him. "Mrs. Drummond Burrell told me herself that she did not hear what you said to her, if anything! Truly! She got it from—from—you hardly have to guess. That blackguard! That vile scoundrel! I wonder that you claim him as cousin."

"Only third cousin," Rob muttered. "Now begin at the beginning and tell me every word. Every word, if you please!" He looked up at her as she stood over him, brown eyes shining, every inch of her radiating excitement and triumph.

The recital did not take long. A waiter popped in to offer more tea—coffee—chocolate. Remembering her lukewarm tea at home, Bets accepted a fresh pot, sat down, and sipped it between repetitions of the previous evening's events.

Rob finally believed there was no more to tell. He could hardly countenance his good luck. After much fruitless effort on his part, this lovely, stubborn, fascinating miss whom he was beginning to like more than a little had come up with the first information that tied the deed specifically to George. On an impulse he rose from his chair, walked around the table, and pulled her up by both hands.

"I owe you," he said softly. "God, what I owe you." His hands dropped hers and went around her shoulders. She was nearly as tall as he. He had to dip only slightly to reach her lips with his. The fit was perfect, he thought dazedly while he could think. His arms moved from her shoulders to hold her face. He pulled away slightly and looked into her eyes, eyes full of surprise—and something else? "Thank you," he murmured, and kissed her again.

Bets could hardly stand. Had Burlingham not been

holding her, she was sure she would collapse. This was nothing like the perfunctory pecks on the cheek she was used to. This was heavenly! She resolved to do more of this—lots more—but Burlingham released her and she fell back into her chair, breathless.

"I do beg your pardon," Rob said gruffly. "I fear I was carried away." He did not look at all sorry.

Bets smiled, a wicked smile. "I must admit I enjoyed your being carried away," she said. "Are you carried away often?"

Rob laughed at that, and the tense atmosphere dissipated. They were friends again.

"If you wish it, I will try to arrange being carried away only in your presence," he said, and gave her a warm smile. "Have I your permission?"

"Oh, yes," she said, and smiled back.

"Now, I must decide what I can do with your information," he said, serious again. "How can I get George Purtwee to admit what he did? There is my reputation to restore if I can. But I am even more interested in *why* he did it. I confess that puzzles me more than anything. What can he possibly gain?"

"I will try to think on it," Bets offered. "Now we really must get on to the museum if we are ever going to. Mama will be worried to death if I am late, what with all the fog." She rose and reached for her cloak.

"Alas, yes," Rob agreed. "Do you really wish to visit the museum? We could go another day when the weather is better."

"For a short while," she answered as she straightened her hat. "Mama is sure to ask what we saw, and I must be able to tell her."

"Ah," said Rob. "Honest to a fault, are you? Can you not remember what you have seen there before?"

"Perhaps, but I shall take no chances," she said. Her heart sank. Honest, was she? What about the monstrous tarradiddle she and her mother were living, pretending they were wealthy? She hated to lie to Burlingham, but her future and her mother's future depended on it.

Perhaps, she thought distractedly, he would forgive her once they were married—if she could get him to the sticking point!—for if he were as wealthy as rumor had it, he would never miss the pittance it would take to provide for Lady Stanbourne.

But what if George Purtwee were right and he was penniless?

Bets decided that must be another of Mr. Purtwee's lies. Lies! They were all caught in a tangle of lies!

"I am ready," she said. "Let us visit the museum."

What with one thing and another, they never got to Astley's.

Chapter Thirteen

Bets was awakened from a troubled sleep late next morning by the voice of her mother. "Bets, dearest? Are you awake, dearest?"

Oh, no, she thought. When Lady Stanbourne addressed her as "dearest," her mother wanted something, probably something next to impossible to obtain. Bets sighed. She preferred to turn over and go back to sleep, but it would be putting off the inevitable.

"Yes, Mama? What is it?" She hitched herself up to a semisitting position and pushed her hair out of her face. It never stayed inside her nightcap.

"Cook tells me the fishmonger was here after his money. Did you not pay him? Our quarter funds cannot be gone already? They came only what—a week or two ago? Dearest, you must be more careful." Lady Stanbourne's faded blue eyes looked close to tears.

A cold fear gripped Bets. She knew in her heart she should never have allowed her mother access to the money they received every quarter day from her half brother Godfrey, her father's heir and trustee of the estate. Lady Stanbourne, reared in luxury, married into more luxury, accepted their penurious state as best she could but had never learned how quickly the money could go when she bought a frivolous bit of lace here, a hod of coal for the fireplace, even in springtime, there.

Each quarter day Bets had learned to list the debts that must be paid—the servants' wages, small as they were; food staples; taxes, and the like. She knew many of the aristocracy ran huge accounts and often failed to pay them, but the tradespeople had been reluctant to offer them credit. No gentleman was at the head of their household, and who could trust two mere women? Bets preferred to avoid credit in any case, for who knew when their situation would improve enough to pay the bills?

"Mama," she said now, "we are hardly half through the quarter, and unless you have been spending foolishly, we should have enough to last until next quarter day. I shall go to the bank today and draw enough to pay the fishmonger. Were you not to do that? Last week, I believe? What happened?"

"I was?" Lady Stanbourne looked blank for a moment, then clasped her hands tightly and stared at the floor. "Oh, now I recall. We were low on coal and I remembered how cheerful a fire can be on a gloomy day. So I sent Molly out to order some. I was right, was I not? Your *friend* Lord Burlingham seemed to enjoy it when he was here the other day. Today does not look to be much better, and the fire will be most welcome when dear Mr. Purtwee visits." She smiled in anticipation.

"Mr. Purtwee? He is coming *today?* But what about the fishmonger?" Bets threw off the covers and searched for her clothes. Prompt action was called for.

"I do not see any connection," Lady Stanbourne said in a puzzled tone.

Bets merely groaned. If she was lucky she would be at the bank withdrawing some of their slender funds when Mr. Purtwee descended on them and basked his hated back at the dearly bought fire.

Then again, she might do well to approach Mr. Purtwee with an account of her talk with Mrs. Drummond Burrell. Or should she leave that to Lord Burlingham? She had not heard from him since that fateful trip to the British Museum, several days ago now. She had no idea whether he had sought out Mr. Purtwee himself.

After a hurried breakfast she betook herself to the bank, only to find their balance was dangerously low. Once she paid the fishmonger they would have thirty-seven pounds seven shillings to live on until next quarter day.

It was imperative that she bring Burlingham—or someone!—to the point of proposing.

"Bloody cold in here," Rob remarked as he donned his shirt, staring at the dead ashes in the fireplace of his bedchamber.

"You were the one to decide no more fires until fall," Geordie reminded him. He handed Rob a neckcloth.

"It is hell being poor, is it not?" said Rob. "You have had more of it than I."

"Indeed, your lordship. Afore I became the Great Geordie, many's the day I had no fire and only the bit of food I could steal," the man confessed. "Never was caught, though. Quick on my feet, I was. Still am, hey? But you're doin' better. Should we have a sparrin' match this mornin'? 'Twould warm you up, sir." Geordie doubled his fists and struck a pose.

"Not today, Geordie. I plan to seek out Cousin George and see if I can persuade him to admit publicly that he made up that scurrilous tale about Mrs. Drummond Burrell and me. And then I must seek out Lady Elizabeth. I must woo and win, Geordie. I had thought to wait until after this scandal was put in its place—it don't reflect well on me and might put Lady Elizabeth off—but damn it, I cannot afford to wait. Will you tell Billy I need the curricle? I'll just have breakfast and be off."

"But, sir—" Geordie handed Rob his socks.

"Yes?"

"Remember? The curricle's gone to get new upholstery. Be a week at least." Geordie looked around for a missing shoe.

"Damn it! Then I shall have to hire."

"Yessir."

Sometime later Rob drew up before the imposing Mount Street mansion that was home to Lord Purtwee and family. His lip curled in disgust at the handsome stone residence, its broad Georgian proportions reeking

of wealth and influence. Cousin Purtwee had it all—
money and all that money could buy. Why did he wish
to destroy a mere third cousin who had never done him
any harm? Rob dismissed the hired carriage and rapped
on the door with its shining brass knocker made in the
form of a giant letter "P."

"Yes?" said a very proper butler.

Rob asked for George Purtwee, only to be told that
Mr. Purtwee was not at home.

"Oh dear," said Rob. "I am his cousin, come from a
distance to see him. Might I ask where he has gone?"

"His cousin?" The butler did not seem impressed. He
glanced past Rob to the street, where no carriage waited.
He eyed Rob from head to toe, measuring the worth of
his clothes. "He left no word with me. Were you expected?"

"Ah—no," said Rob. "Surprise visit. Could you tell
me when he is expected back?"

"Mr. Purtwee is much involved in his research," the
butler said stiffly. "When he is working on his book one
never knows when to expect him."

"His research?"

"Yes, sir. On timepieces, sir."

"Oh, of course," said Rob. "Thank you. Please tell
him his cousin called." He left his card, ran down the
steps, and walked briskly along the street before the butler had closed the door. He did not look for another
hackney until he was well away from Mount Street.

A second hackney carried him to Knightsbridge Terrace, where he recognized George Purtwee's rig parked
in front in the charge of a gloomy groom.

Was Lady Elizabeth entertaining his cousin behind his
back? Rob's heart fell for a moment, but by the time he
had paid off the hackney he realized she could be acting
on his behalf, trying to get Purtwee to admit his wrongdoing. Even so he faced a dilemma. He had no wish to
see the lady and the cousin at the same time, for he had
very different matters to settle with each. He braced
himself. This could prove interesting.

* * *

"Oh," said Molly, looking astonished to see Rob at the door. "She ain't here, sir—I mean, your lordship." She glanced back toward the sitting room, then faced him again. "You're here to see Miss Bets, ain't you? She ain't here."

"May I wait? Will she be long?" Rob started to edge inside, but Molly stood firm.

"She ain't here! Her ladyship's entertaining a gentleman, sir. That's his rig out front." She looked with satisfaction toward Purtwee's elegant cabriolet, standing at the curb.

"Quite so. Thank you, Molly. I know the gentleman."

Molly snickered at that. Probably knows every detail of our comings and goings, Rob thought in disgust.

"I wish to pay my respects to Lady Stanbourne," he continued. "I shall go right in, shall I?"

He did not wait for an answer. Shoving his hat into her hands, he pushed past her to stride purposefully toward the sitting room. He could hear murmured conversation and the crackle of a fire. A fire! He quickened his step.

The sitting room door was open. Opposite it was the fireplace, and blocking the fireplace, absorbing the heat, stood George Purtwee. His fingers caressed the clock on the mantel. His face was turned toward Lady Stanbourne. Rob had rarely seen such a fatuous expression.

"—interesting, is it not, how the horologists have been able to miniaturize works such as these and put them into a timepiece that fits into a man's pock—" Suddenly Purtwee caught sight of Rob and he stopped in midsentence. The fatuous expression became bland.

"Ah, my dear cousin," said Purtwee, "I did not hear you announced."

"What would you have done had you heard?" Rob shot back. "Disappeared into the woodwork?" His hard look softened as he turned to Lady Stanbourne. "Good morning, madam. I trust I find you well?"

Lady Stanbourne's chin quivered as she took in the

new arrival. "Oh," she said tremulously. "Lord Burling-ham. Would you care for some tea? Let me just tell Molly." She rose, stared behind her for a moment at the split blue silk upholstery of her chair, and dropped her shawl on it in a seemingly careless gesture. She hurried out.

Rob advanced into the room and stood before his cousin. "Purtwee," he said, "you are reckoned an expert at measuring the passage of time, are you not? Then I give you two minutes. Two minutes before Lady Stan-bourne returns. What in the *hell* did you mean by that tarradiddle with Mrs. Drummond Burrell? She admits herself she failed to hear me say a word. You made it up out of whole cloth, did you not? Why? For God's sake, *why?*"

Rob felt a strong desire to knock Purtwee's teeth out, but he refrained. He stood with fists clenched, almost toe to toe with Purtwee.

"Tsk, tsk. You are in a snit, ain't you?" Purtwee stood, a small smile on his face, with his back to the fire. As if to keep Rob from the heat, he spread his arms to catch every last current of warm air. "Should have thought of that before you acted the ass," he said. "Falling in a heap before a patroness at Almack's! Simply not done, you know."

"You know that I know. You also know how I came to be in that condition, do you not? Tell me. How much did you give Tessie?"

"Tessie? Who might Tessie be?" Purtwee seemed to be nonchalant, but Rob thought he detected a note of fear in his cousin's voice.

"Tessie the barmaid, you dunce. Never mind how I know. Not your usual haunt, was it? You stood out like a gold sovereign in a mudhole. No wonder Tessie remem-bered you." Rob stared grimly at Purtwee.

"But you go—never heard of Tessie the barmaid," said Purtwee, abandoning his spread posture in front of the fire and sidling away from his adversary. He sank into a chair.

"But I go where?" Rob persisted. "Aha! You mean I patronize the place, and because I am of the first stare, and accepted, then your presence there should not be remarkable. Am I right?" Rob moved to face Purtwee once again.

"No! No! I do not know what you are talking about!" Purtwee's voice rose. It ended in a squeak as he heard footsteps in the hall. Lady Stanbourne trotted in, waving her hands.

"I have no idea what Cook is about, but tea should be ready shortly," she announced. "Dear Mr. Purtwee! Are you unwell? Let me hurry the tea if I can. It will set you to·rights." She trotted out again.

"We will conclude this conversation later," said Rob. He backed up to the fire and let its soothing warmth help calm him. "I mislike airing our dirty linen in front of Lady Stanbourne. So tell me. How is your horological study progressing?"

Taken aback by Rob's sudden about-face, Purtwee could only mutter imprecations in a low tone. Finally he roused himself and said, "What do you care? You ain't interested in clocks. I suppose Lady Elizabeth has told you of my research? She still goes about with you, does she? More fool she!"

"You are referring to me?" said a new voice. Bets had returned from the bank.

Rob lost no time in going to meet her, a smile on his face. He gently took her hand and raised it to his lips. "So glad to see you," he began, but his voice was drowned out by that of George Purtwee.

"Lady Elizabeth! Lady Elizabeth! That I should have to share your company with this oaf! May I assure you that he barged in not ten minutes ago, and your gracious mother could do naught but accept him. You will recall, I hope, that you had agreed to go out with me to—to—to call on my aunt? I have been waiting this age, but I forgive you. Shall we go?" Purtwee rose and held out his arm for her to take while carefully skirting Rob, who continued to hold Bets' hand.

"Gentlemen!" Bets gasped. "Mr. Purtwee, I made no such engagement with you, and you know it. Your aunt? Pah! You have never mentioned an aunt. Lord Burlingham, I am pleased to see you. May I have my hand back, if you please?" In truth, she was in no hurry to reclaim her hand. His fingers were cold, but they shot a warm tremor through hers. He released her hand reluctantly.

A wave of excitement tinged with fear swept over Bets. Here were the two cousins, bitter enemies, in her sitting room. What a setting for a confrontation! She noted her mother's shawl draped carelessly over a chair and knew Lady Stanbourne must not be far away; were these two planning to have it out in front of her *mother?*

Purtwee dropped his proffered arm with obvious reluctance and moved back to the chair he had occupied before. He was about to sit when he hesitated, waiting for Bets to be seated first. Rob, meanwhile, again sought a place by the fire and stood, one hand tracing the columns on the mantel clock. His face, Bets thought, was a picture of unholy glee. That must mean he was getting the better of Purtwee. Good!

Bets looked from one man to the other. She must stave off any violence. Let them beat each other up somewhere else.

"Quite a gloomy day today, is it not?" she said calmly. "I should think a cup of tea would not be amiss. I allow I would love one, after more than an hour on my errand. The wind has a chill." She managed to produce a smile. Oh, if she could just keep the peace until these two took their leave!

"Lady Stanbourne is, I believe, arranging for tea," said Rob, trying to keep a straight face. Purtwee slouched in his chair and stared at his boots.

"And here we are!" Lady Stanbourne emerged triumphantly from the hall with Molly, who was bearing the tea tray in her wake.

Though the next twenty minutes were filled with light conversation as the four drank their tea, the atmosphere was charged with tension. The tea calmed no one. It was hot, true, but it was so weak as to be little better than colored water. Cook, or more likely Molly, had failed to add fresh leaves to the once-used batch remaining from breakfast. Bets was full of embarrassment and chagrin. If the gentlemen noticed, they did not show it.

"Is this a different blend?" Lady Stanbourne asked, peering into her cup. "I declare, I do not favor it. I shall have to give Fortnum and Mason a piece of my mind."

"Yes, Mama," said Bets. She gritted her teeth.

"I do believe your half hour is up," Rob addressed Purtwee. "Do not let me detain you. May I make an appointment to discuss our business further? We must not be talking business when in the presence of two such beautiful ladies." He grinned at his cousin.

Purtwee had been chafing under the necessity to keep a calm outward appearance in the face of Burlingham's gloating. Burlingham's effort to get him out of the house while he, himself remained was galling.

Purtwee jumped from his chair and shouted at Rob. "Damn you, Burlingham! You tell *me* what to do, you nobody! You lack two shillings to rub together! Tell 'em, dear coz. Tell 'em how you had to sell the great London town house the Marquesses of Fleet had owned for generations to get enough of the ready to live on. Tell 'em how your parents have to rusticate in Dorset because they have nowhere else to go. There ain't room in that little box you live in! Tell 'em how the only servants you can afford are a broken-down fugitive from Newgate and a boy you got out of the workhouse. Tell 'em how you're putting up a front in London just so you can snare some poor, unsuspecting heiress. Tell 'em how you are so foxed most of the time you have no idea what you are doing. Tell 'em how you had to give up your bit of muslin only because you could not afford to keep her! What a man! Go on, Burlingham, tell 'em!"

Rob grew white as he saw his world tumbling down about him. Why, oh why, had he the bad luck to meet up with Purtwee in front of Bets and her mother, of all people! He steadied himself and took a deep breath.

"You forgot Mrs. Burket," he said, forcing himself to seem calm.

"Who the hell is Mrs. Burket?" Purtwee sneered.

"She is my utterly respectable cook and housekeeper," said Rob. "I wonder, as you know so much about me, how you could miss knowing of Mrs. Burket."

Rob spared a glance at Bets. She had gone as white as he, and tears were threatening. She pulled a handkerchief from her reticule and dabbed at her eyes, then patted the handkerchief over her face in an effort to disguise her intention.

Purtwee was too incensed to stop. He was standing now, staring at Rob with hatred in his eyes. The effect was somewhat spoiled because he had to look up at his cousin, who was taller than he. Every muscle was tensed; he was almost quivering with rage.

Rob, on the other hand, adopted an easy stance, seemingly relaxed although he was far from it. He looked down at Purtwee as if the man were a noxious insect he was about to step on.

"Tell 'em!" Purtwee cried. "Go on, tell 'em! You are on your uppers and no mistake. I felt it my duty before God to warn poor Lady Elizabeth, but she must not have believed me, else she would not have had anything to do with you. I did warn you, did I not, Lady Elizabeth?"

"You failed to convince me," Bets said in a small voice.

"Just let him deny it!" Purtwee railed. "You do not see him denying it, do you?"

Bets turned to Rob, a suspicious glisten in her eyes.

"No," said Rob in a resigned tone. "No, I cannot deny all of it, though George is painting an exaggerated picture to be sure. I have recently come into some funds, however. I am not penniless. I assure you, I am not penniless."

"Funds? Ha! Taken to thieving, have you? Where would you get funds?" Purtwee demanded.

Rob was about to answer when Lady Stanbourne interceded. "I do not like this manner of talk in my house," she announced. "Mr. Purtwee, I thought you a gentle-man. I have so enjoyed our little discussions on time-pieces! Such a brilliant man you are, with your knowledge of horology and the book you are writing. Never did I dream you could be so vindictive toward your cousin, and in my house too! While I allow that Lord Burlingham may have his faults, this is not the place to enumerate them."

"Thank you, madam," Rob said gravely. He left Purtwee gesticulating in his rage, and repaired to a chair as near the fire as he could manage. He rubbed his hands. "The fire is most welcome," he said.

George was not to be stopped. He had worked himself up to a point that brooked no retreat. "Damn you, Burlingham!" he cried, turning toward Rob's chair. Then he caught sight of Bets, looking at him in horror. With visible effort he calmed himself and smoothed his impeccable yellow waistcoat.

"I—I beg pardon," he said, addressing her. "Cannot think what came over me. 'Struth, though, you know. M'cousin's a wastrel."

With slow deliberation Purtwee took the few steps to Bets' chair and carefully, so as not to damage his pan-taloons, knelt before her. He cast her a soulful look and reached for her hand. She quickly withdrew it. Some-what disconcerted, he continued with what seemed to be a part learned for Drury Lane.

"Lady Elizabeth!" he said. "Will you do me the honor of becoming my wife? I would wish to take you away from all this and give you all that you deserve. I want only the best for you. What a happy marriage we can have! You may even take some small part in my studies of timepieces should you wish it. I offer you my heart and all my worldly goods. Please say yes!"

Bets was thunderstruck. What an incredible time to re-ceive a marriage proposal! Of course she had no inten-tion whatever of accepting, for living on the parish would be preferable to becoming this man's wife.

She was trying to formulate a polite refusal when

Burlingham came to his feet. He was seething but held it in as best he could. He walked slowly to where Purtwee knelt before Bets, looking into her eyes. With one hand Burlingham tipped his cousin over. Purtwee, taken unawares, toppled on his side in an undignified sprawl on the Axminster rug. Burlingham knelt, wrapped his hands around Purtwee's waist, and shoved. His astounded audience heard an ominous rip as a seam in Purtwee's tightly fitted pantaloons gave.

"I see that it is time I speak," said Rob, moving on his knees to the spot Purtwee had occupied. "Lady Elizabeth, will you marry me? I offer you my heart. I may not have this bumptious paperskull's bounty of worldly goods, but we will manage, and some day you will be the Marchioness of Fleet. What say you, my dear?" He reached for her hand, and she gave it to him gladly. He kissed it reverently and smiled his devastating smile into her eyes.

"Yes!" Bets cried. "Oh, yes, yes!" She beamed on him and clasped the hand that had held hers. At last! Oh, at last!

"No!" Lady Stanbourne thundered.

They stared at her in awe. Even Purtwee, engaged in trying to rise to his feet and restore his dignity, was struck dumb. No one had ever heard Lady Stanbourne, delicate, dainty Lady Stanbourne, thunder.

"No," she said again.

Chapter Fourteen

"Neither one of you is worthy of my daughter! Her father was the Earl of Stanbourne! No scandal has ever attached to her name! She deserves no less than one of the royal princes. For shame, both of you! I do not wish to receive either of you in my house again." Lady Stanbourne did her best to look intimidating but her lower lip quivered.

Bets, her mind in a whirl—so much had happened in the last few minutes that she could hardly take it in— dropped Rob's hand and skirted his kneeling figure to reach her mother. She put her arm around Lady Stanbourne's shoulders and gave her a quick hug. "There, there, Mama," she said softly. "Calm yourself. Royal princes indeed! They are all old enough to be my father, and they have their own wives or—or—you know."

Lady Stanbourne's face crumpled and she began to cry, small, broken sobs with much sniffing. Bets gave her ineffectual pats on the back as she looked down at her two suitors, both on the floor.

"Shall we arise, cousin?" Rob was the first to recover his equanimity. He regained his feet in one fluid motion and held his hand down to help Purtwee, who was now sitting up and scowling. "You may give me a ride in your handsome cabriolet while we discuss our differences away from Knightsbridge Terrace. Up, my good man. Up."

Purtwee batted Rob's hand away and carefully pulled himself up by holding on to the chair Bets occupied. The strain on his pantaloons, despite his care, had been too much. It was apparent to all when he finally stood that the inseam in the right leg had given way for fully six inches near the knee. Purtwee looked down at the gap and turned purple.

"Damn you, Burlingham!" he roared. "All your fault! You get no ride from me."

"I do not recall ripping your unmentionables," Rob said smoothly. "Very well. When, then, may we meet?"

"Never!"

"I see I shall have to take matters into my own hands," said Rob. "Lady Elizabeth, would you be so kind as to ask Molly to fetch our hats? Because my hands may be full, perhaps she would be willing to deliver them to Mr. Purtwee's fine cabriolet."

Rob snatched his cousin by the back of the neck, utterly crushing his neckcloth, to hustle him out the door. Purtwee writhed and twisted, attempting to get a hold on the man behind him, but Rob was too quick for him. He dodged back and forth while shoving Purtwee inexorably onward. The ladies could only look on in wonder until Bets remembered the gentlemen's hats.

"Molly!" she called. "Quickly! Open the door!"

Molly was parked just outside the sitting room, listening. She hurried to open the door while Bets collected the hats. Just in time too. Rob had almost reached the threshold when the door was opened for him.

Bets followed closely, carrying the hats. She watched Rob march his cousin down the steps and along the walk, and her heart nearly burst with pride.

Purtwee's groom looked up in amazement at the procession bearing down upon him.

"Here, sir! Whatcha doin' with the master?" he asked belligerently.

"I believe he has had some kind of a fit," said Rob, frowning. "Has this happened before?"

"Damn you, Burlingham! Let loose!" Purtwee shouted. He tried again to twist out of Rob's grasp.

"He has quite lost his head," Rob told the groom. "I fear for him. I am not sure that you can hold him yourself. I am his cousin, you know, and I believe it my duty to see him safely home." He took a firmer grip on Purtwee's collar, then moved around to give his cousin smart slaps on both cheeks. "I cannot seem to bring him out of it," he continued gravely.

The groom studied his master for a moment and shook his head. "Never seen the like," he said. "Wot should I do, sir?"

"Let me go! Damn you, let me go!" Purtwee was in a frenzy.

"Pay him no attention," Rob said. "I fear he may froth at the mouth, but I have him under control now. It is best I get him away as soon as possible. Could you perhaps take a hackney and precede me so that you may prepare his family?"

"Oh, sir, with him in that state you'll never to able to drive," the groom said, looking worried.

"Try me," said Rob grimly. "Lady Elizabeth, our hats, if you please. And you, groom, would you kindly put up the hood on the cabriolet? I do not wish to embarrass Mr. Purtwee by letting the world see him in this state—if he is aware, that is." He gave Purtwee a shake and slapped his cheeks again.

By this time Purtwee did indeed look mad. His clothing was awry, the rip in his pantaloons had traveled down to his boot, his hair was in wild disorder, and his eyes were rolling as he sputtered and twisted. Rob took his cousin's hat from Bets and clapped it on its owner's head, donned his own, and shoved Purtwee into the cabriolet, pushing him across the seat so that he could get in himself.

"Hand me the ribbons," he ordered the groom. The man complied and Rob drove off.

Once well away from Knightsbridge Terrace, he released his hold on Purtwee and looked wonderingly at his hand.

"You nigh tore it off," he mused, flexing his fingers. "Had no idea you had so much iron in you, George."

"You bastard!" said Purtwee.

"Now, George! My mother would take exception to that. What do you say to a little drive? I would like to clear up a few points."

"I have nothing to say to you!" Purtwee turned on his cousin with a look of loathing.

"Oh, no? Should I then deliver you straight to Bedlam? Your groom and the Fortescue ladies, not to mention my humble self, would be glad to testify that you are prone to dangerous fits. Fits that require restraints, you understand. Perhaps your poor brain has been addled with the weight of your horology? That must be it." Rob turned a face full of grave pity on his cousin.

"Ha!" said Purtwee, unconvinced. "You would never get away with such a Banbury tale. M'father can speak for me. *He* knows I'm all right in the upper story."

"But your father is a mere baron. I, on the other hand, am an earl, heir to a marquess. What is his word against mine? Not to mention that of a dowager countess? Lady Stanbourne will be happy to testify if necessary, I am certain."

"Damn you! Damn your hide! Throw that up to me, will you? You think I do not *know* you are heir to a marquess? Known it all my life. Just because of an accident of birth. *I* should be the heir to a marquess, not you!"

"What? What are you talking about? You are so far down in line you would never succeed to the title. You could kill me today and probably innumerable other cousins as well, and you still would never be marquess." Rob looked askance at his cousin, by now sitting dejectedly, his head in his hands. Maybe the man *was* touched in the head. Could this farfetched idea be behind Purtwee's hatred and nasty tricks?

"Your great-grandfather and my great-grandmother were brother and sister," Purtwee said slowly.

"Yes?"

"But my great-grandmother was the elder! She should have been a man! Damn it, she should have been a man!"

"What? Was there something havey-cavey about her? I never heard it. You surely do not mean she . . . ?"

"Oh, no, you bastard. She was a perfectly fine woman as far as I know. But do you not see, she was the *elder*. Had she been a man, she would have become the marquess, and my grandfather, and my father, and I . . ."

"Oh, my God," said Rob. He pulled the carriage over to the curb and stopped.

He had been driving aimlessly, aware enough only to avoid collisions with drays and carts and carriages and thread his way through narrow streets. Now he found himself on an unfamiliar street. Raucous cries and shouts of drivers, pedestrians, hawkers, and onlookers resounded all around him. Unpleasant smells were near to overpowering. This was not the best part of London. It was hardly the place to have it out with George Purtwee.

"We shall go to the park," he announced to his sullen cousin. "We shall find a quiet spot, and you shall tell me this entire sorry story. Will you be able to get to your home alone afterward? With no groom . . . Why in hell did you have a groom along, George? A cabriolet hardly needs a groom."

"To watch over the rig, of course," said Purtwee. "Never know when some light-fingered nodcock will take into his head to make off with a fine new carriage and horse such as these." He looked down with pride at his cabriolet, running his fingers lovingly across the leather squabs. Then he looked up at Rob.

"I will gladly drive you home if you like, then I must be on my way. Sorry, no time today to have a meeting; perhaps some other time. I have appointments . . ."

"It will not fadge, George," Rob said sternly. "We go to the park and you will remain as long as I say. If you do not wish to drive me home afterward, I will walk."

Rob watched his chance to pull out into the line of traffic again and before long, thankfully, found himself on familiar streets. He drove to Hyde Park, pulled off on a little-used path, and drew the cabriolet to a halt.

"George," he said, "you are about to tell me what has

been festering in your brainbox all these years. You are about to admit you arranged that little episode with Mrs. Drummond Burrell at Almack's. You are about to bare your soul, or by God, you will be on your way to Bedlam."

When Purtwee hesitated, Rob faced him and put a strong hand on his arm. "Begin," he said.

"You were always so damn arrogant," Purtwee burst out. "Older than me, and bigger than me. Those times when the esteemed marquess"—he sneered—"and marchioness were at their fine London town house with their son and their servants and all. Remember? Our families used to visit back and forth. You treated me like dirt. That was the beginning."

"Treated you like dirt? When was that? I distinctly remember your whining and sniveling because you failed to get the lion's share of the tarts Cook made. I wanted to plant you a facer but my mother had taught me to be polite to guests. I dreaded to see you coming, George. You were the greediest boy it has ever been my misfortune to meet. And another thing . . ."

"And another thing!" Purtwee shouted. He stood up in the cabriolet, which shifted under him. He sat again. "Yes, another thing! Do not forget the cricket! You refused to let me touch your bat. Talk about greedy! A guest in your home, but oh, no, little George must not touch dear Robert's cricket bat. Talk about selfish!"

"You had just broken my best bat, you fool. Remember how you lost your temper? You banged it and banged it on that iron railing near the pitch until it looked like it had been chewed by an elephant. Why did you do that, George? I forget."

"I never did! It was hardly scratched!"

"George, we are squabbling like two ten-year-olds. We could go on like this all day and never solve anything. Settle back and relax, cousin."

Purtwee leaned back and glared.

"We will pass over all the imagined slights when we were boys," Rob said. "Now we come to this business of your great-grandmother and my great-grandfather. For God's sake, why blame me because she was female instead of male?"

"Because you are not at all what a marquess's heir should be," Purtwee said bitterly. "You have every vice known to man and not a feather to fly with. I, on the other hand, know how to dress"—he looked ruefully at his disheveled clothing—"and neither drink to excess nor gamble. I have kept no mistresses and I have never been challenged to a duel. I do not throw away my blunt on foolishness. I—"

"What in hell do you do with your time, then?" Rob asked, looking at his cousin with something akin to pity. "Oh, do not tell me. You delve into horology, do you not?"

"And what is wrong with horology? What worthwhile thing have you ever done?"

Rob thought for a moment. What, really, had he ever done? Loved his parents, tried to be a dutiful son, laid plans to save the family's fortunes with an advantageous marriage. That did not seem to count for much, measured against his rakehell years.

He gave a somewhat embarrassed laugh. "Something will come to me, I am certain," he said.

"You see my point," Purtwee said with a smirk.

"Even so, you are far down in the line to inherit," Rob emphasized. "I cannot change the rules, George, you know that. I shall become Marquess of Fleet, assuming I survive, whether you wish it or no. So why take out your spleen on me?"

Now he thought of it, Rob could understand what bedeviled his cousin. George was not as good-looking as Rob, no matter how much attention he paid to his neckcloths and waistcoats. George did not attract the attention of young ladies, for he was boring and pedantic, with no gift for light conversation. He had few male cronies, for men found him as boring as did women, and he did not take part in cards or betting at White's, or attend boxing mills, or cockfights, or horse races. Poor sod! He probably would find a wife, for his family had money. But would she love him?

Some of his fury at Purtwee began to dissipate.

Purtwee just looked at him, disgust in every line of his face.

"Very well," said Rob with a sigh. "I am willing to put this all in the past if you are. We will never see eye to eye but surely we can be civil to one another. I have only one demand, George. You will admit that you misheard my speech to Mrs. Drummond Burrell. You will noise it about that I was suddenly taken ill after arriving at Almack's, which led to my collapse. It happened so soon after my arrival that I had no chance to say a word to Mrs. Drummond Burrell. If you wish, you may admit that you made up that 'speech' out of whole cloth. You will indicate that in the many years you have known me, you have learned that never would I have done such a thing. Is that clear, George?"

"How can I do that?" Purtwee whined. "It will make me out a liar."

"Well?"

"Robert! I cannot do it!"

"I think you can. I think you will. I think you will find it much easier than the prospect of Bedlam."

"Bedlam." Purtwee stared off into the park, fixing on a plane tree nearby. "You cannot really send me to Bedlam."

"You think not? Do you wish to try me?"

"But you have no money! You cannot grease any palms. That is what it would take, you know."

"Perhaps. Do you wish to take the risk? I would sell my curricle, sell my house even, if necessary. Remember, I have witnesses who will gladly testify that they saw you in a mad fit."

"Very well," Purtwee said at last. "For the future good relations of our families, I suppose I must manage it. You will give me time, will you not? I cannot undo this in a day."

"Shall we say a sennight?"

"A sennight! I am not sure I . . ."

"A sennight it is, George."

Purtwee gave Rob a long look. "A sennight. Then you will be in clover, will you not? Still lacking two pennies to rub together, your fancied betrothal to Lady Elizabeth up in the air. I wish you joy of it."

"Thank you, George. Do you wish to drive me home?"

"You may crawl," said Purtwee contemptuously. "Get out of my cabriolet, Burlingham."

"Gladly." Rob hopped down. As Purtwee moved to take the reins, Rob smiled, dusted his hands, and started home.

"Mama!" Bets cried. The two gentlemen and Purtwee's groom had left and they were again in the house. Molly hovered over them in a poorly concealed attempt to learn more of her mistresses' doings. "Whatever have you done? Lord Burlingham is blameless! It was entirely Mr. Purtwee's fault. Why ring a peal over Burlingham when he had *just* asked for my hand? Oh, Mama! I fear you have sent him off and I shall never see him again!"

Despite her jubilation at Burlingham's clever mastery over his cousin, she felt she had been left in limbo. Not a kind word, not a farewell, not a promise to meet again had he given her when he departed. He was fully occupied; she would give him that. But surely he could have said *something* beyond asking for their hats!

"Fiddle, my dear," said Lady Stanbourne. "That one is not the man to be frightened off by anything I say. Even so, I doubt he is the man for you. You heard what Mr. Purtwee said. You notice that Lord Burlingham did not deny it.

"I always wondered why the Fleets' London house was sold," she mused. "The word around town was that Burlingham found it too big for a bachelor. Monstrous big thing, it is. I believe the Cripforths have it now. I must ask Lady Stafford. She always knows what is going on."

"Mama, you are getting off the subject," Bets remonstrated. "This is my *future* we are discussing. I want Lord Burlingham. Is that clear? I have accepted his proposal. I intend to marry him. If we must live frugally, then we shall live frugally. Without my mouth to feed, I believe you should be able to manage on what you receive each quarter day from Godfrey. I am so sorry I will not be able to provide for you!"

Lady Stanbourne led the way back to the sitting room and ordered Molly to bring fresh tea—"Not that pale kind from Fortnum's, Molly! Tell Cook it must be strong!" She sank into the ripped chair and rubbed her forehead.

"Tell me," she said. "What exactly do you know of Burlingham's fortunes? He said he had 'come into some funds.' Has he mentioned what they are? How would he come into funds?"

"On the 'Change, perhaps," Bets hazarded. "I have no knowledge of what they are, or how much."

Lady Stanbourne sighed. "I shall have to ask him if I ever see him again," she said. "Not that I would understand. Those dealings on the Exchange are Greek to me. But as your only parent I suppose it is up to me. Do have some tea, dear."

Molly had entered with tea and seemed disposed to remain, even making motions to pour.

"Thank you, Molly, I will pour," said Bets. "You may go." Molly left reluctantly. They heard her footsteps briefly in the hall and then, silence.

"I will lay you a farthing she has gone no farther than the other side of the door," Bets said in an undertone.

"Bets!"

"Just let me look." Bets set the teapot down soundlessly and crept to the sitting room door. She threw it open with a flourish and peeked around the frame. Molly was plastered against the hall wall next to the doorjamb.

"I said that would be all, Molly," Bets said firmly and

returned to the sitting room. "Oh, that girl!" she mourned as she took up the teapot again.

"If you were to change your mind and marry Mr. Purtwee, we could hire a dozen maids better than Molly," Lady Stanbourne suggested.

"Mama! You forbade him entrance to this house!"

"Perhaps I was a little carried away. Oh, dear. I shall miss him and his remarkable knowledge of clocks," said Lady Stanbourne.

Hourly Bets expected word from the Earl of Burlingham. Whatever he intended to do with George Purtwee could not take long. Bets did not think for a minute that Burlingham meant to send his cousin to Bedlam, but if Mr. Purtwee believed the threat, so much the better. She chuckled as she remembered the incensed Purtwee struggling in the grip of his cousin. Burlingham could not have known in advance that Purtwee would be present, so his plan to get Purtwee into his clutches must have been made on the spur of the moment. She had every confidence that Burlingham would find out everything he wanted to know and reduce Purtwee to an abject idiot if he wished. But where was Burlingham? Luncheon and afternoon tea passed; supper was served; the sun had long ago set and the candles lit, and still no word. Maybe tomorrow.

Bets went to bed and resolutely concentrated on visions of what their married life would be. That kiss they had shared had wakened feelings of want that seemed to be with her all the time now. She shivered. When they were married he would expect much more than kisses. Or so she hoped! She loved him. She wanted to spend the rest of her life with him, whether in wealth or in poverty, she did not care. Did he love her? Surely he did! He had said he was offering her his heart, had he not? Or was that merely the usual wording of a proposal? As she remembered, Mr. Purtwee had said very much the same thing. Bets felt confused as she drifted off to sleep.

Not until the next afternoon did she get word from

Burlingham, and she considered it entirely inadequate. It was a note, delivered by Billy, and it said, merely:

> I must go to Dorset. Will return as quickly as possible. *Ab imo pectore,* my devotion.
> Burlingham

"He tells me next to nothing, but then he has to put part of it in Latin!" Bets groused to her mother. So sure had she been that Burlingham would appear today that she had spent more than an hour on her toilette, twining her hair this way and that, adding and subtracting ribands, polishing slippers. Her gown was one of her newer ones, only two years old, a pale lavender print. And no one to see it but her mother and Billy, no longer wearing a toga but ordinary clothing, proudly entrusted with his master's missive.

"Billy said the earl left at first light this morning," Bets said in explanation to her mother, who only raised her brows. "He knew no more than that, or was not telling. Fudge! Mama, what does "*ab imo pectore*" mean?"

"You are asking me? *Me?* Perhaps you can find that Latin dictionary of your father's. Or did we leave it behind? I cannot imagine why we would have brought it to London."

Bets left the breakfast table to spend a fruitless half hour searching for a Latin-English dictionary. Whom did she know who could translate for her? If the phrase was something personal, she did not wish to entrust it to a stranger. Was it complimentary or otherwise? She feared she would have to wait until she saw Lord Burlingham again—if she ever did—to learn the truth of it.

The waiting began.

Chapter Fifteen

Rob was gleefully recounting the details of his meeting with George Purtwee to Geordie at the supper table. Mrs. Burket puttered between stove and table—they were eating in the kitchen, as usual—drinking it all in and murmuring, "My, my!" at intervals. Billy was out scouring the neighborhood for the cat; he was not to have his supper until Caterine Purr was safely home. Rob had got as far in his tale as the collaring of George Purtwee when he heard someone banging on the front door. The someone was obviously intent on pounding the door from its hinges.

"I'll go," said Geordie reluctantly, "but don't go no further! I mustna miss a bit of it!"

Soon loud voices were heard in the hall and Rob's old friend Tom Hazleton burst into the kitchen.

"Where have you been keeping yourself, you scurvy knave?" Tom demanded. "And why do I fail to see a tot of brandy awaiting me? Good God, man, just because I could not learn any more at the Friend at Hand—not that I have ceased trying to sweeten Tessie up—you give me the cut direct. Explain yourself, sir." Tom reached for a slice of bread and chewed vigorously. "Damn good bread, ma'am," he said, nodding at Mrs. Burket.

"Have you supped? Will you join us?" Rob jumped up to fetch another chair.

"Just brandy, if you please. Where is the brandy? In your library?"

After sending Geordie after the brandy, Rob explained to his friend that the need for pumping Tessie for information was past. "It is all over," he said gleefully. "I am exonerated. I have George Purtwee where I want him. I was just telling the tale when you arrived. If you like, I will start again."

The recital took some time, particularly when Rob had to backtrack once again for Billy, who arrived clutching an angry Caterine Purr. The cat was pacified with a saucer of cream.

"Cor," said Billy, impressed. His estimation of Lord Burlingham increased twofold. "Wish I could o' seen you and that goosecap into Bedlam! Now we're rid o' 'im, ain't we?"

"He is not really in Bedlam," Rob explained. "I just threatened him. I need him out in circulation to take back the stories he told about me!" He stretched and got up. "Let us go into the library, Tom, and you can advise me what I should do next."

"Next? It seems simple to me. You marry Lady Elizabeth, get your hands on her considerable fortune, and live happily ever after."

"Perhaps. Come along."

Tallow candles for a guest? Hardly. Rob brought out one of his newly purchased beeswax tapers and set it in lonely glory in his five-branch candelabrum, leaving the tallow stubs in the other branches unlit. He poured brandy for Tom and himself and settled before the empty hearth.

"I have an ominous feeling in my gut," he confided. "After numerous visits to Knightsbridge Terrace it strikes me that the Fortescue ladies may be hiding signs of penury just as I have been. Can it be true, Tom? Have you heard anything? Good God, if they have no blunt I cannot marry Lady Elizabeth."

"Are you certain? I have heard nothing," his friend replied. "What makes you think so?"

"Little things. They seem to have only two servants, and one of them worse than useless. No carriage. They both seem wrapped up in their garden, but I wonder whether it is to hide the fact they have no gardener. They

have one cursed chair in the sitting room that is split all
to pieces—the fabric, that is—and Lady Elizabeth takes
care to sit in it herself to hide the splits. I could go on
and on."

"Looks suspicious, does it not?" Tom agreed. "Have
you got to the point of discussing dowries and settle-
ments?"

"No, of course not. I proposed only today! Which reminds me. They served us tea, as usual, and I could have
sworn it was made with reused tea leaves. Of course,
that foolish maid could have been to blame, but I wonder . . ."

"Best find out quickly, old friend. Once this betrothal
is common knowledge you cannot cry off, you know.
Your reputation would sink into the depths, and it is poor
enough already." Tom grinned. He found it perfectly acceptable to chaff Burlingham now that his friend's contretemps with Mrs. Drummond Burrell was to be shown
for what it was. "I may be able to help you there, you
know—put out that George Purtwee has confessed all, in
case he misses mentioning it to anyone."

"Funny thing," Rob mused, staring at his brandy,
"George never did actually confess anything. But we understood each other, all right. That bastard!"

Tom rose to pace the room. "Yes, yes, I understand
how you feel," he said, "but we must get back to Lady
Elizabeth. Can you not ask her point-blank? Or would
that be amiss? You must do something quickly, Rob, or
it will be too late and you may be leg-shackled to a pauper. If she is a pauper, you would do well to get out of
that betrothal immediately—you can think of something—and set your sights on some other chit."

"But I have decided I wish to wed this particular chit,"
said Rob. "Therein lies the problem."

Tom stopped his pacing and stared at his friend.
"Oho! That is the way the wind blows, is it? What do
you intend to live on?"

"Heavens knows. Pour me another tot, will you, Tom?

We might as well drink up my good brandy before I go to debtors' prison."

"That is hardly likely, you being an earl and all. Come, come. You are the heir of a marquess. Your father owns a large part of Dorset, does he not? You tell me he is on the brink of ruin, but how can that be? An estate that large must produce some blunt, must it not? What does he do with his riches?" Tom smoothed his bright green waistcoat with loving fingers.

"What riches?" Rob looked morose. "Papa has not the least notion of running an estate. He and Mama barely get by. I set out on this quest for a rich wife to save them. You know all that."

"Better you should look to saving the estate yourself, you cawker," said Tom, frowning. "When have you done anything about that? It will be yours someday! You have taken no more interest in it than your father has."

"Mayhap I should visit Dorset and see for myself," Rob said slowly, mulling it over in his mind. "Running an estate is not my dish of tea, I fear, but still . . . Are you free? Would you go with me?"

As the idea began to take shape, Rob thought quickly of all the arrangements that would have to be made. A note to Lady Elizabeth; Mrs. Burket and Billy left behind to take care of the house and Caterine Purr while Geordie would go along. No. He would leave Geordie here—always best to have a man in the house—if Tom would accompany him.

"I suppose I might go," Tom allowed. "When would we start?"

"Tomorrow!"

"Impatient as ever, I see. Very well. I had best go home and pack. How do we travel?"

"Horseback. How else? M'curricle is in for repairs. Unless you wish to provide a travel coach?"

"Horseback it is. I will be at your door at dawn. Meanwhile, shall we finish this decanter? It might go bad during our absence."

Solemnly they drank, to the success of the trip, to the

imagined fortune of Lady Elizabeth, to the health of the Marquess and Marchioness of Fleet, to Caterine Purr, to each other. Once the decanter was empty, Tom wove his way home while Rob went to notify his servants and pen a note to Lady Elizabeth. Geordie, crestfallen at being left behind, nevertheless packed a few necessities for his master's journey.

Dorset was clothed in springtime splendor. Even Tom Hazleton, who usually felt distinctly uncomfortable away from the city, remarked on it. Rob's usual impatience was heightened when he realized how much he had missed Dors Court in springtime, with the trees in fresh new leaf, the chalk downs covered with their special wildflowers, and most particularly, the house itself, sturdily built of Purbeck stone.

They had reached Dorchester in late afternoon. Rob was torn between an overwhelming desire to finish the journey and a realization that their horses needed rest. He was riding Fortiter, a chestnut noted more for endurance than speed (its name, he was happy to explain to those ignorant of Latin, meant "resolutely"), but even Fortiter was tiring. Hazleton, a splendid and experienced rider, rarely had occasion to travel so far on horseback with no more interruptions than the eager earl permitted. He demanded an overnight stop.

"But we stopped last night," Rob demurred. "It is not much farther. Please, Tom."

Suddenly it came to Tom why Rob wished to go on. "We will stay at the nearest inn and you will be my guest," he announced. "I insist." He turned his horse toward the stables of a prosperous-looking inn down the street of the little town. "I would not wish to surprise your unprepared parents so late in the day," he explained as he dismounted and handed over his horse to a waiting boy.

Rob gave in and insisted on paying for a good meal. So it was that they set out early next morning, the sun behind them warming their backs, for Dors Court.

"I have not been home in so long I shudder to think

how it will look," Rob confided as they rode. His glance swept over the familiar countryside, savoring the fresh air, the ploughed fields, the sight of a skylark poised, motionless, high above them, singing its heart out. As it swooped down to light on a low post, he wondered why he had ever wanted to leave Dorset.

Tom Hazleton murmured something soothing and fell silent.

Their way took them past Maiden Castle, and Rob remembered how he had offered to show it to Lady Elizabeth sometime. Would that day ever come?

Then they were approaching Dors Court, set in an expansive parkland and reached by a tree-lined approach. Grass grew unchecked in the parkland except for an area to the right where a flock of sheep nibbled. At the first turn of the drive the house became visible, and Rob pulled up his horse.

"Ah," he said. The house looked the same, though somehow smaller than he remembered. The sun warmed the east-facing front, where giant stone urns flanked the steps. Usually they were kept full of flowers; now they were bare. Shrubs planted around the perimeter had grown ragged. The house itself, however, seemed unchanged, standing foursquare and proud, its windows reflecting the early sun.

"The stable is round at the back," Rob said softly. No human was visible and he had a strange need to talk in whispers. "We can leave the horses and go in by the garden door." He led the way around the house.

The stable was presided over by a man he had never seen before. The man looked up in inquiry as they approached.

"I am Burlingham, the marquess's son," Rob explained. "Are my parents at home?"

"Yessir, your lordship," the man said, tugging at his forelock. "They won't be up yet, I should think. Take your horses?" He reached for their reins and led the horses away. They could hear him muttering, "The son's home, eh? 'Bout time," as he disappeared into the stable.

The two men made their way to the garden door by a path that ran alongside the kitchen garden. A flourishing crop of weeds almost hid the stalks of last year's brussels sprouts. Rob sighed. "This will take years," he lamented. Tom smiled and said nothing.

The garden door, halfway along the north wing of the U-shaped manor house, yielded to his touch, and they entered a long hall that connected the family quarters with the kitchen and servants' domain. It was darkly oak-paneled and got little natural light from its one north-facing window. Rob led the way forward to the entrance hall, well lit by its east windows, and started up the broad, curving staircase.

"Dorcas? Is that you? Would you bring—" a feminine voice came from above, and stopped. "Robert? *Robert!* Oh, my, oh, my, Robert is here! William! Robert is here!"

The tall, gray-haired lady, wrapped in a somewhat tattered robe, flew down the stairs and clasped Rob in her arms. "Robert!" she cried again, a tear running down her cheek. She hugged him tightly for a moment. Then, recalling herself, she turned to Tom Hazleton. "I must apologize," she said, pulling her robe more closely around her. "We are not dressed for company. You are . . . ?"

"This is my dear friend Tom Hazleton," Rob explained, patting his mother's arm. "Kept me company on the trip. Is Papa upstairs?"

"Just getting dressed, I believe. He had to let his valet go, you know, and he does have trouble with his buttons when I am not there to help. His fingers no longer work as they should."

"Excuse me, Tom," said Rob. He took the stairs two at a time to reach the stooped figure looking down on them from the upper landing. "Father!" he cried, grasping the man's hand to shake it cordially. His father winced, then smiled.

"My boy," he said. "Here at last. How goes it? Have you brought a wealthy young fiancée to meet us? Who is the young buck with you?" He looked again at his wife and the man with her, both of them staring up at him and his son. Nervously he fingered his collar, shy of any neckcloth. "I—I am not fit to receive company, I fear," he said in embarrassment.

"Never mind," said Rob, "it is only Tom Hazleton, who knows all about us. How are you, Father?"

"Doing the best that I can," the marquess answered. "You did not answer my question. Where is the wealthy young fiancée?"

"Ah, that requires some explanation," said his son. His smile faded.

"Then we will go to your mother's morning room and you can tell us over tea. I tell you, it is a blasted nuisance, this house. We are living in the south wing, downstairs, so as to get the sun, but your mother will not give up her usual bedchamber in the north wing—and the only way for the servants to get from the kitchen to the south wing is by way of this north corridor." The marquess frowned as he surveyed the dim hallway. " 'Twould make more sense to close off one wing or the other. Two of us rattling around in this pile! But come. I wish to hear all." He moved cautiously down the staircase, still fingering his collar. "Coming, Jane?" he addressed his wife.

"Heavens!" The marchioness was indignant. "Looking like this? And I must order the tea. Dorcas!" She walked quickly toward the kitchen. "Dorcas! Tea in the morning room!"

A young maid appeared, took the order, and returned to the kitchen. Lady Fleet fled upstairs to dress, calling, "Please do not start without me!"

"Do you wish to change?" the marquess inquired. Told there was no hurry, he led the way, slowly, to the morning room in the south wing. Rob noted with sadness that his father had aged badly since last they had met more than a year earlier.

The morning was taken up with Rob's recital of his life since he had seen them. He had written a few times, but "only enough to stir our interest and want more," his mother reported. She and his father looked grave when Rob told of his suspicions about Lady Elizabeth's wealth.

"Why did you not bring her along?" the marquess asked. "Your mother would have ferreted out the state of her income to the penny, would you not, my dear . . . ? Is she a comely wench, Robert? Is she biddable? Perhaps you should look elsewhere, just in case."

"Yes, I consider her comely, and no, she is not particularly biddable," said Rob. "But I have decided to choose her. Whatever her fortune, I choose her. The problem is, should she lack a fortune, what do we live on? We all know *I* have no fortune."

His parents looked mutually glum. "It is not too late to change your mind," his mother ventured.

"You say she accepted your proposal?" his father asked. "How can you be certain, considering the situation you described? She could have said yes to avoid having to contend with George. Never did trust that lad, come to that. Shiftier than his father, and that is going some. Even if they are our relatives. Cannot believe George is blaming his great-grandma. I remember her well. She was a good sort; never would have occurred to her to want to be the Marquess of Fleet. My Great-aunt Ivy, you know." The marquess was lost in the past.

"I believe Lady Elizabeth returns my regard," Rob said, sounding more certain than he felt. "We have had no opportunity to talk further. It seemed more honorable for me to learn exactly what the family financial situation is before I pursue this matter. That is why I am here."

"You have only to look around you," said his father, frowning. "Nothing has changed since we left you in London; it has only become worse."

"What of your steward?"

"He tells me we are headed toward ruin if we do not improve our breeding stock and invest in new strains of corn and I do not know what all—things we have no money to do." The marquess looked hopelessly at his son, his fingers picking at his collar.

"Who keeps the books?"

"He does, of course. Never was any good at accounts, myself. Why? Do you wish to see them?"

"Indeed I do, Father."

"In the library. I shall fetch them." Lord Fleet pushed himself painfully up from his chair and left the room.

"When did he become like this?" Rob asked his mother in a hushed voice. "I can hardly believe the change."

Lady Fleet moved her chair closer to that of her son. "I did not mention it in a letter because he reads what I write you," she said. "He finds it too painful to write himself, you understand. It is his joints. They grew much worse over the winter, what with the cold and damp. I had hoped—now spring is here—oh, Robert! He is no better, and I worry so." She blinked back the tears and busied herself with pouring another cup of tea.

Rob felt himself covered with guilt and remorse. In his pursuit of an heiress and his efforts to clear his name he had neglected his parents shamefully. He knew his father, even when in the best of health, had neither talent nor experience in running an estate; until recent years the marquess had lived as aimless and spendthrift a life as he, Rob, had been doing. Why had not his father's father drilled some sense into him instead of letting him do as he pleased? Rob caught himself. His father had done no better by him. But he, now at the advanced age of eight-and-twenty, had realized the error of his ways and meant to do something about it—if it was not too late.

Lord Fleet returned with the estate books clutched in his gnarled fingers and dropped them into Rob's lap. "Here," he said. "See what you can make of them."

"This will take some time," Rob said, glancing at the cramped handwriting within. "Let me take them with me. Can you put Tom in the chamber next to mine? I trust mine is still mine? We can go over these together." He rose, beckoned to Hazleton, bent to kiss his mother, patted his father's shoulder, and left the morning room for the long trip back to the north wing where his bed-chamber sat on the second floor.

Rob and Tom, fortified by a scant nuncheon and later by a bottle of his father's brandy, spent the afternoon poring over the Dors Court books. Hazleton proved an invaluable ally, grasping the meaning of obscure entries that had Rob completely at sea.

"Where did you learn all this?" Rob marveled. "We never learned it at Cambridge."

"A younger son has to do *something*," Tom laughed. "M'father thought it would be useful if I could help keep the Hazleton brass under control, even if I get little enough of it." He bent over the books again. "Look here. A hundred forty-seven pounds three shillings tuppence for *breeding ram*. I thought your father said he could not afford new breeding stock! And why try to improve the sheep? Sheep are not the moneymakers in Dorset; crops are. Any fool knows that."

"Is that so? I did not know that. I thought sheep could be raised anywhere."

"Of course, and the Dors Court sheep are being raised just outside the window, if you care to look. Do you note any prize rams?"

Rob wandered to the window, stretching to get the kinks out of muscles atrophied from sitting too long over the books. The little flock of sheep he had noticed on their arrival had moved so close to the house he could hear their bleats, though the window was closed. He opened it and stared down at them. How to recognize a prize ram? He had no idea. They all looked the same to him, varying only in size. Stupid creatures.

"Any other peculiar entries?" he asked Hazleton.

"I am not sure. May I mark up the book? I would like to confer with your father about some of these. I will tick the questionables if it is all right with you."

"Please do."

Rob and Hazleton spent the better part of two days going over the Dors Court accounts, dating back nearly

ten years. It had been ten years since the Marquess of
Fleet, his wife, and son had made a semipermanent re-
moval to London, where life was livelier and more
suited to the flamboyant tastes of the marquess and Rob.
During all that time the fate of Dors Court was in the
hands of Jonas Dyer, steward. So long as the money continued to flow from Dorset to London, Lord Fleet and
family lived a life of ease. The decline was hardly noticeable at first. When it became alarming, Lord Fleet
had returned to the estate to hear a tale of woe from his
steward. Nothing could be done to make the estate prof-
itable without an infusion of capital, Jonas Dyer had explained, showing Lord Fleet the carefully kept accounts.
They had meant little to Lord Fleet, but he knew something had to be done. It was then that he decided he and
Lady Fleet would have to remove to Dorset; the big
house in Mount Street would be sold and Robert would
be permitted to have the proceeds, from which he could
buy a smaller house. With luck, the personable young
man could find a wealthy heiress to wed before the re-
mainder of the house sale money was gone.

Ten years of accounts. Tom Hazleton and Rob had de-
veloped headaches from deciphering page after page of
numbers and cramped writing. Copious brandy supplied
by Lord Fleet was little help. Neither was Lord Fleet
himself; his knowledge of going prices for crops, for a
new ploughshare, for a new roof for a tenant farmer, was
nil. Rob began to realize for the first time what a compli-
cated undertaking it was to run an estate.

To get the cobwebs out of their heads, on the third day
the two young men closed the books, snuffed the candles, and mounted their horses to survey the estate. It
was in sorry condition, no doubt about it. Little as he
knew about farming, Rob could see it.

He was greeted in friendly fashion by several of the
tenants, ploughing the fields, planting grain, or busy
about some task around their own small holdings. They
knew who he was, even though he had made only brief

visits in the last ten years. No doubt the groom had spread the word of his arrival.

"We should talk to some of the tenants," Rob suggested, squinting into the bright sunlight that turned the heath to red-gold. "Perhaps Amos Tuttle, if he is still around. Used to know him well when I was a boy. His wife made the most delectable treacle tarts! I shall ask." He summoned a man who was attempting to dig out a clump of gorse nearby.

"Amos Tuttle still about?" he asked.

"Yes, indeed, your lordship," the man answered. "Just down this lane, turn right—"

"I know where it is," Rob said, suddenly eager. "Come along, Tom."

Amos Tuttle was at home, nursing a broken finger he had caught in a well chain a few days before. His wife invited the gentlemen in.

"Burlingham! Your lordship!" Tuttle jumped from his chair, holding out a thickly bandaged hand. "Oh, sorry, I keep forgetting. Can't shake your hand, can I? Do sit down." He indicated chairs in the small, neat kitchen-dining-sitting room.

Once Tom had been introduced, Tuttle had explained his finger injury, and Mrs. Tuttle had been urged to find a treacle tart if any were left, Rob told him of their study of Dors Court's books.

"How is Dyer to work for?" he inquired. "Seem to know what he is doing? D'you think he is honest?"

"Lazy, that's what," Tuttle answered. He attempted to pack his pipe with tobacco and found one hand was not sufficient. "Damn," he said, "I keep forgettin'. Now, Dyer started out well enough, back when he first came— what was that? Nine, ten years ago? But with your pa and you away in London, nobody to keep an eye on him, he just let things slide. Honest? I wouldn't know, your lordship. You find anything havey-cavey in them accounts?" He handed his pipe to his wife. "Can you stuff a pipe, Vinnie? Sure could use a draw."

"Get along with you, Amos," she said in embarrassment. She laid the pipe on a shelf.

"Let me," said Tom. He found Tuttle's tobacco pouch and set about carefully filling the pipe, handed it to Tuttle, and looked around for a spill. Mrs. Tuttle handed him one, he lit it from the cookstove, and held it while Tuttle drew great drafts. Tuttle smiled.

"You're a good lad," he said. "You'll do. Now. About Dyer. He's let things go to ruin, and when one of us needs somethin', he says he ain't the money for it. Y'see that window? Been cracked for a year at least! Piece o' glass came out and we had to plug it up with greased paper. Like they done in the Middle Ages! Turley's needed a new roof for two year. Has to put pots around to catch the leaks. Yet Dyer never put in no barley last year at all! Never got around to gettin' the seed. Y'see what I mean."

"Dyer will have to go," said Rob with finality. "We will need someone else, however. M'father and I know next to nothing about running this place, damn it all. Tuttle, what say you? Would you like to be steward?"

"Me? Your lordship! I'm past fifty! Not too many years left. What would you want me for?" Tuttle's round face held a look of wonder tinged with regret. He puffed madly on his pipe.

"Amos, I have known you most of my life. I cannot think of a better man. Are you able to keep accounts? You do read and write, do you not?" Assured that he did, Rob asked, "Will you not at least try it?"

"What do you say, Vinnie?" Tuttle asked his wife. "Should I do it?"

"You can do it," Mrs. Tuttle assured him. She patted him on the shoulder. "Of course you can. Would we live in the steward's cottage, your lordship? So much finer than this one." She frowned at the cracked window.

"Yes, indeed," Rob assured her. "It is settled, then. Come up to the house this evening and we will talk it over."

"What about Dyer?" Tuttle asked.

"I will take care of Dyer. Shall we go, Tom?"

"But the treacle tarts!' Mrs. Tuttle cried. "You must have one of my tarts!"

The two gentlemen obediently had a tart apiece and left with lighter hearts.

Rob and Tom went together to confront Jonas Dyer, who vehemently denied any wrongdoing. Rob, nevertheless, believed the steward was not surprised at his accusations. It was as if he had expected them.

"Look at the accounts books! I accounted for every penny!" Dyer cried. Hastily he pushed aside a pile of papers and an unsavory mug that had once contained coffee so his visitor could sit down. Dyer was a widower, and obviously lacked any housekeeping skills. The sitting room of his cottage was a shambles.

"I see no evidence of many of the items you say were purchased," Rob rejoined. "Mr. Hazleton here, who is a dab hand at the accounts books, assures me that many of the entries *smell*. What have you been doing, Dyer? Lining your pockets at our expense?"

"Hardly, sir," said Dyer. "There weren't nothin' to line 'em with." He forced a laugh. "You see any signs of me rollin' in wealth? Ha!"

"Your attention to the crops, to the tenants' needs, to the upkeep of the manor house is a disgrace," Rob went on. "Dyer, you are dismissed. Amos Tuttle will take your place. You will be out in"—Rob looked around at the disorder—"three days. But just in case, Mr. Hazleton and I shall search this rat's nest. Immediately, I believe. Dyer, please leave the premises for a few hours."

"You can't! You have no right!" Dyer protested. "I swear, you won't find nothin'!" He looked worried, but not as worried as a man guilty of hiding away his employer's money should be, Rob thought.

"I have every right," Rob said sternly. "This cottage is my father's property, not yours. Out with you!"

Dyer left reluctantly. Hazleton watched out the wir

dow as the steward saddled his horse, mounted, and rode away.

"Did you see that horse?" Hazleton asked. "Mighty fine horse for a steward. You should trade him for Fortiter."

"Another cause for suspicion. Come on, Tom. Where could that devil have hidden his hoard? We will take this place apart if need be."

For three hours, during which there was no sign of Dyer, the pair ransacked Dyer's cottage, examining it for loose floorboards, false walls, hidden compartments. It was an arduous task because of all the debris scattered about. Their only discovery was a small cache of coins in a dirty cup in the cupboard. Rob had thought Dyer might have kept a duplicate set of books revealing the true nature of his accounts, but the only books in the cottage were a Bible and a violent diatribe on the plight of workingmen ground under the heel of the ruling class.

Finally the two men gave up in exasperation.

"We will have Dyer up to the house to explain his method of accounting to Tuttle—and may God grant that Tuttle is honest!—and then I hope never to see Dyer again," Rob said with a sigh. "Thank you for all your help, Tom. Never could have done it without you."

Events moved swiftly thereafter. Rob and Hazleton gave up on the books; what was past was past, and could not be undone. A diffident Dyer explained to Tuttle his methods of keeping accounts, and Tuttle grasped them without difficulty. The session in Lord Fleet's library was short and uneasy; it was clear the two men did not like each other. Dyer, maintaining his innocence to the last, nevertheless seemed strangely unperturbed. He glanced around the tiers of leather-bound books with seeming disinterest.

Later Lord Fleet listened to his son's plans and made a show of interest and understanding, but Rob believed most of it went over his father's head. Tuttle had made no promises of early recovery; it would take years.

Penny-pinching would have to continue for the foreseeable future.

What were they all to live on meanwhile? It came to Rob that his father's library might hold more books that he could sell, now that he knew something about the subject. He spent hours counting the volumes and sorting them according to the condition of their bindings.

His father found him there one afternoon. When Rob told him what he intended, Lord Fleet was enthusiastic.

"Already sold off most of the paintings," he admitted. "As you probably noticed. Never thought of trying to sell those old books."

"I have not found anything particularly valuable," Rob confessed. "Fine bindings, but little of interest inside. That is no doubt why they are still here. I took the best to London." His face fell.

"Maybe you could sell 'em to someone who just wants his library to look good," Lord Fleet suggested. "There are such gulls, you know. Remember Lord Thistlethwaite? We were having a drink in his library one evening when he was called away for something, and I started looking through his books for something to do. Half of 'em had blank pages! The spine would say 'Dryden' and there would be nothing inside! What do you think, boy?"

"It is a possibility," Rob agreed. "I could advertise in the newspaper—no need to go through a bookseller—the buyer would not want his name known, for who would admit to having finely bound trash in his library?"

"I would," said Lord Fleet. He laughed. "I freely admit it. Never look at it."

"No, you never were a reader. These were all Grandfather's, or maybe Great-grandfather's. Perhaps age will add to their value. I shall try it. Thank you, Father."

Rob made arrangements to have nearly nine hundred books carted to London and he felt a desire to leave. They had been gone for nearly a week. Had George Purtwee cleared his name as promised? What of Lady Elizabeth? She must be monstrously perplexed by this time. He conjured up her face, the delight on it when she accepted his proposal. Surely she meant it? He felt an overwhelming desire to kiss her. He had not even kissed her when she said yes. His preoccupation with George Purtwee was no excuse. What must she think of him?

"We are going home, Tom," he told Hazleton. "I mean London. Much remains unresolved here, but even more remains unresolved in London."

"I wondered when the fair Lady Elizabeth would come to your mind," said Tom, laughing. "I will be delighted to go back. This bucolic life is all very well, but it is not London."

Spending one night on the road, they reached London eight days after they had left.

All was well at Rob's town house. He took time only to wash, change clothes, and warn Geordie of the imminent arrival of two cartloads of books before jumping into his newly upholstered curricle for a trip to Knightsbridge Terrace.

Would Lady Elizabeth receive him? Would prospects of a revived Dors Court—possibly far in the future—make up for his current lack of fortune? Would Lady Elizabeth even permit him in the house? His warm reunion with his love—yes, she was his love, no doubt about it—had been the goal driving him since he had set out for Dorset. Now that the time had come he felt strangely hesitant, fearful that his dream would come tumbling down like a house of cards. He slowed his horses.

The space in front of the little house in Knightsbridge Terrace was already occupied. A familiar groom waited with a familiar cabriolet.

Purtwee.

"Damn!" said Rob. He pounded his fist on the newly upholstered seat.

Chapter Sixteen

Rob had to go through the usual verbal battle with Molly to get into the sitting room. He felt like pushing the maid, who for once wore a clean apron, into the woodwork. Instead he handed her his hat and brushed past her toward the sound of voices.

"—recently decided I must visit Wimborne in Dorset to study its early fourteenth century clock. It shows the sun and moon orbiting the earth! Dare I hope you would accompany me?"

The calmly uttered words in Purtwee's voice threw Rob into a rage even before he entered the sitting room, pursued fruitlessly by Molly.

"No!" he cried, storming across the threshold. "No! I will not have it!"

Three pairs of eyes in surprised faces stared at him.

"The prodigal returns," Lady Stanbourne murmured.

Rob looked around. Purtwee, again a picture of elegance, stood in his favorite place by the mantel, his fingers caressing the clock. Lady Stanbourne was seated in the chair with the split upholstery, facing Purtwee. Bets was seated at one side next to the tea table, holding a cup half full of tea.

Slowly it penetrated Rob's brain that Purtwee apparently had invited Lady Stanbourne, not Bets, to accompany him to Dorset. *Lady Stanbourne?* She was twice Purtwee's age. But that was none of his business.

"I beg your pardon," he said stiffly to Lady Stanbourne. She nodded.

An uneasy silence fell. Rob could think of a hundred

things to say, but not which to say first. Finally Bets spoke.

"A cup of tea, your lordship?"

"Ah. Um. Yes, thank you."

"We shall need another cup. A moment, please, while I summon Molly." Bets rose and left the room.

Rob decided to wade right in. "Have you done as you promised?" he asked Purtwee.

"I believe Lady Stanbourne made it clear that our differences should not be aired in this house," said Purtwee primly. "I withhold my answer."

Rob's imperfectly banked anger rose again. He tamped it down as best he could. "You could answer without 'airing any differences,' could you not? I suggest you do so." He glared at his cousin.

"Not in front of the ladies," said Purtwee as Bets walked in carrying a cup and saucer. "Must not upset their sensibilities."

"Your tea, my lord," Bets said hurriedly. She could see Burlingham growing angrier and angrier.

"Thank you," he said, accepting the cup. He looked down at her, seated quietly by the tea table. Her eyes were downcast, refusing to meet his. Lines of worry marred her brow. Despite a most becoming lavender print gown and smoothly arranged hair, she looked tired and dispirited.

Rob tipped up her chin with one finger. "Look at me," he said softly. When she did, he smiled warmly and said, "Soon." Then he walked over to an empty chair, sat down, and drank his tea.

When he had finished, he rose, set the cup and saucer carefully on the tea table, and turned to Purtwee.

"George," he said, "you are making every effort to arouse my ire. You have succeeded!"

He lunged at his cousin, catching him once again by the collar at the back of his neck. Putting his mouth to George's ear, he said quietly, "No Bedlam until later. We will have this out now. How well do you spar, coz?"

Purtwee writhed and twisted. "Not here!" he said breathlessly. "Not in front of the ladies!"

"Very well. In the garden, perhaps? Out in the street? Or Hyde Park? It is not so far. You may ride in my curricle." He gave Purtwee a shake.

"Very well! Very well! I will answer," Purtwee struggled no longer and seemed to shrink into himself. "I—I have been ill. I fully intended to follow your instructions, but I had such a bad throat I could hardly talk." He cleared his throat. "But I promise! Immediately! Truly!"

"Has this man shown signs of illness since I have been gone?" Rob demanded.

Lady Stanbourne looked upset but said nothing.

"We have seen him only thrice," Bets offered. "I noted no problems with his voice."

"Did he know I was away?"

Bets and Lady Stanbourne exchanged glances. Lady Stanbourne finally admitted she might have mentioned it.

"As I thought," said Rob. "Come, George."

"Where are we going?" Purtwee quavered. Rob's strong hand had him by the back of the neck again.

"Outside."

In deference to the ladies, Rob thrust his cousin out the door, down the steps, along the walk, and finally across the street before the house of a stranger. Removing his hand from Purtwee's neck, he faced his cousin and put up his fists.

"No!" Purtwee cried. "I am no pugilist! No!"

It was too late. Two quick punches and Purtwee was on the ground, moaning.

"He is all yours," Rob told Purtwee's groom, who had watched the proceedings with awe. The groom hauled the prostrate Purtwee to the cabriolet and with some difficulty got him into the seat. He drove off with Purtwee's moans fading in the distance.

"Bully!" cried Billy, who had seen the whole thing from Rob's curricle. Billy waved the skirts of his toga in celebration.

Rob smiled briefly and returned to the house. The two ladies were standing in the doorway, with Molly jumping up and down behind them in an effort to get a better view.

Rob took Bets' hand and led her inside, back to the sitting room. "Are we still betrothed?" he asked.

"Are we?" she countered. She sat down again at the tea table. She seemed dispirited.

"I hope so. We must talk."

"I agree." Bets tilted her head toward her mother, who had followed them in, and raised her eyebrows in question. "Where?"

"May I have the honor of your company for a drive in my curricle? We might perhaps inspect the park."

"Ah, yes, the park. It has, perhaps, one or two blades of grass I have not seen before. I look forward to making their acquaintance . . . your lordship."

"I believe," said Rob, frowning, "that you were to call me Rob, or Robert, if you prefer. No more 'your lordship' please."

"Certainly, your lordship. As you wish, my lord."

"Why so grumpish? What have I done now?"

"Have you the day free? That might give me time to list your shortcomings." She gave him a scathing look and turned away to give all her attention to her empty teacup.

Ah, more fences to mend, Rob realized. Going off to Dorset with nothing more than a brusque note to his betrothed had been a bigger gaffe than he knew.

"We go to explore the beauties of the park," Bets told her mother in a bored voice. "I am sure they shall all be new to me." Reluctantly she fetched her bonnet and reticule.

"Now, please tell me what this is all about," Rob begged when they were under way. "I can see I have offended you in some manner."

"Surely you cannot believe I would find offensive a departure for more than a sennight—eight days!—immediately after your so-called proposal—I assume it was truly meant as a proposal?—without a word—not a word!" Bets' voice rose as the uncertainty and worry of the last week came to a head. "Leaving Mama and me to the tender mercies of your cousin? Three visits he has made! Three times I must act the hostess, and pour the tea, and listen to him go on about his precious clocks! O-o-oh!" She drummed the curricle seat with her fists.

"Please calm down!" Rob thought he might have been in the wrong, but only moderately—not enough to occasion such an outburst. He put a hand over the ear nearest her and attempted to guide the horses with the other hand. "You have scorched my ear. I do beg pardon," he said stiffly. "I was so taken up with George, and then I had to go to Dorset without warning . . ."

"I hope none of your family was ill?" Bets calmed at the thought. In a summons on account of illness, all would be forgiven.

"Not exactly. I will explain in a moment. First, though, please tell me about George. I had his promise to admit his lies in the Drummond Burrell affair to all the *ton* in a sennight. Yet he has not done so, evidently. Has he said anything to you or your mother?"

Bets brightened. "No, but the word is out that something monstrous has happened! We understand that people are taking sides everywhere. Some truly believe Mr. Purtwee had a fit and had to be restrained. Molly got it from a maid of the gentleman across the street that he actually saw foam coming from Mr. Purtwee's mouth! Several people vow they remember Mr. Purtwee having fits regularly in his childhood, but thought he had outgrown them. Mama heard from someone else that Lord Purtwee, George's father, was prepared to spend up to ten thousand pounds to keep George out of Bedlam and place him in a private asylum. Many are shaking their heads and comparing him to King George. I should warn you, however, that some are scandalized that you, his older and bigger cousin, should use force on him for no apparent reason. And in public too! Right in the middle of Knightsbridge Terrace! I fear they are acquainted with your rakehell ways, my lord."

Rob chuckled. "My setdown today should give them some more to talk about," he said. "Once George admits his part in that plot, I trust the *ton* will forgive me."

"I think," said Bets, "that he called on us in an effort to demonstrate that he is in his right mind. But your lor—I mean Rob—he is so *tedious!* Of course we never mentioned what had happened the day you marched him out, nor did he. He only prosed on about his eternal clocks. Mama seems fascinated. Poor Mama. I suppose she needs a new interest to fasten upon."

"Could you not have left them to it? Excuse yourself to tend to some needlework or something?" Rob felt uneasy at the idea of Bets in the company of another suitor, even if he had been rejected.

"Mama, I fear, wishes to keep two strings to her bow. She insisted I be present, for Mr. Purtwee supposedly is calling on me, not her, and Mama believes she is holding him in reserve should you not come up to scratch."

"Then it behooves me to come up to scratch," Rob said firmly. "That, in truth, is why I journeyed to Dorset. Oh, Bets, I fear I have bad news. Dors Court is not doing well. M'father is no manager; never has been. It seems our steward was a lazy lout who let everything slide, and cheated us besides. M'friend Hazleton and I went over the books and found suspicious entries, but they are hard to prove. We searched his cottage inch by inch for money or anything else he might have stolen, and found nothing. I have a new steward now, but it will take years to bring Dors Court back. Meanwhile, I hope to put some nine hundred old books on the market, but I cannot guess what they will bring. So, my love, we may have to live on your considerable fortune for the nonce. Do you mind terribly?"

Bets gripped Rob's arm with both hands so tightly that he had to stop the curricle just as he was about to guide the horses into the park. Shouts and catcalls, threats and curses came at him from behind. The driver of a cart immediately behind the curricle left his horse untended to run forward and shake his fist at Rob.

Harried, Rob wrenched his arm loose and guided them forward.

"Say that again," said Bets.

"Say what? Please, ma'am, permit me to stop in a more suitable place," Rob begged. In a few minutes he reached a quiet stretch and pulled over. "Now."

"You called me 'my love,' " said Bets. "Did you mean that?"

"Of course! Did I not tell you I offered you my heart? Do you wish to tell me you were not listening when I proposed? And I made a special point of including a phrase in my note that I believed you, though not everyone, would understand. '*Ab imo pectore,*' if memory serves."

Bets reddened. "You credit me too highly," she confessed. "I have wondered ever since what it means."

"Loosely translated, it means 'from the bottom of my heart' and that is precisely what I meant," said Rob, taking her hand. "Dear Bets, indeed I love you, from the bottom of my heart. Can you doubt it? I fear I am not practiced at sweet talk. Fisticuffs? Yes. Racing? Yes. Old books? Yes, I think. Sweet talk? No."

"What, then, did you say to your mistress? Or should I say, mistresses?" Bets colored. Surely she had the right to ask this, if they were betrothed?

It was Rob's turn to redden. "I should have guessed you would ask that," he said. "I do not remember. That was so long ago."

"Long ago? It was common knowledge during my second season. Have you forgotten so soon, sir?"

"Oh, my dear Bets, I have had neither the blunt nor the inclination. That is all in the past. Forgive me? I must say I find it interesting that you should remember. You knew I was alive, then, two years ago? I am flattered."

"Only because I was horrified at such profligate living. My family never lived that way and it made me wonder. No one ever saw you; you never attended any parties or balls; you just lived your rakehell life."

"But that is all changed, my dear. I have seen the error of my ways. I shall be such a model husband I will bore you to tears. You will wish you had married George Purtwee to gain a little excitement in your life." Rob laughed but his look was serious as he stroked Bets' hands. "Do you think you can put up with me?"

"Oh, yes! But first I must make a terrible admission. Rob, I have no considerable fortune. We have the Knightsbridge Terrace house, which Mama inherited from her father. My father was indeed wealthy, but apparently he lost most of it before his death. My half brother Godfrey as executor sends us Mama's and my share each quarter day, but it is little enough. That is all we have. I was to have a dowry, of course, but Godfrey says we have been using up that amount just to live. Oh, Rob! That is why Mama has been after me to find a wealthy suitor! After four seasons she was ready to give up when she hit upon you! She believed we could stomach your rakehell ways, if we could gain enough to live on."

Bets glanced timidly at Rob's face, grown thunderous as she explained her mother's plan. "But it was not that way!" she cried. "Truly, it was not that way!"

"So, your tumble in the park was prearranged, was it?" he roared. "An unconventional but very successful way for you to meet the wealthy rakehell? Let me tell you, madam, you had me fooled. As, for that matter, I had you fooled, for I am no wealthy rakehell. As I have just explained." He had loosened her hands and again gripped the reins, looking bitterly at his horses. "Hoist by my own petard. I should have known."

Rob had clucked at his pair and started up again when Bets put her hand on his to detain him. "Wait!" she cried. "No! Listen to me!"

He stopped.

"Truly, it was coincidence that you appeared after I tumbled that day," she went on. "How could I have known you would be there? And once I came to know you, I could see you were a far better man than gossip would have it. Rob, I fell in love with you! If I were seeking only a man with money, I could have accepted your cousin. I have worried ceaselessly that you would discover our lack of the ready. But do you not see? We are two of a kind. Both seeking to marry money. I think we should do famously together!"

As Rob pondered her words, they began to make sense. Good sense. She loved him! He could not imagine life without her, fortune or no fortune. Her little deception was no worse than his.

He smiled.

"Let us go tell your mother and talk about a wedding," he said joyously. "If we must live on love alone, at least we have plenty of it." Whereupon he drew her into his arms and kissed her, a long, lingering kiss that removed any doubt in either heart of their feelings for each other.

As Rob's firm lips came down on hers, Bets reveled in their taste, their texture. It was as if they opened a vista of delight that led she knew not where. Then Rob murmured disjointed phrases of love and desire in her ear as he moved to kiss the side of her neck. She wrapped her arms more tightly around him, and when he started to draw away, she held him fast.

"My dear, the entire *ton* may be watching," he reminded her gently. "I fear the park is not the place for this. I apologize. I am being talked about too much already, and I have no wish to draw you into the gossip. Shall we proceed?"

Reluctantly, Bets released him. "I obey you in all things," she said, "as a proper prospective wife should. That is, if it suits me!" She gave him a roguish smile.

"As I told my father," said Rob with mock severity. He urged his horses into a sedate trot. "He asked if you were biddable, and I had to admit that you were not. Never would I want a biddable wife. I have had enough boredom to last me without the burden of a namby-pamby female. You are certainly not that!" He tucked her arm in his.

"Surely you have wondered *why* George dislikes me so," he said a little later. "Let me tell you as he admitted it to me." He repeated Purtwee's entire conversation as well as he could remember it, even to the destruction of the cricket bat.

"I find Mr. Purtwee despicable, but I can almost—*almost*—feel some pity for him," was Bets' judgment.

It was Thursday, and Bets was eager to attend Lady Stafford's weekly At Home. She hoped to learn whether George Purtwee had at last admitted to his plot against the Earl of Burlingham. The younger women rarely bothered with what Bets privately referred to as Tittle-Tattle Tea, but this was an unusual situation.

In the intervening days, Rob had called often but had never stayed long. He wished to be available should anyone answer his newspaper notice offering a library of books for sale. No one had yet. Lady Stanbourne was in a constant state of nerves at the prospect of planning a wedding, one that would not look too cheese-paring, yet would not take every penny they had. She was barely reconciled to her daughter's choice of bridegroom. A man with no money, a man of dubious reputation! Surely Bets would do better with George Purtwee? She brought up Purtwee's name frequently, recalling his devotion, his impeccable wardrobe, his spotless reputation. She could not bring herself to believe that he had harmed Burlingham. Why would he? She could see no reason for it; therefore it could not be true.

Heartily tired of her mother's innuendos, Bets suggested the outing to Lady Stafford's. Hearing it from someone else's lips might finally persuade Lady Stanbourne of the truth when her own or Rob's protestations were dismissed.

Bets donned her lavender print, lavished now with a new white lace ruffle at the neck, and prodded Lady Stanbourne into her best dress of rose silk. They arrived in a hired hackney and were welcomed effusively by Lady Stafford.

Once the eight middle-aged ladies and Bets were seated in their hostess's gilt chairs and tea and cakes had been passed, Lady Stafford called for silence.

"I have the best tittle-tattle in months," she announced gleefully. "We have all heard, I am sure, of the mystery surrounding young George Purtwee—whether he is fit for Bedlam, or whether he was the innocent victim of the Earl of Burlingham." She paused, glancing over her rapt audience. "Now I have the right of it. You will never be able to guess!"

"Get on with it," Lady Grace Simpson murmured.

"It seems that Burlingham had just cause!" Lady Stafford continued. "George Purtwee attended Almack's last night, and would you believe it? He apologized to Mrs. Drummond Burrell. He said he misheard Burlingham. Said Burlingham was *not* foxed, but had suffered some sudden indisposition—food gone bad, perhaps. Said as Burlingham's cousin he had known the earl most of his life, and whatever one might say about the earl, he would never have insulted a patroness of Almack's. Mr. Purtwee must have made up the tale from whole cloth! One wonders why. Mr. Purtwee always has seemed such an exemplary young man. A dead bore, perhaps, but hardly the man to malign his own cousin for no reason. It must be true, then, that—how shall I say it?—something is amiss in his brainbox."

As murmurs and exclamations broke out among the audience, Bets raised her voice.

"I have some knowledge of this," she said clearly. "Mr. Purtwee has been jealous of his cousin for many years, and believes but for an accident of birth he, not Burlingham, would be heir to a marquess. Mr. Purtwee believes himself to be the better man for the title."

"Accident of birth?" Lady Stafford asked sharply. "How can that be? They are only third cousins, I believe."

Bets explained the twisted reasons for Purtwee's actions, as Burlingham had explained them to her. "Sometimes I believe he is truly a candidate for Bedlam," she added.

Lady Stanbourne looked ready to cry.

"How do you know this, my dear?" their hostess inquired. "It is common knowledge that you have received the attentions of both of them. How do you know which one to believe?"

"Mr. Purtwee admits it, as you have just told us, and Burlingham confirms it," Bets answered. "What is more, Burlingham is certain that Mr. Purtwee caused something to be put in Burlingham's drink just before he visited Almack's. He has made a thorough investigation. I believe him."

Bets rose and looked around the faces turned to hers. "And what is still more, Burlingham and I have become betrothed," she said. "I trust you will wish me happy." She sat down again and patted her mother's hand.

Lady Stanbourne dabbed at her eyes with her handkerchief.

The buzz of comment grew louder. Mixed with the felicitations were a few remarks of dismay, but on the whole Bets felt the ladies' sympathics had turned toward Burlingham rather than Mr. Purtwee.

She fended off numerous questions about the date of the wedding and the couple's plans, saying little had been decided.

"Will you be living in Burlingham's town house?" Miss Bascomb asked. "Such a shame that the earl sold the big house in Mount Street and bought that little one in Grosvenor Row."

"I do not mind," Bets began when she was interrupted by another of the ladies.

"Speaking of the big house in Mount Street, I hear the new owners—what is their name?—are completely doing it over," she said. "I hear it was not in the best condition when they bought it. Much to be done, it seems." The lady, whose name Bets could not recall, looked smug.

"The Cripforths," Lady Stafford supplied. "Upstarts."

"I called once," another lady remarked. "Out of curiosity, you understand. Hopeless. No idea how to go on. Not a book in that huge library! Nothing *there* but money, I vow." She seemed affronted.

No books! Bets could hardly wait to see Rob.

Rob was beginning to wonder whether anyone had even noticed his advertisement of books for sale. Not a single nibble had he had. The books were occupying an unconscionable amount of space in his small house. He had most of them stacked in neat piles along one wall of his central hallway, but the hall was so narrow that anyone moving quickly along it was almost certain to dislodge a pile or two. Perhaps his grand plan was a pipe dream and he would have to use them as protection for his roses over the winter. It certainly would be too expensive to send them back to Dors Court.

On the Thursday he was morosely retrieving a fallen pile when a messenger arrived. With surprise he realized the messenger was one of his father's servants, a man he had seen the week before at Dors Court. He felt a cold chill. Had something happened to his father?

"What is it, Catton?" he demanded. "Is it . . . my father?"

"From your father, yes," the man replied. "Oh, no, sir," seeing the stricken look on Rob's face, "he's all right. Just said this were too important for the post." He handed Rob a letter.

Rob tore it open with trembling fingers.

My dear son,

Quickly, I beg of you, do *NOT* sell that lot of books until you have examined each one!

Amos Tuttle came to the house to go over the books with me after supper last night. A good man, Amos Tuttle. I am so grateful you thought of him. We entered the library, he first and I behind him with a candle, only to discover that Jonas Dyer was there before us! He must have just come in through the window, for it was open and he was standing near it, holding a lantern. Tuttle did not hesitate. He leaped upon Dyer, but had difficulty subduing him because of Tuttle's bandaged hand. He had a broken finger, if you remember. So I had to enter the fray. I seized the lantern and hit Dyer over the head with it. I regret to say there is a large charred spot on the carpet as a result.

While Tuttle sat upon Dyer, I finally got out of him that he had been in the habit of hiding bank notes in the books in my library! He had free access to the accounts books, and he knew your mother and I never opened those old volumes. He was stupefied to discover the books all gone, the shelves bare, and that is how we discovered the connection between the books and his thievery and pressed him on it. He has given us no idea of how much may be hidden thus. Meanwhile he has been remanded to the magistrate.

Search those books immediately, Robert! I pray this does not reach you too late!

I am well, though pained in the arm from my exertion. Your mother has rubbed it down with one of her fool concoctions. She sends her love. (She had to write this for me and objects to 'fool concoctions.')

> Yours,
> Fleet.

Rob finished the letter and let out a yell. He read it again, his hands shaking. "Geordie!" he roared.

When Geordie came running, Rob was already fumbling through a pile of books, holding them by their spines and shaking out the leaves. No showers of bank notes came forth. He frowned.

"Here. Read this," he ordered Geordie, forgetting his faithful servant read only with difficulty. Geordie shoved the letter back to him, saying the handwriting was impossible to decipher, so Rob stopped his mad search and explained.

The messenger Catton looked on with fascination. "I could help, your lordship," he offered.

"Indeed you shall," said Rob. He straightened and eyed the piles of books lining the hall. Nine hundred books! This would take a while. In addition to those in the hall were dozens more in his library, replacing those he had sold earlier.

"We will start in the library," he decreed. "Over a glass or two, perhaps? This calls for a celebration." He led the way.

Geordie unobtrusively poured brandy while Rob began on the library's volumes. No bank notes were forthcoming until he opened a copy of Plutarch's *Lives*. The book was a dummy; no print on its pages, but two hundred pounds in notes fell out. Rob whistled.

The next discovery, made by Catton, was in a volume by Pope. It held three hundred pounds.

"He must of liked the 'P's,' " Geordie remarked idly.

"Of course!" Rob shouted. "Of course! 'P' for pounds, perhaps. When Dyer was ready to flee with his money, which he most certainly meant to do eventually, he would want to know exactly where to look for it. Watch for the letter 'P.' "

Catton did not read but learned to recognize a "P" in no time.

Hours later, the library and hall a chaos of books lying helter-skelter, the brandy gone, the men reeling with weariness, Rob reported the last book had been examined.

The result was a grand total of thirty-eight thousand pounds.

"I shall bank it in the morning," Rob announced. "Catton, you will spend the night and carry the good news to my father tomorrow. We are saved! By God, we are saved!"

Within two days Rob had called upon the new owner of the Mount Street house, bringing a few samples from his stock of near nine hundred volumes, and had struck a bargain. The new owner had met Rob when the house changed hands, and greeted him affably. Once the purpose of Rob's visit was made known, Cripforth's florid face, liberally bedecked with whiskers, broke into guffaws.

"These are valuable volumes," Rob assured him. "Lately I have let Hatchard's have a small number, and they brought a thousand pounds." He showed Cripforth the Hatchard receipts.

"Just what I needed but never knew it," said Cripforth. "O' course! Books! That'll make 'em sit up and take notice. My boy, you came in the nick. I'll take the lot."

The next day a cartload of books was delivered to Mount Street and Rob went home, richer by four thousand pounds.

Now only one thing remained to be settled: the dowry.

"I fear this is highly irregular," Rob remarked to Lady Stanbourne and Bets. Full of excitement, he had called to tell them of his successful book sale. "Ordinarily m'father would have met with the Earl of Stanbourne and come to an agreement, most likely without our knowing anything about it. But m'father cannot come to London; he is so crippled in the joints he is confined to Dors Court. Besides, he has no more idea of what he can afford to settle on me than a leghorn chicken. In truth, he can settle nothing on me, nor on you, dear Bets.

"As to the dowry, I trust you stand in your late husband's place?" He addressed Lady Stanbourne. "Perhaps the three of us, for I believe Bets must be consulted, can come to some conclusion. Or is the dowry money already gone?"

"Oh, you poor children!" cried Lady Stanbourne. "I have to wonder what you will live on. Our quarter day payments are small enough, and I must think of myself, of course . . . Whenever Godfrey writes, which is not above twice a year, he proses on about how we must be more careful, and about how he is having to dip into the dowry money to provide for us, and . . . and . . ."

"But surely your late husband provided for the dowry in his will?" Rob asked. "You heard the reading of the will, of course? Godfrey cannot go against its provisions."

"Oh, yes, we heard it. It seemed very generous. Did you not think so, Bets? But I was so distraught—we were at sixes and sevens, you understand—I wished to move here to my own house in London as soon as possible, as we were not comfortable with Godfrey—we left it to Godfrey and his man of law to take care of it." Lady Stanbourne's pale blue eyes filled with tears as she relived that sad time when her beloved husband had died.

"Then we must summon Godfrey to London, or beard him in Suffolk," said Rob. "I believe it would be best to go to Suffolk, for we can talk to his solicitor as well."

"Oh, you will never get Godfrey to London," said Bets, frowning. "He will never consider the marrying off of his half sister worth the effort. We shall have to go to Suffolk. You will go with us, Rob?"

"Indeed," said her betrothed. "I look forward to it."

Chapter Seventeen

They set out by mail coach for Ipswich, where Rob would hire a carriage to carry them north to Coddenham and the Fortescue estate, a few miles beyond Coddenham.

It was May now, and the day was soft and warm. The farther they got from London the more Bets reveled in the sights and smells of the countryside. Lambs gamboled and bleated for their mothers in fields lush with grass. Oats and barley were sprouting in neatly ploughed squares separated by stone walls or in some cases, hedgerows alive with birds. Occasionally they rode through green tunnels where forests on either side met overhead.

Farther into East Anglia the land grew flatter, the forests, copses, and spinneys became fewer, and the view was a vast ocean of planted fields. Rob, accustomed to the rolling terrain of Dorset, much of it still wild heathland, found little in Suffolk to recommend it. He kept his thoughts to himself, however. It would be natural for Bets to believe Suffolk the Eden of England only because she had been born and brought up there.

Having decided to spend the night in Ipswich, the three travelers alit tired, cramped, and dusty, and arranged to stay in the inn where the mail coach changed horses. It was clean if noisy, what with coaches coming and going at all hours, teams being changed, and travelers arriving and departing. They felt themselves fortunate to obtain a private room for supper.

Rob was enjoying a single brandy after supper—with

the ladies in attendance, for where else were they to go?—when a sudden thought came to him. He rapped his head with his knuckles in chagrin.

"What is the name of the solicitor?" he asked. "He is most likely to be in Ipswich—the county town—we could see him before we go on to see Stanbourne. Why did I not think of that before?"

"Heverham, is it not, Bets?" said Lady Stanbourne. "Or is it Heveringham? Or Hevlingham? Something '—ham,' for this is 'ham' land in central Suffolk. Oh!" She covered her face with her hands in confusion. "I tend to forget you are a 'ham' also, are you not, Burlingham? Perhaps your family originated in Suffolk."

"I could not say," said Rob, "though I think I have distant cousins here somewhere. I tend not to look too closely. I have not had the best of results, dealing with distant cousins."

"Besides, your family name is Farnsworth, is it not?" said Bets. "Even so, I suggest you say 'Burlingham' very clearly to the solicitor. If he believes you are from a Suffolk family, however far back, he might be more kindly disposed."

"Point taken," Rob agreed. "I shall ask the innkeeper immediately."

Excusing himself, he ran down the steps to the common room, where he ordered another brandy and proceeded to ingratiate himself with the innkeeper.

"It is indeed Heverham," he reported happily forty-five minutes later. "Has his office not ten minutes' walk from here. Does he take care of sending your quarter-day funds, or does Godfrey do it himself?"

"Oh, Godfrey does it," Lady Stanbourne assured him. "It is as if Godfrey wishes us to know how good he is being to us, as if he were beggaring himself to make sure we have enough to live on. Pah! How could my sainted husband the earl have spawned such a one?"

The hunted look in her eyes told Rob what he had never realized before. She lived in mortal fear of her

stepson. Lady Stanbourne worked nervously at her handkerchief, folding and unfolding it.

"Tomorrow we shall call on Mr. Heverham," Rob announced. "Lady Stanbourne, you may remain behind if
you like. Bets and I can—"

"No! I must know where we stand!" she interrupted.
"My future is at stake as well!" She dabbed at her eyes.
"Why did I not accept Mr. Purtwee's kind invitation?"
she wondered as if to herself. "I could be in Wimborne
this minute looking at a fourteenth century clock."

She rose hurriedly, cast an agonized look at her
daughter, and ran into the bedchamber she and Bets were
to share. The door slammed behind her.

"I had best go to her." Bets, alarmed, got to her feet.
She paused a moment, looking at Rob with concern.
"Did you hear that, about Mr. Purtwee? I cannot under-
stand it."

"She is frightened, I think," said Rob. "Your brother
has never struck her, surely? I suppose his power over
her has become too much to tolerate. Remember, my
love, we have each other, but with you soon to be gone,
she will have no one. Unless she wants George
Purtwee!" Rob laughed at the thought. "I would never
wish that on her!"

"Never that," Bets agreed, and went in to comfort her
mother.

Three people, two of them calm and assured, the third
a bundle of nerves, waited in the anteroom of Mr.
Charles Heverham's office next morning. Lady Stanbourne fidgeted and played with a fresh handkerchief.
Rob and Bets sat straight as ramrods and talked quietly
together. Eventually a clerk told them that Mr. Heverham would see them.

"Lady Stanbourne!" Charles Heverham greeted her
enthusiastically, taking both her hands in his. "It has
been much too long! Surely five years at least! I am delighted to welcome you back to Suffolk." His long, pale,
deeply lined face lit up. "Would this be your beautiful

daughter? Dear lady, I cannot believe you old enough to have a grown daughter. You grow younger as the years pass."

Still clasping Lady Stanbourne's hands, he backed into his office. "Do be seated," he said. He indicated several upholstered chairs scattered about the comfortable room, where three large windows provided a view of the busy street below. "Now what may I do for you?" He moved behind his desk, waited for the trio to be seated, then sat down himself.

Lady Stanbourne seemed quite overcome. "This—this is indeed my daughter, Bets we call her, and her betrothed, the Earl of Burlingham. They will tell you why we are here. It is good to see you again, sir."

Heverham acknowledged the introduction and looked pointedly at Rob.

"Burlingham," Heverham mused. "From Suffolk, your lordship? I believe I have heard the name."

"Possible relatives, sir," said Rob. "Unfortunately I was born in Dorset. Had no choice in the matter, you understand."

Heverham seemed to think that statement was hilarious. He laughed so hard his thin frame shook. Just as quickly he sobered and said, "What brings you here, my lord?"

"It is the matter of Lady Elizabeth's dowry. The present Earl of Stanbourne has intimated that his stepmother and half sister have cost him so much in living allowances that he has had to dip into the dowry money for their support. Surely that cannot be! We would like to consult her father's will, if you would."

Heverham was clearly scandalized. "I do not believe it!" he insisted. "Have you talked to Stanbourne? There must be some explanation. Stanbourne is doing very well. He is a good manager and has a good mind for figures. Just a moment. I will have a copy of the will brought in."

He summoned a clerk and asked for Lord Stanbourne's will. While he waited, drumming his fingers on his desk, he asked after Stanbourne and his younger brother.

"We have not been to Coddenham yet," Lady Stanbourne explained. "I rarely hear, so I cannot tell you anything about them."

"I gather the younger one—Will, is it?—is quite a trial," said the solicitor. "Has never figured out what to do with himself, and drowns his sorrows in gin. Stanbourne has had a bad time with him. The boy gets into fights when he is half-seas over. But he is hardly a boy, is he? Must be past thirty. Ah, well. You will no doubt get the straight of it when you reach Coddenham. Now, here is the will."

There it was, plain as could be. A dowry of ten thousand pounds and a settlement of five thousand on each of any children his daughter might have. And for his dearly beloved wife, the earl had specified a jointure of eight thousand a year plus rents from two manor houses he had owned in Essex, these two funds to revert to his younger son, William, on his wife's death. Godfrey got everything else.

"The visitors were stunned. "But how—" Bets began, then sank back, trying to reconcile the written words with the careful way they had been living.

"You heard the reading of the will," Heverham pointed out. "Do you not remember? Everything was clearly stated; there are no ambiguities here. I drew it up myself, carrying out the earl's wishes, of course."

"Then why did you not make sure those wishes were implemented?" Rob demanded. He looked keenly at Heverham. The solicitor appeared surprised, but Rob could see no evidence of guile.

"Certainly I did!" Heverham said, affronted. "Indeed I did. The present earl carried out the bequests under my constant supervision. I am a busy man, you must understand. I have many clients to satisfy. I had no reason to suspect his lordship of any wrongdoing, but he made sure I saw evidence of every disbursement, every penny involved. The terms of the will have been carried out to the letter. I am sure of that." He looked down again at the parchment pages as if they could solve the mystery.

"Eight thousand pounds," Lady Stanbourne murmured. "Eight thousand pounds! And the Essex rents! Why have we not seen all that money?"

"Are you certain you have not, dear lady?" Heverham asked gently. " 'Twould be easy to fritter it away without realizing it. Eight thousand pounds is no fortune today."

Lady Stanbourne's rounded jaw jutted. "I beg your pardon," she said. "My daughter knows to a farthing where we stand. That would be—what, Bets?—two thousand every quarter day? Plus the Essex rents? What have we received?"

"It was a thousand every quarter at first. Remember, Godfrey wrote that the investments were doing poorly and he had to reduce it to nine hundred—and then eight hundred a quarter? We were told we were receiving the interest on the sum in Papa's will, just as the will stated. Was that not the way of it, sir?" She looked appealingly to Heverham.

"Good heavens, no!" Heverham cried. "You must be mistaken! I saw the disbursements myself! Something is definitely amiss." He frowned and stared again at the papers in front of him.

"I would suggest that you accompany us to Coddenham," said Rob. "It is your responsibility to see the will's provisions carried out. When can you leave?"

Flustered, Heverham called for his clerk. "What appointments have I today?" he asked. As they were recited, he made notes.

"Nothing I cannot put off," he decided. "Tell Carkenham I will call on him Wednesday. Give Bilham his deed; it is all prepared. Shall we leave now?" He rose and looking inquiringly at his callers. "Have you a carriage? If not, we can use mine. Let me get my hat."

Rob had not yet arranged to hire a carriage, so they accepted a ride in Heverham's worn but spacious coach. He arranged his passengers so that he could sit next to Lady Stanbourne.

"It is such a pleasure to see you again," he told her once they were under way. He smiled ingratiatingly. "How have you been keeping?"

"It has been hard, since my husband . . ." said Lady Stanbourne, sniffing. She straightened, looking at her daughter sitting opposite. "If it were not for Bets, I wonder what I would do. She has been such a comfort to me!" She smiled warmly at Bets, completely missing the fact that Bets' hand was held in that of the Earl of Burlingham.

"A daughter must indeed be a treasure to her mother," said Heverham. "My late wife and I had only sons, you know. Both of them thought they had to go off and fight Boney. I pray for them nightly." He sighed.

"Oh!" said Lady Stanbourne, her interest quickening. "I was not aware you had lost your wife. You have my sympathy."

"Thank you." He gazed in bemusement at Lady Stanbourne's hands, covered in pale pink gloves, as they twisted her handkerchief.

Rob and Bets exchanged knowing glances.

Bets' self-confidence reached a new low as they approached Spolia Opima, the Earl of Stanbourne's estate. Even though she was now a grown woman and had the Earl of Burlingham at her side, she felt an uncertain seventeen again, as she had been when she and her mother had left Suffolk. Burlingham had divined her mother's fear of Godfrey. Her own fear was nearly as strong.

The coach paused at the gate, where two wrought-iron leaves were closed but unattended. Rob jumped out to open them and saw the name of the estate in stiff iron letters across the top.

When he returned to the coach, leaving the gates open behind them, he remarked on the name. " 'How sweet it is.' You never told me your home was named in Latin."

"Mostly the people hereabouts call it 'Spoila,' " Bets reported. "or 'Spoily.' I doubt anyone remembers what it means. Godfrey is very proud of it, however."

"Of course." He cast about for other inconsequential subjects to take the ladies' minds off the meeting ahead. He could see how much they dreaded it. "What fine old trees. They must date back to your grandfather's time, or before."

"Yes, yes, I am sure of it."

The talk died as they rolled down the drive. Heverham seemed wrapped in his own thoughts. At last they reached the house.

And a fine house it was. Rob compared it with Dors Court and found Dors Court wanting. Built of warm reddish stone, it gave the impression of a collection of windows laced together with slim columns of stone topped by an incredible number of chimneys. Surely even the servants' rooms had fireplaces! A chimney sweep could grow rich here, Rob decided. Well, no, not likely with the likes of Godfrey Fortescue in charge.

"Peterham!" Bets' face was wreathed in smiles as she greeted the elderly retainer with the pronounced paunch who opened the door at her knock. "How good to see you."

" 'Tis Miss Bets! Is your mama with you? Ah, yes, my lady. Welcome home, my lady." The butler bowed them in.

"We must see Godfrey," Bets told him. "Is he here?"

"Oh, yes, miss. In his study. I'll tell him you're here." He hurried faster than dignity would allow to notify his master.

He returned more slowly and drew Bets aside. "Shouldn't be tellin' you, miss, but he didn't seem best pleased," he said in a hoarse whisper. "Watch out for 'im. He's been cross as crabs lately."

"Thank you, Peterham," said Bets. She steeled herself and led the way to the study. Rob took her arm and gave it a gentle squeeze. Lady Stanbourne followed and the solicitor brought up the rear.

"Good afternoon, Godfrey," Bets said as calmly as she could.

The tall man dressed all in brown rose from behind

his desk. Rob scrutinized him carefully for any resemblance to his half sister. Other than his height and a certain way of moving, there was little. His eyes and hair were brown; so was his skin. He might have been handsome except for deep pouches under his eyes and a permanent crease between his eyebrows. It would seem that he frowned often.

"Elizabeth," he said gravely. "And, Stepmama. And a stranger. And my solicitor. How goes it, Heverham? What brings you here?"

"May we sit down?" Heverham asked. "This may take a while."

"You realize it is near time for luncheon, do you not? I regret I am not prepared to entertain you. Mabel and the children are away and Cook is taking the day off as a result." He frowned. He had not invited them to sit.

"We will survive," said Bets, taking the nearest chair. "Godfrey, this is Robert Farnsworth, Earl of Burlingham, my betrothed. We have come to discuss my dowry with you. Please sit down, Mama, everyone. You too, Godfrey."

Despite his tan, Godfrey turned white as a sheet. Rob nodded, acknowledging the introduction, and watched the man closely. He seemed taken aback by his half sister's calm assumption of authority. Rob silently saluted his bride-to-be's courage. Did he detect a momentary look of panic in the other man?

"Very well. What about your dowry?" said Godfrey. He glanced at Heverham briefly and turned back to Bets.

"Papa's will says I am to get ten thousand pounds," Bets said. "There is no mention of our right to have any of it to live on before I marry. Why have you told us you have had to dip into the dowry to provide us with a living?"

"Oh, my dear," said Godfrey, suddenly the loving, caring brother. "I own it was not exactly true, but I did it for you and Stepmama. In my better judgment I realized as two innocent ladies you were unable to fathom the need to spend your money wisely. If I held over you the threat of having to use some of your dowry, you might curb your natural tendency to spend your money on fribbles. That is all, my dear. Truly all. Your dowry is untouched."

Godfrey smiled. What a terrible smile, Rob thought.

"Very well," said Bets. "I am glad to hear it."

"Then we may part friends?" Godfrey rose again as if to usher them out. "I am sorry you had to make the journey for such a triviality. I wish you and your earl all happiness."

"Sit down," said Bets.

Godfrey, startled, sat down again.

"There is the little matter of Mama's eight thousand pounds a year and the rent from the Essex manors," Bets continued. "How do you plan to squirm out of that one?"

Rob could not help himself. He clapped his hands with enthusiasm. He saw Heverham and Lady Stanbourne smile.

Godfrey did, indeed, squirm. At long last he pulled himself together and folded his hands on the desk. Looking at his hands rather than his audience, he said in a pained voice, "You must think me unfeeling, but that is far from the case. I knew you had that fine house in Knightsbridge Terrace, Stepmamma, and for all I know your father probably left you a tidy sum to run it. On the other hand, I have been at wits' end to bail William out. He has a taste for blue ruin. I cannot break him of it. Will gets into brawls—he broke a man's collarbone just last week—lawsuits—doctor's bills—damages in the public house—the burden is incredible. Incredible, I tell you! You know if you have consulted the will that Papa decreed William should get your share, Stepmama, after you are gone. I realized William needed it more than you, but I have never failed to send you your bank draft every quarter day, have I? Have I?"

Godfrey broke down and put his head on the desk, his hands over his eyes. His audience heard deep sobs.

Bets looked at him with loathing. "You are trying to tell us that Mama's money went to the rescue of those

Will has beaten?" she asked. "We are to accept that and go away nicely? We are to let Mama live in poverty while Will drinks himself to death? He was well on the way when we left Suffolk more than five years ago. Godfrey, it will not wash."

Heverham, impressed by the way this young lady forced the bare truth on her half brother, believed it time to intervene.

"Lord Stanbourne," he said, "it is evident you counterfeited the records of payments to Lady Stanbourne here. Whatever the reason, Will Fortescue or any other, that will not do. It simply will not do. I am well aware of your assets. You can afford to get Will out of his scrapes and never miss the cost. I must insist you give Lady Stanbourne what is rightfully hers—with interest, mind you!—or I shall have to see you hauled into court."

Godfrey raised his head and glared at Heverham.

"The Essex manors don't bring much," he said. "They need work."

"Then for heaven's sake, send Will down there and let him fix 'em up!"

"And have him brawling all over Essex? No, thank you."

"We digress. I shall not leave, your lordship, until this matter has been settled. You have wronged Lady Stanbourne and Lady Elizabeth. You have wronged Burlingham as well, for he is about to become part of the family. I shudder to think how your father would have felt to learn of your treachery."

"Oh. Burlingham." Godfrey sneered in Rob's direction.

"You will not speak of him so!" Bets cried. "He will be Marquess of Fleet one day, Godfrey, and I will be marchioness. We shall make it a point never to speak to you again."

"*You* a marchioness? Your grandfather was in trade! Tell your fine earl that! You are not fit to shine his boots. Of course," Godfrey continued sarcastically, "I am crushed that you should spurn me. It will break Mabel's heart as well, I assure you, not to mention the children, your little nieces and nephews. We have five now, you know."

Rob could take no more. The man could say what he would about Rob, but no one must speak so of Bets! With a mad roar Rob leaped over Godfrey's desk, pulled him from his chair, turned him around, and faced him. "What will it be?" Rob demanded. "Fisticuffs? Swords? Pistols?"

"You are challenging me to a *duel?*" Godfrey gasped in amazement. "Duels went out in Suffolk long ago."

"They have just returned," said Rob.

Godfrey laughed, but it was shaky. "Not a sword in the house," he reported. "Pistols perhaps, but not a matched pair. I suppose it must be fisticuffs. When? Tomorrow at dawn? Where? In my barley field?"

"What about right now, in your study?"

"No seconds. Must have seconds."

"Heverham, will you serve as my second?" Rob asked.

Heverham nodded.

"Summon a servant for yourself, then," Rob told Godfrey. "A footman perhaps? Your butler Peterham?"

Godfrey thought a moment, then pulled the bell. When a sturdy footman in deep wine livery appeared, Godfrey told him he was to be the second in a—duel? Mill? Bout? Match? Godfrey did not know what to name it. He appeared game though not eager. Rob eyed him speculatively and believed himself to be the better man.

"Oh, no, sir, not me!" the footman demurred, trying to back out of the room.

"It is only for show," Godfrey explained. "Stand there." He indicated a spot at one end of the study. I will stand here," he said, moving to a place near the footman, "and you, your esteemed lordship, may stand yonder." He waved toward the other end of the room. "Heverham, stand wherever you damned please, and you ladies, leave the room!"

The ladies would have none of it. They took refuge behind Godfrey's desk.

"I cannot think exactly how we should do this," Rob muttered to the solicitor. "Do we go back to back, step off, then turn and rush back together again? One cannot fight from twenty paces. I doubt fisticuffs constitute a proper duel."

Heverham was having the time of his lawyerly life. He laughed and slapped Rob on the back. "It won't matter," he said. "Go to it, my lord."

It was at that point Rob made a decision completely out of character.

"I withdraw my challenge," he said. "I would fight for my lady"—he threw a warm glance at Bets—"at the drop of a hat, but I do not believe it is necessary this time. My lord Stanbourne, I leave you to live with your guilt. Though I do not intend to mention it, the story of your perfidy toward your stepmother and half sister is bound to become common knowledge, probably within hours. They may wish to sue, but I believe the disdain of righteous men will punish you enough. However," his voice rose as he pinned Godfrey with a look, "should you ever attempt to cheat them again, you will have to deal with me."

Everyone in the room save Godfrey applauded.

Godfrey slumped into a chair. His footman crept out of the room, no doubt to begin spreading the tale.

Heverham gripped Rob's hand. "I suggest you take the ladies back to Ipswich for a late luncheon and a look at the sights of the town while I make sure Stanbourne comes up with the money," he said. "You may return for me this evening."

Rob nodded and motioned the ladies out. They did not look at Godfrey, and he did not look at them.

"You were so brave," Bets said. She and Rob were "seeing the sights" of Ipswich, which mostly consisted of looking at each other over a very late luncheon in their private parlor at the inn. Lady Stanbourne, overcome, had taken to her bed.

"No, *you* were so brave!" Rob corrected her. "The way you stood up to your brother—I was so proud of you!"

"I was really frightened inside," she confessed. "I never could have done it without knowing you stood behind me. But I was sure you would knock Godfrey down. I could have kissed you when you refrained, even though he deserved it."

"You may do it now," he offered.

She complied.

The wedding was small but beautiful. It took place in the home of the bride's mother, in Knightsbridge Terrace. The bride was given away by an Ipswich solicitor, Charles Heverham by name, who seemed to be a close friend of the bride's mother. The bridegroom had a single groomsman, Thomas Hazleton, who actually remembered to produce the wedding ring at the proper time. The guests were an odd mixture; they included a man with a crooked nose, who gossip said had once been a pugilist, and a scrawny fourteen-year-old boy, as well as members of the *ton*. After the ceremony two new maids in frilly white aprons served refreshments to the assembled guests while another, named Molly, who was supposed to remain in the kitchen, popped in and out to see what was going on. After the festivities the bride and groom rode to the groom's home in his curricle, attended by a tiger rigged out in a blinding white toga adorned with three rows of gold braid around the neck, the sleeve openings, and the hem. Some noted a close resemblance to the lad at the wedding.

The newlyweds made a trip to Dorset to visit the groom's parents, who were charmed with the bride. The groom spent some time with his father's new steward and came away looking satisfied. They returned to London after a week to settle into their small house in Grosvenor Row.

To their surprise the bride's mother had sent a wedding gift during their absence. They found it displayed on the mantelpiece of the library—a black lacquered antique clock, more than two feet tall, with Corinthian columns, much gilt trim, and the name of the maker on the back: Henry Jones, London.

"Oh, no," Bets groaned. "Mama's prize possession. Has she forgotten how I hate that monstrosity?"

"Shall we sell it?" her husband suggested eagerly. He had been thinking for far too long what that clock might bring. He checked himself. They were no longer on the edge of poverty.

"No." He answered his own question. "Your mama would notice its absence. We cannot do that to her."

Their only disagreement came about over the cartloads of the books from Dors Court. Bets mourned their loss to a man who apparently never would open them. Rob tried to explain that his house had no room for them.

Within the year, however, he heard that Cripforth had lost all his money in a canal venture gone sour. Before he faced the specter of bankruptcy, which could mean the loss of the house and all it contained, Cripforth put it on the market. Asking price: sixty-six thousand pounds. Rob smote his brow. What an opportunity! He still had the thirty-eight thousand secreted by Dyer in his father's books, but some of that had to go to his parents. What could he get for the house in Grosvenor Row?

He could get forty thousand pounds, three thousand more than he had paid for it, he learned to his delight when a buyer appeared. He sold the Grosvenor Row house and bought back the old house in Mount Street. Its only drawback was its nearness to the home of Lord Purtwee, but they could live with that.

All nine hundred volumes, unopened, untouched, came with it.

Rob even read some of them when he was not busy teaching Bets to play cards. He came to regret those lessons. She soon won two games out of three.